EVERSONG

THE KINDRED

DONNA GRANT

XOXO!

Donna Grant

Eversong (November 20, 2017)

Coming April 2018: Book 2

Coming December 2018: Book 3

CHIASSON SERIES

Wild Fever

Wild Dream

Wild Need

Wild Flame

Wild Rapture

LARUE SERIES

Moon Kissed

Moon Thrall

Moon Struck

Moon Bound (January 2018)

WICKED TREASURES

Seized By Passion

Enticed By Ecstasy

Captured By Desire

Wicked Treasures Box Set

A Dark Seduction

A Forbidden Temptation

A Warrior's Heart

DRUIDS GLEN

Dragonfyre (connected)

Highland Mist

Highland Nights

Highland Dawn

Highland Fires

Highland Magic

SISTERS OF MAGIC

Shadow Magic

Echoes of Magic

Dangerous Magic

Sisters of Magic Boxed Set

THE ROYAL CHRONICLES NOVELLA SERIES

Dragonfyre (connected)

Prince of Desire

Prince of Seduction

Prince of Love

Prince of Passion

Royal Chronicles Box Set

MILITARY ROMANCE / ROMANTIC SUSPENSE

SONS OF TEXAS

The Hero

The Protector

The Legend

CONTEMPORARY / WESTERN / COWBOY ROMANCE

HEART OF TEXAS SERIES

The Christmas Cowboy Hero (October 31, 2017)

STAND ALONE BOOKS

Mutual Desire

Forever Mine

Savage Moon

ANTHOLOGIES

The Pleasure of His Bed

(including *Ties That Bind*)

The Mammoth Book of Scottish Romance

(including *Forever Mine*)

Scribbling Women and the Real-Life Romance Heroes Who Love Them

1001 Dark Nights: Bundle Six (including *Dragon King*)

This is a work of fiction. All of the characters, organizations, and events portrayed in this novel are either products of the author's imagination or are used fictitiously.

EVERSONG
© 2017 by DL Grant, LLC
Cover Design © 2017 by Charity Hendry

ISBN 10: 1635760844
ISBN 13: 9781635760842
Available in ebook and print editions

www.DonnaGrant.com
www.MotherofDragonsBooks.com

EVERSONG

Dear Reader –

I began reading romances at twelve after finding one of my mother's. I was hooked. Instantly. It was an addiction that has only grown over the years. While I don't remember what that first book was, I do know it was a historical. There was just something so beautiful and magical about being transported back in time and living through those characters.

For years (and really I mean over a decade) I only read historials – but ALL historicals. I didn't care what time period, I wanted them. No, I *needed* them.

I devoured anything by Johanna Lindsey and Julie Garwood, just to name a few. That's why when I began writing it was natural for my books to be historicals. Though, I liked to sprinkle magic throughout mine.

Historical paranormals hadn't really taken off when I started writing. There were a few, but they were difficult to find – and they didn't do well. (Marketing, people. It's all about marketing.)

I can't tell you how hard it was to find an agent willing to try and sell the Dark Sword series. I was told repeatedly that it was a great story but impossible to sell. Then, I finally found someone willing to take a chance. Even had that not happened, I would've continued with the small press I was with.

I had a desperate need to write those stories. And while I took a detour (okay, okay. It was a rather looooong detour) I've been planning to give you a new historical paranormal series for some time.

So, now I'm introducing The Kindred. I'm *in love* with this series, lovelies. And it's been a real treat to dive back into the medieval world.

While this book – and the series – will have all the elements you've come to expect from me (strong heroines, sneer worthy villains, and alpha heroes), there will be a few different things.

Unlike my other series, this is heroine driven. Unlike my other books, my main characters aren't the paranormal element – they're fighting it.

I hope you fall as madly, deeply, and crazily in love with The Kindred as I have. And I think you're in for a few surprises.

xoxox,
DG

West Morland, England
September 1349

It was a good day for hunting witches. Then again, Leoma believed every day was a good day to hunt.

She kept the hood of her cloak pulled forward to conceal her face as she meandered through the crowd. The few days of fair weather they'd enjoyed, allowed the soggy ground a chance to dry so that mud no longer squished beneath her shoes. The market was filled with people, and while she detested the crush of bodies, it gave her cover.

Chickens squawked, men yelled, women haggled, and even a dog or two barked. The smell of freshly baked bread and raw fish, along with rank body odor, clung to everything. Leoma ignored all of it, including the children that ran through the market without a care or worry—picking pockets when they could.

With her pace unhurried, it was easy to blend in with the crowd while her gaze was focused on her quarry—Brigitta. The witch was easy to pick out with her flagrant beauty that she happily showed off.

Leoma battled the rising hatred within her. Edra, her mentor, warned her about letting anger rule. But it was becoming more and more difficult to keep it at bay.

While Leoma had begun learning to battle witches the day Edra and Radnar found her starving on the streets, it hadn't been until Brigitta cruelly and viciously killed Leoma's closest friend that she truly understood vengeance.

"Ease your mind."

Leoma inhaled deeply as Edra's words came back to her. While releasing her breath, Leoma centered herself. It had been six weeks since she left the safe haven of the abbey ruins Edra and Radnar had made into a home.

All those years of training with various weapons and learning how to fight against witches were being put to the test. This wasn't the first time Leoma had gone hunting, but it *was* her first time alone.

For weeks, she had been steadily closing in on Brigitta. Two days ago, Leoma finally found her. It was obvious by the way the witch traveled with determination that she had a specific destination in mind.

It was really too bad she would never make it.

Leoma smiled, her hand on the hilt of her sword hidden beneath her black cloak. She couldn't wait to sink the blade into the witch's heart. Or better yet, slice off her head.

Meg's face popped into her mind. Leoma had to close her eyes against the assaulting image of her best friend's decapitated body.

If only Leoma hadn't insisted they split up in order to corner the witch. If only she'd realized that Meg was terrified. If only....

There were so many regrets that haunted her, and Leoma was sure they would remain until her dying day.

She touched the inside of her left forearm. Before she left her family, another tattoo had been added to her body. The Vegvisir.

The Icelandic word meant signpost, but the magical stave was much more than that. It helped the bearer find their way and never become lost. The Vegvisir would not only help Leoma track Brigitta, but it would also bring Leoma back to her family.

She dropped her arm and moved away from a cart to continue following the witch. It was only Brigitta's habit of remaining right in the mix of people that kept Leoma from attacking. Because Leoma wouldn't have the weight of any more innocent deaths on her conscience.

If she had to track the witch for a year in order to get her alone, then that's what Leoma would do.

Brigitta suddenly halted and looked over her shoulder. Leoma ducked behind a building. She peered around the corner, her gaze taking in Brigitta's stunning face with her long, black hair up in braids, and bright blue eyes that seemed to hold everyone entranced—everyone except Leoma.

A few moments later, the witch continued on. Crowds parted without Brigitta ever saying a word. It was as if others recognized the power within her without understanding what they felt.

While men stared after Brigitta in a lust-filled haze, none were brave enough to approach. It sickened Leoma that so many were so easily manipulated by a beautiful face. Couldn't they tell the witch could end them with a thought? Did they even care?

To Leoma's surprise, Brigitta stopped again and simply looked around as if searching for something.

Or someone.

Leoma remained hidden, wondering just what the witch was up to. Had it not been for Edra, Leoma would never know that there was magic in the world, or that there was a Coven who recruited the most powerful witches in order to grow.

For what exactly, no one knew. Yet.

But that knowledge was something Leoma hoped to bring back to the abbey.

The Coven once sought Edra. They had hunted her for seven years until Edra took a stand. With the love of her life, Radnar, by her side, Edra defeated the witches sent to either bring her into the fold or kill her. That's when Edra decided to create her own coven—a Hunter's Coven.

Leoma was the first of the homeless, abandoned, and starving children that Radnar and Edra found. Some trained like Leoma, and others, like Meg, found different duties at the abbey.

No one was forced to do anything they didn't want to do, but everyone pulled their weight. It allowed Radnar and Edra to supply a safe place for anyone who wanted or needed it.

Leoma couldn't imagine growing up any other way. While Radnar had been her first teacher, he hadn't been her only or her last. Other knights and warriors found their way to Radnar and helped train those wanting to be a part of the Hunter's Coven.

The sword Leoma carried had been designed by Radnar and created by Berlag, their master blacksmith. And then Edra had filled it with magic so Leoma could kill witches.

Because a witch could survive a normal blade. It took something special to make sure a sorceress remained dead. And Leoma would make damn sure Brigitta never hurt anyone again. It might very well cost Leoma her life, and she accepted that.

As soon as she saw the witch move, Leoma scanned the crowd, looking for anyone who could be meeting up with Brigitta. Leoma might get lucky and find a second witch. It wouldn't be the first time she fought multiples.

She had the scars—and the tattoos—to prove it.

Leoma counted to twenty before she slid from her hiding spot to follow Brigitta. To her surprise, the witch walked into the Three Moons. Leoma flattened her lips as she eyed the tavern.

It wasn't that she minded going into such establishments, it was just that she spent most of her time fending off advances from drunken idiots who thought that anyone with breasts was fair game for a tumble into bed.

But she wasn't going to let that stop her from discovering all she could about Brigitta, just in case Leoma did survive the battle and made it back to the abbey. Any information—no matter how inconsequential—was needed.

She made her way around the building made up of small stones and wooden pillars to make sure the witch didn't sneak out the back. Then Leoma waited until she found a group of men walking into the pub. She snuck behind them and went unseen by most.

The tavern was packed. Loud, boisterous groups singing and laughing occupied several long tables. Those enjoying food and drink took other, smaller tables.

Leoma noted the hearth and roaring fire, as well as the shadowed parts of the interior. She quickly found a smaller table with an elderly couple who didn't bat an eye when she sat with them. Leoma gave the woman a nod and set a few coins on the table before sliding them toward her.

The woman took the money and didn't look at Leoma

again. That allowed Leoma to let her gaze wander the tavern as she inhaled the delicious aroma of food, which was probably why the place was so popular.

With little effort, Leoma picked out the men she knew could be trouble. Danger filled the air around them like a dark cloud despite their laughter and noise—or perhaps *because* of it. They drank too much and made sure everyone could hear their boasting. But so far, the men were content to focus on imbibing instead of fighting.

Just before her gaze moved away, she spied someone she had somehow previously overlooked—twice. He sat motionless in a shadowed corner with a mug of ale before him and his gaze directed toward the stairs.

She eyed him, wondering how she could have missed him in her perusal of the occupants. She put his face to memory. Dark hair, thick with just a hint of wave, that fell loose to his shoulders. A lean, rugged face that had sharp cheekbones and a square jaw with a slight indent in his chin ensnared all her senses.

His lips were wide and sinfully full. Thick brows slashed over piercing eyes a deep color she couldn't quite discern from the distance.

Leoma couldn't remember ever encountering a man with such a striking face before, and the fact that she didn't want to look away disturbed her greatly.

But it wasn't just his features that captured her attention. There was an air about him that declared he and battle were well acquainted. If he were a knight, his plain brown cloak and leather jerkin beneath hid the chainmail. He reclined in the chair as if he didn't have a care in the world, and yet his expression told a different story. He was intent on something.

Perhaps he was hunting, as well.

She regretted that she wouldn't find out for sure because

igued. And she almost felt sorry for whoever the ... er. He seemed the type who would not give up ... his target to ground.

... ulled her gaze away and looked at the table. This ... e time when Meg told her to flirt. Meg had always ... na to do the things she watched others do. Her ... her a part of the world instead of just someone ...

... na was better at watching. The few times she tried ... rs did, it hadn't turned out well. It's why Leoma ... to witch hunting. It was a solitary business. And ... was damn good at it.

She began to wonder how long she would have to wait for some sign of Brigitta when the witch walked down the stairs with a young woman. Their heads were close together as they whispered.

Leoma saw Brigitta pass a small bag to the woman before they reached the bottom step. The woman hugged Brigitta and hurried to the back of the tavern with a bright smile in place as silence fell over the occupants.

Brigitta's grin was coy and sly when she caught men staring. She gave them a little wave before walking out. Leoma glanced at the back of the tavern. A part of her knew she needed to see what the witch had given the woman, but Leoma didn't want to lose Brigitta.

Yet, if Leoma found her once, she could again. Leoma waited until the conversation in the taproom resumed, and then she discreetly rose and made her way to the back.

"I got it," came a feminine voice.

Leoma leaned around the corner to find the woman showing the bag to a man.

"We can have a child now," the woman said excitedly.

The man eyed the bag. "I'm not sure about such methods."

Leoma knew the risks involved with using magic for such things. The couple would be indebted to Brigitta forever. And the witch wouldn't hesitate to take what she wanted from them—most likely their firstborn child. There was no way Leoma could allow that to happen.

She put a smile on her face and walked toward the couple. "My apologies. I don't mean to interrupt, but I think I'm lost."

The woman set the bag on a table near the hearth as she turned to Leoma. "It sometimes happens. Would you like something to eat?"

The tavern owner hurried out to the customers when someone shouted for more ale, leaving Leoma with his wife. The first thing Leoma had learned in her training was to be swift of hand.

She walked closer while the woman spoke. "This is a wonderful place. I'm glad I stopped in."

"That pleases me greatly to hear," the woman beamed.

When the wife glanced out the doorway, Leoma swiped the bag. "Can you show me the way out, so I do not get lost again?"

The woman's smile grew tight, most likely irritated at being interrupted, but she replied, "Of course."

Just before Leoma followed the woman out, she tossed the bag into the fire.

Leoma began searching for Brigitta as soon as she was out of the tavern. She caught a glimpse of the witch heading west and made to follow when the same gorgeous man from the tavern snared her attention. She allowed herself a moment to stare while he saddled a horse. But it was the way his gaze kept returning to Brigitta that made her frown.

Leoma hoped the man wouldn't interfere. She'd hate to have to put him on his arse, but she'd do it in a heartbeat. The witch was her prize.

2

Envisioning his hands wrapped around Brigitta's slim neck was all that kept Braith trudging through each day. He thought he had put blood and death behind him, but one woman changed everything in a single night, with one vicious act.

He mounted his horse and patted the steed's neck before clicking to him. The dapple gray stallion began walking. Braith allowed Brigitta to have a long lead ahead of him. He'd actually debated catching her in the village but decided against it. Because what he planned for her didn't need an audience.

Ever since he discovered Josef, Braith had devised many ways to torture the murderous bitch before he finally ended her life.

As he travelled down the road, he thought of how he'd found his ward and heir lying dead in a pool of his own blood. The image replayed over and over in Braith's mind.

In didn't matter whether he was sleeping or awake, the scene never left him. But it gave him focus. The single-mindedness would eventually deliver the woman's death that he needed as retribution.

He glanced down at his hands. Years of service to the king had coated him in blood that never seemed to wash off no matter how many times he scrubbed.

Only a year earlier, he had been given a fresh start. He eagerly left the life of battle behind without a second's hesitation. For the first time in years, Braith had been able to look down at his hands and see them devoid of dripping blood.

That lasted only a few short months before he came upon Josef. Braith had tried everything he could to stop the bleeding as he shouted Josef's name, but it was to no avail. His ward was already dead.

The sight of Josef's blood covering his hands and clothes made Braith feel as if someone dragged him back to Hell. After he had clawed his way out the first time, he knew the ghosts of the men he killed wouldn't allow him to get free again.

The bellow he'd issued that day was part grief, part regret.

And all vengeance.

He'd taken a few days to ready Josef's body for burial, and then as soon as he was entombed, Braith rode away from the small keep and its plot of land, which had been given to him by the king for his services.

He didn't expect to return. Whether Brigitta killed him or not, the path Braith was on was one of death and destruction.

His gaze lifted to the gray sky above. More rain was coming. The scent hung heavy in the air. After several days of sun, the clouds returned to hang low and dark. The storm would be fierce. No doubt it would force Brigitta to find shelter.

That's when he would make his move.

Braith held the reins in one hand while the other rested on

his thigh. Brigitta disappeared over a rise on the road ahead, but he wasn't worried about losing her or the fact that the road cut through a forest. Capturing her was something he could do in his sleep.

Once he had Brigitta, he was going to find out why she took Josef's life. His ward might have been reckless, just as Braith was at that age, but Josef was also loyal and honest. Women flocked to him, willingly giving him their bodies, so Braith knew Josef hadn't tried to force himself on Brigitta.

What irritated Braith was that the raven-haired beauty had deceived him. Nothing had warned him that she was there to do his family harm or that she intended to kill anyone.

While he acknowledged Brigitta's beauty, he hadn't been enamored with her as Josef was. Then again, she had gone directly to his ward. Looking back, Braith guessed that Josef was her target all along.

But why?

The question rolled loudly through his mind. He would have answers.

One way or another.

To be one of the most feared knights in all of England, only to have a woman come into his home and kill someone he cared about without hesitation was something that would have hold of Braith until he sank his blade into Brigitta's cold, black heart.

Braith moved his mount to the side of the road as a man stooped with age held onto a walking stick with one hand and the reins of the oxen attached to his cart with the other.

They nodded to each other as they passed. Braith wasn't sure what made him look over his shoulder at the man, but he did. Nothing struck him as out of place, but he wasn't going to take any chances. His instincts had sent a warning. He would listen.

When he finally crested the rise and looked down the road, there was no sign of Brigitta. Braith pulled back on the reins to halt the stallion. His head turned to the right to stare into the thick woods beside him.

He scanned the area leisurely, listening for anything. Then his head slowly turned forward and to the left. Several moments passed before he dismounted and began to look for tracks on the ground, anything indicating that the woman had left the road.

There was no sign of anything for the next league. It was as if she'd disappeared entirely. But Braith knew that couldn't happen. She was out there somewhere, and he was going to find her.

He stood in the middle of the road and looked right and then left, trying to decide which way Brigitta could've gone. It wasn't until he walked to his right and stood just a few yards into the forest that he heard the stillness.

It was much too quiet. Someone was out there, and he would happily bet his sword that it was Brigitta. Braith issued a short whistle that had his horse coming to him. He opted to remain on foot to continue looking for traces of the woman.

With the stallion's reins in hand, Braith gradually made his way farther into the dense woodland. The trees were massive, alluding to hundreds of years of growth. Ferns lined the forest floor in thick batches.

The only sound was the shuffling of the leaves above him as a soft wind moved through the trees. No birds sang, no squirrels chirped.

His gaze jerked to the left when something orange flashed. A big, fluffy tail was all he saw before the fox disappeared. Something was frightening the animals, and it wasn't him.

The stallion snorted and jerked up his head, causing Braith's arm to pull back. He immediately turned to soothe the steed, moving to stand at the animal's shoulder and stroking down his neck as he spoke softly to calm the gray.

"Easy, lad. All is well."

As quickly as the horse had spooked, his fear subsided. Still, Braith didn't move for several moments. Then he walked deeper into the forest that seemed to go on forever before him and to either side. Brigitta could be anywhere.

That didn't deter him. After all, it had taken him over a month to find her after she fled his lands. If he found her once, he could—and would—find her again.

His path through the forest zigzagged as he scoped out the ground for hints that he was on Brigitta's trail, but it slowed his progress. All too soon, the thick canopy of trees blocked out what little light the clouds let through.

Braith doubled back to a cave that he'd spotted earlier and used it for cover. He unsaddled the stallion and tied the reins to a low-lying branch so the horse could graze before Braith gathered wood and built a fire.

He ate some food he'd gotten from the village, and then wrapped his cloak around him for added warmth as he thought of all the ways he would hurt Brigitta.

Finally, he closed his eyes and tried to get a little rest. Not that he would sleep for very long. He dreamed of discovering Josef each night, waking with his heart pounding against his ribs as helplessness consumed him.

His senses were attuned to listen for anything that meant danger, so he was in turns alarmed, shocked, and angry when the cold steel of a blade pressed against his throat. His eyes flew open to find a cloaked figure before him.

"You've no idea what you're getting into."

The husky, feminine voice was as much of a surprise as the metal against his skin. "You're going to have to be more specific."

She moved to stand before him, the sword never wavering. The hood of her cloak fell away from her heart-shaped face, and he was held speechless by the stunning beauty revealed.

The firelight sparkled in her liquid brown eyes framed by thick lashes. Her high cheekbones gave way to wide lips that looked as if they rarely—if ever—smiled. Her dark locks were braided and pulled over one shoulder.

But it was the black pants and leather he spotted beneath the cloak that snagged his attention. She wore the outfit of a warrior, of someone who was comfortable in the attire since it fit her like a second skin. Her tall, black boots came up to her knees, and he spotted the glint of metal peeking from the top of one. Mostly likely a dagger.

His eyes returned to her face. He was drawn to her serious and silent features. Their gazes held as they sized each other up.

While she was of average build, he had no choice but to take into consideration the blade she kept at his throat. Her arm didn't shake, which meant she was used to holding the weapon. And that indicated that she was most likely trained in the use of it, as well.

It would be an oddity for sure, but for some reason, that excited him.

Finally, she spoke again. "Stop tracking the woman."

"Sorry. That's not going to happen."

"You're walking into a trap."

"How do you know?" he questioned.

Her lips thinned as if in frustration. "I thought I could reason with you. Perhaps I should've just slit your throat."

"You're not a killer. I know what one looks like, and while I might not know who you are, I do know you are no murderer."

One slender brow lifted. "I'm going to tell you this one time. Leave. Go back to wherever it is you came from."

"Why are you protecting Brigitta?"

Anger flashed in the woman's dark eyes. She pressed the point of her sword against his neck. Braith clenched his teeth as he felt the tip pierce his skin.

"I'm not protecting her. I'm hunting her," the woman announced.

Every time she spoke, Braith was more surprised. The entire time they had been conversing, he'd been slowly moving his hand beneath his cloak until he grasped the hilt of his sword.

He lifted one shoulder. "I'm sorry, but she's mine."

As soon as the words were spoken, he rolled to the side and jumped to his feet as he unsheathed his weapon. He barely had time to raise his blade to stop hers.

She jumped over the fire as if she had battled around such things all her life. And the way she moved, he had never seen anything in all his years. She was quick and fluid. Catlike.

He had a hard time keeping up with her movements, but somehow, he managed to block her time and again. Yet he wasn't getting any hits in himself. He should've had her on the ground by now. Instead, she was the one in control.

His mouth fell open when she did some kind of flip through the air and landed on her feet, all without getting tangled in her cloak. That thought barely processed in his head before he spotted both of her feet coming right for him.

There was no time to get out of the way. The hit landed in the middle of his chest and set him backward, slamming into a rock. Pain exploded in his head as he dropped to his knees.

No matter how hard he attempted to hold onto his sword, it fell from his numb fingers. Something trickled down the back of his head as he fell sideways and rolled onto his back.

He forced himself to remain awake, even as black dots clouded his vision.

The woman stepped between him and the fire. He struggled to move his gaze upward to look at her. This couldn't be how he died. Not after everything.

She squatted beside him and blew out a breath. "I'm killing Brigitta to save lives, and that means yours as well. I can't have you walking into something you know nothing about. Forget her. Forget me. You might actually live if you do."

His eyes closed of their own accord. He could still hear her speaking, but her voice grew more distant until blackness claimed him.

3

Leoma felt no regret as she walked from the cave and out into the darkness. She had seen enough innocents slaughtered by witches because they didn't recognize the evil around them. The knight, whoever the hell he was, wasn't going to be added to those numbers.

She realized he wasn't the type to stop following Brigitta with just a warning. Leoma had to take drastic action, but even now, she wasn't sure it was enough. She probably should've tied him up or something, but she wanted to reach the witch.

After a league of travel, she stopped. Her gaze lifted skyward as she made out the twinkling of the stars though the trees. By the time the man woke, the witch would be dead.

Leoma drew in a deep breath and looked straight ahead. Mist rolled through the forest as if alive. It unfurled like the gnarled fingers of a crone.

A chill ran down Leoma's spine.

There was an invisible line between her and the copse of

trees ahead. Within that tree line was a Witch's Grove. Only one other time had she ever ventured into such a place.

Before, she had been surrounded by other Hunters—and had Edra by her side. Now, she was going to face whatever was within alone.

A Witch's Grove was a sacred place to a sorceress. It was where they went to transition from one tier within the witch hierarchy to another. It was also a location where they could communicate with other witches within their coven, as well as sacrifice others for their cause.

The reason for Brigitta entering the Witch's Grove was of no concern to Leoma. And it did not matter if it was just Brigitta or several others with her...all the witches had to die.

Leoma ran her hand down the side of her thigh. There was no denying the thread of fear that quickened her blood, tightening around her like a noose.

There was a chance Leoma could be walking into a trap. Despite their years of hunting witches, no one—not even Edra—had figured out how many were in the Coven. What they did know was that the power of the Coven continued to grow year after year. That could only be done by a growth in numbers.

It terrified Leoma to think what the world might be like if Edra hadn't gotten away from the Coven. And it made Leoma wonder how many other women had been snatched by the witches.

The soft flap of wings caused Leoma's head to snap up. Looking around, she spotted the little owl as it landed on a branch near her. Its big, yellow eyes locked on her before they blinked once.

"Hello, Frida," she whispered to the owl.

Knowing that Asa sent Frida to locate her allowed Leoma to steady her nerves. Asa had been born in Norway, but made her way to England, searching out the abbey Radnar and Edra took over.

Asa's Norse heritage added another element to the Hunters. It was Asa's steady hand that put the tattoos on each of them. More importantly, like Edra, Asa was a witch fighting against the Coven. With Asa's ability to communicate with animals, Leoma could pass on a message.

"Tell Asa I've found another Witch's Grove. Brigitta is inside. If I don't make it out, they'll know why."

The owl turned its head toward the Grove before flying away. Leoma watched the bird until she lost sight of it in the trees and darkness. At least now, her family would know where she was.

Her heart was slamming against her chest when she finally lifted her foot and took the first step toward the Grove. Magic ruled within its confines. Things few could comprehend called it home. Those beings were mostly neutral in the war, but Leoma had to be prepared for any eventuality.

The closer she got to the Grove, the more she wanted to turn back. But that wasn't an option. She held fast to her courage and continued onward.

From the moment she began training as a Hunter, she knew her days were numbered. The witches had magic in abundance, while Hunters only had their skills and weapons forged in magic to get them through each encounter.

One thing Leoma never worried about was getting old. She understood—and accepted—that she would one day die by a witch's hand.

Leoma's steps brought her to the mist, right on the edge of the border to the Grove. While her fingers itched to draw her sword, she kept it sheathed. For now.

Unrecognizable whispers bombarded her from all sides. She ignored them. If she fought too hard to understand them, there was no telling what they might do to her. Even when a whisper came from right beside her, she refused to acknowledge it.

The deeper into the Witch's Grove she went, the darker the night became. She couldn't see her hand in front of her face, but that didn't stop her.

The witches had implemented many things to keep others out. The silence and eeriness was enough to frighten even the most stalwart of people. If Leoma didn't know that magic had generated all of this, she would never venture into such a place.

It didn't matter how bright the sun or moon was, a Witch's Grove was always gloomy, as if a multitude of clouds continuously blocked light from entering.

One foot in front of the other, with her eyes straight ahead. It was how she moved. Nothing halted her steps or made her pause—not the whispers or the feeling of things brushing against her.

She put one hand on the hilt of her sword, ready to draw the weapon in the next heartbeat if needed. It didn't go unnoticed that she felt as if she were walking straight into the hands of the Devil and to her death.

The mist finally began to clear, and the inky blackness lessened enough that she could make out a clearing ahead. The closer she got to the glade, the clearer things became.

And that's when she spotted Brigitta.

The witch knelt in the middle of the clearing. Her cloak was puddled at her feet as her face lifted toward the sky. Her arms were bent in front of her, her palms face up.

Suddenly, the mist slunk towards Brigitta like a snake. It coiled around her with flashes of bright green. Since there was no way of knowing if the mist was a magical barrier or not, Leoma decided not to attack. Yet.

She ducked behind a fallen tree and watched, putting to memory everything she witnessed. None of the stories she'd been told or books she read mentioned the mist turning green.

If she made it back to the abbey, this was certainly a story that needed to go into the journals Edra and Asa kept to record things that could help fight future covens.

Of course, Leoma had to take out this one first. The Coven was the strongest and the largest in all of England. It worried Edra, and frightened Asa, and that was enough for all the Hunters to know that something had to be done, quickly.

Not even the pounding in his head when he woke could stop Braith from wanting to find the slip of a woman responsible. Never had he been taken down by a female, much less someone so quick.

He wanted to know where she'd learned to move like that so he could train there. It wouldn't be useful with armor, but if he could twist and turn his body in such ways, he wouldn't need the protection.

Braith put his hand on the back of his head and winced as he felt the stickiness of drying blood. With a curse, he got to his knees and looked for his waterskin. Then he poured the liquid over the back of his head to wash out the wound and rinse the blood from his hair.

A glance outside the cave showed that dawn was fast approaching. Moments after that, he put out the embers of his fire and gathered his things. He saddled the stallion but chose not to get on his horse since he was scouting for a sign of where the warrior woman had gone.

The fact that it took him over an hour to find any trace of

her told him that she went to great lengths to cover her tracks. But all it took was one slipup for him to find a trail.

His rejoicing was short-lived since he quickly lost her path again. He backtracked and tried different routes. Finally, he found a soft indentation, as if she had stood in one spot of thick leaves for a long time.

He knelt beside the depression and touched his fingers to it. Then he lifted his gaze and looked toward a thicket of foliage that looked as uninviting as an enemy's camp.

Braith slowly stood. Though he couldn't explain it, it appeared significantly darker within the forest. Yet, he knew the woman had gone in. Though she'd been hesitant. That in itself gave him pause.

What had she said to him?

"I'm killing Brigitta to save lives, and that means yours as well. I can't have you walking into something you know nothing about. Forget her. Forget me. You might actually live if you do."

He had no idea what she was talking about, but he intended to find out. And in order to do that, he had to go into the darkness.

"Shite," he mumbled.

He'd faced all kinds of foes, and not once had he faltered. Why was he now? Because this place looked a little imposing? Scary even?

Braith clenched his teeth and took a step. Only to be drawn up short by his horse rearing and trying to retreat. The next few moments were spent calming the animal down after moving the gray away.

Finally, the stallion quit trembling. Braith kept rubbing the steed as he tried to come up with how to proceed. It didn't take him long to realize that the horse wasn't going anywhere near the copse of dark trees.

He removed the saddle and bridle, hiding them in a bush.

Then he gave the stallion one last pat. Hopefully, the animal would be near when he got back.

"It's all right, lad. I'll go it alone from here."

Braith walked back to the spot the woman had stood in. He glanced over his shoulder to find the horse staring at him with his unblinking, black eyes. Once Braith turned back around, he decided it was now or never.

In three long strides, he was within the thicket. Mist he hadn't noticed before covered the ground in a thick carpet. Just as he suspected, it was significantly darker within the place. But most alarming of all were the whispers he could hear.

His gaze scanned the surrounding trees, looking for some-one, but he saw nothing. At least, not at first. After a few more steps, he saw something in his peripheral vision. When he jerked his head to the side, he saw a naked woman with skin and hair like bark lean away from a tree and hold out her arm to him.

Braith forced his gaze away, but the whispers increased. No longer was the movement out of the corner of his eye. He saw them everywhere. It looked as if they were part of the tree trunks, overlooked by their camouflage until they chose to move.

The trees themselves swayed, creaking loudly in the unnerving stillness, even though the leaves didn't rustle with wind.

This was a place unlike any he'd seen. He would've given it a wide berth if he weren't looking for the warrior woman. He needed to find and stop her because he planned to be the one to take down Brigitta. And he was prepared to halt anyone who tried to beat him to it.

The females from the trees never left their posts, but their curious black gazes were locked on him. He glanced at the ground, finding it disconcerting that he couldn't see what he was stepping on because of the mist.

He briefly thought about turning around and retracing his steps, but then he recalled how the woman had said she was going after Brigitta. He fisted his hands and continued forward.

It felt like an eternity before he saw a clearing through the trees. But it was the glowing green light from within the mist, moving in a circle around Brigitta that made him pause.

"What the bloody hell," he murmured.

4

There was no preparation for finally finding the murderous bitch. The rage that consumed Braith was all-encompassing. Never before had he wanted to kill something as badly as he did at that moment—and his sights were set on Brigitta.

He glanced around, looking for the warrior woman who'd attacked him, but she was nowhere to be seen. Which was fine by him. He could get to Brigitta now and return for his horse before the other female knew anything.

The only thing that gave him pause was the mysterious...beings...he'd walked through to get here. He didn't know what they were or if they meant him harm. But that was something he'd deal with on the way out.

He slowly unsheathed his sword. The way Brigitta knelt in the middle of the clearing with her eyes skyward was odd, but the green light in the mist was more so.

Then again, it was just mist.

At least, he hoped it was.

One of the reasons he had survived so many years of

battle was because he wasn't rash or reckless. He studied and contemplated. But now, he was throwing away everything that had kept him alive, driven by the cold bite of vengeance.

He kept to the trees and slowly made his way to the left to get behind Brigitta. The ground was more uneven, causing him to walk at a more sedate pace to keep from tripping. He hated not seeing the ground.

After catching himself when his ankle began to roll, Braith waved his hand at the mist to clear a spot so he could see the ground. As soon as his gaze landed on the skull and other bones, his mouth fell open in shock.

What was this place? He had seen all kinds of graveyards, but this wasn't one. This area felt...wrong. Foul, malevolent. Wicked.

The quicker he got out of there, the better.

He set his gaze on Brigitta once more and squared his shoulders. Then he walked into the clearing.

"Unbelievable," Leoma murmured when she saw the knight step into the clearing.

At least the imbecile had enough sense to come up from behind Brigitta. Not that it would do him much good. He had all but sealed his fate by following her into the Witch's Grove.

While Leoma didn't want to see him die, she had warned him. It wasn't her fault that he chose not to listen. His arrival —and the imminent attack he planned—might give her time to sneak up on Brigitta and kill her before the witch even knew Leoma was there.

Leoma's gaze returned to the knight. His gaze scanned the area warily. Perhaps he wasn't as stupid as she thought. But he had walked into the Grove during the day, which meant he had seen the Gira.

She shifted, her knee slamming into a bone.

She wondered if he noticed what littered the ground. The first time she had come upon a Witch's Grove and saw the floor of the forest after the mist moved, she had tripped over herself trying to get away.

And then she got sick. Twice.

The bones that lay at her feet and over the rest of the Grove were victims of the witches' spells. Or other witches who refused to join the Coven and then were subsequently used for a spell.

The coiling of the mist suddenly stopped. The green light grew so bright that Leoma had to raise her hand to shield her eyes. When that wasn't enough, she turned her head away until it dimmed.

When the flare faded, she found two other witches holding a bound woman between them. They pushed the female to her knees, her long, dark red hair falling over her shoulders.

Brigitta lowered her arms and smiled as she looked at the arrivals. Then she rose to her feet and glared down at the woman, the mist slinking away.

"Join us or die, Helena," Brigitta said.

Leoma gasped as she realized what she was seeing.

Helena lifted her head defiantly. "I'll never join the Coven."

"Then you die," Brigitta announced.

One of the other witches looked up then and noticed the knight.

The appearance of the three women seemingly out of thin air

caused Braith to halt. He could only stare in shock and wonder at what was before him.

His instincts told him to help the bound woman, but something held him back—a shout of worry in his mind that cautioned him to remain where he was.

The exchange between Brigitta and Helena only made him frown. Who or what the bloody hell was the *Coven*? And why did Brigitta want the woman to join them?

His thoughts came to a halt when one of the new arrivals noticed him. Her eyes widened, and her expression hardened as she said something in a dialect he didn't understand. The next instant, all four of the women were looking at him.

"Braith," Brigitta said, a smile curving her lips. "I knew you would find me, earl."

He tightened his grip on his sword that hung at his side. "If you wanted me dead, you should've killed me when you murdered Josef."

Brigitta laughed, the sound both seductive and evil. "Of course, I *could* have, my lord. But you're needed for something else."

"Whatever you have planned, forget it. Now, release the woman."

The two females behind Brigitta smiled as if in anticipation. Helena eyed each of them, seeming to size up the situation to see if she could escape.

Braith was going to give her that and more. He couldn't believe these women, without a single weapon between them, thought to stand against him. They would be slaughtered.

And he would enjoy sinking his sword into Brigitta's body.

The metal hummed with the anticipatory song of blood—Brigitta's. Many enemies had died upon his blade, but there was never one more deserving than the black-haired female before him.

"You callously took Josef's life," Braith stated. "Without thought or care. I opened my home to you, and you took advantage of my hospitality by murdering my ward."

She lifted one shoulder in a shrug. "You can continue your rant, but it will not change what has been done." Brigitta took a step toward him. "The fact is, you know the ultimate blame is yours. You welcomed me into your home. You're the one who foolishly believed that a woman would not dare harm a man."

The fury inside him was becoming harder to control, more so because her words were true. He had looked at her and thought that she could do no harm. It was a mistake he wouldn't make again.

"I almost wish you had remained at your keep," Brigitta said. "But I knew you would find me. It was planned all along."

"What are you talking about?"

"You."

"I'm no one."

Brigitta cackled and spread her arms wide. "Oh, how little you know. But you're about to find out, my lord."

He lifted his sword, the tip pointing to the sky as he held it before him. No longer would he listen to nonsense. "Release the woman. Either way, you're going to die this day."

"It's a pity I cannot kill you," Brigitta said with a sigh. "However, another fate awaits you."

Before he could comprehend her words, he saw smoke curl up from the hand that held his sword. Almost immediately, his skin began to burn. The longer he held onto his weapon, the more his palm sizzled.

"The more you resist, the more it will hurt," Brigitta stated.

He couldn't believe that she was the one doing this, but

there was no other explanation. He gripped his wrist in a bid to keep hold of the hilt.

The two women behind Brigitta moved to stand on either side of her. While they might be fair of face, there was an evil air about them that no beauty could conceal.

Suddenly, from his left, a figure stood from behind a fallen tree. He immediately recognized the warrior female from the previous night.

She reached up and unclasped her cloak. Then, she stepped on the tree and unsheathed her sword while flipping forward and landing deftly on her feet before tossing a knife to Helena.

Braith gazed in wonder at the leather-clad woman standing so defiantly behind Brigitta and her companions. The warrior woman hadn't said a word or issued a sound, but her appearance shifted the tide.

Her gaze met his. In her soulful brown eyes, he saw an unwavering determination. With a bow of his head, he silently agreed to work with her.

There was the slightest stirring of the air as she lifted the blade of her sword upward. One of Brigitta's companions turned and saw her. An instant later, the warrior plunged her sword into the female.

Just as Braith was about to look away, he saw that the soon-to-be dead woman began to burn from the inside out. It was the sound of the woman's screams that caught Brigitta's attention.

The heat from Braith's sword lessened. As soon as Brigitta looked elsewhere, he tossed his weapon into his left hand. A glance at his wounded palm showed blistered skin, red and puckered.

As Brigitta and her friend faced off against the now freed Helena and the warrior, he was forgotten. There was a pause as the four women stared at each other. The warrior was calm, her stance ready.

The flame-haired Helena had anger flashing in her green eyes. "The Coven has gone too far," she said.

Brigitta spread her fingers at her sides. "Oh, we're just getting started." Brigitta's head shifted to the warrior. "Who are you?"

"Vengeance."

That made Braith smile. He might not appreciate the warrior's attack on him, but he acknowledged her courage.

The air crackled with tension. Ignoring the pain of his hand, he took two steps closer to Brigitta. He noticed the mist creeping back into the clearing.

"You're in the wrong place, Vengeance," Brigitta said. "But I'm going to enjoy killing you."

Helena's smile grew. "Oh, you stupid woman. You think I killed your friend?" She shook her head before looking at the warrior.

Braith was confused. Why wouldn't Brigitta think the warrior killed her companion? There was an element he was missing, one that seemed to be right before him that he couldn't grasp.

"Hunter," Brigitta said in a low, strangled voice.

The thread of fear he heard brought him immeasurable joy.

The warrior grinned. "You and every other witch in the Coven will pay for your crimes. We'll begin with penance for the beheading of my friend."

In unison, Helena lifted her hands, palms out, while the warrior gripped her sword with both hands and brought the weapon up to her shoulder. Not one to let an opportunity pass, Braith saw that Brigitta's concentration wasn't on him, so he used the opportunity to sneak up behind her and plunge his sword into her spine.

It wasn't how he wanted to kill her. He'd wanted her to suffer first, but it was enough that her life would end.

To his shock, she didn't so much as cry out. Her head lowered as she watched the tip of his sword exit her chest. His mind reeled when she walked forward until she was free of his blade.

She whirled around so fast that he was unprepared. Blood covered her blue gown, but it didn't faze her. She curled her fingers and lashed out at his face.

Braith shifted, raising his shoulder to block her blow. Her nails, sharp as any blade, slashed through his leather jerkin and tunic to sink into his skin before sliding downward.

Leoma lunged toward Brigitta as Helena went after the other witch. Braith's face was contorted with pain, but he had enough wherewithal to swing his sword back toward Brigitta. While it wouldn't kill her, every wound he delivered inflicted pain. And that was exactly what Leoma wanted.

He fought like a man possessed, like someone who needed revenge for what had been done to his ward.

When Leoma heard his words about what Brigitta had done, she understood why he was so intent on tracking the witch. She recognized it as the same motivation that drove her.

Brigitta moved just before Leoma's sword made contact. Leoma spun, using her momentum to deliver another blow, but Brigitta was waiting. The force of the magic that slammed into Leoma's chest knocked the wind from her as it propelled her back.

Leoma struggled for breath. She lifted her head to see Braith swaying on his feet, his body under attack by the magic that was unleashed through Brigitta's nails and delivered straight into his bloodstream.

A gasp tore through Leoma as air filled her lungs. She rolled onto her side, happy to know that she'd kept hold of her sword. She pushed herself to her hands and knees. Using a tree for help, she got to her feet in time to see Helena press her palms together before shoving her hands outward.

Coils of purple-tinted lightning flew from Helena's palms and straight into the witch who screamed as soon as they wrapped around her. The tendrils sank into the witch's skin, leaving black marks.

Everyone watched as the witch began to convulse before falling to the ground and bursting into flame.

Leoma pushed away from the tree and started toward her target the same time Helena turned her gaze to Brigitta. The witch glanced at Braith, trying to decide if she had enough time to get to him before Leoma and Helena reached her.

"Until next time," Brigitta said and waved her hands before her.

In a blink, she was gone.

Leoma turned to Helena, but the witch didn't wait around. She ran off through the Grove. Leoma almost went after Helena, but she couldn't leave the knight. If he didn't get treatment, he would die.

Or worse, Brigitta would return for him.

"Damn," Leoma murmured and sheathed her sword.

She retrieved her cloak and dagger then hurried to Braith, who had fallen to his knees, only staying upright because he'd anchored his sword tip in the ground to help hold him up. Sweat covered him, rivulets running down his face. Between the injuries to his right hand and his left shoulder, he must be in tremendous pain.

His gaze was filled with agony as he stared at her while he tried to remain vertical. For the first time, Leoma got a good look at his eyes. They were a deep, fathomless indigo, like the sky right before sunset.

"You should've stayed away," she said.

He gave a shake of his head and parted his lips.

"Nay," she said when he attempted to talk. "No need to waste your energy. We have to get out of here. Now. Before Brigitta returns. The witch has plans for you."

Braith clamped his teeth together and issued a single nod. When he tried to stand, she took his right arm and slung it over her shoulder. Even then, he kept most of his weight from her.

"We need to move, and fast. I'm sturdy, so lean on me as much as you need," she said after he sheathed his sword.

She led him toward the path she had taken into the Grove. The Gira shifted away from the trees as she and Braith walked past. His breathing quickened when he saw them.

"Do not look," she whispered.

He gave a grunt. Whether that was agreement or not, she didn't know. The Gira seemed to be taking a curious interest in Braith, not that she blamed them. He was strikingly handsome. And strong. But in his weakened condition, it would take very little for them to call him to them.

And once in the clutches of a Gira, there was no coming back. The tree would surround him, consuming him for the Gira to play with or torture as they pleased.

The tip of Braith's boot caught on his other foot and pitched him forward. Leoma managed to move quickly enough to get in front of him, catching him before he fell. He was heavy, and they still had a ways to go.

"We're almost out," she told him. "You have to stay upright until we get out of the Witch's Grove. Can you do that?"

It took him two tries, but he managed to straighten. She

gazed at his ashen face and knew her time was running out. If she didn't stop the magic in his blood soon, it would be like a beacon for Brigitta—or another witch.

Worse, the longer the magic remained in his system, the more damage it would do. It would continue to weaken him, and could eventually kill him if left untreated.

He gave her a nod. Leoma draped his arm around her shoulders again, and they set off once more. She moved him as quickly as she could without causing him to trip and fall. With her gaze on the border of the Grove, she watched her goal get closer and closer.

"Nearly there," she told him.

His arm tightened, causing her to glance his way. That's when she saw the mist on either side of them closing in. No doubt, it was behind them, too.

It was Braith who quickened their pace. She gladly matched his steps. Unable to stop herself, Leoma glanced behind her. It was a mistake. As soon as she saw the mist rising up to take shape, she knew that whatever it was, intended to keep them trapped in the Grove.

The Giras' whispers had gone silent. That should've been a warning, but she had been too intent on getting Braith out to notice.

She and Braith burst through the Grove's barrier and were soon drenched in sunlight. There was a smile on her face, but it vanished when Braith fell forward. Leoma tried to catch him again, but his unconscious body was too much for her. He ended up dragging her down with him.

Giving herself a moment to catch her breath, she rolled him onto his back and pushed herself up before rubbing her shoulder that she'd jammed into a rock when she fell.

She rummaged through the bag attached to her waist and pulled out a small leather pouch. As she knelt beside him, she began talking, more for herself than him since he was unconscious.

"These are herbs," she said. "I hate to say this since you've just been introduced to this unknown world, but you've magic in your blood thanks to Brigitta. This will draw it out."

She unfastened his leather jerkin and pushed it aside, along with his sliced linen tunic so she could pour the herbs into the four wounds.

"This is Edra's magic. It's going to burn a little, but that's the herbs fighting to cleanse you."

Leoma put away the pouch when she finished and wiped his brow before looking around. They were still much too close to the Witch's Grove for her liking, but she wasn't sure how far she would be able to drag Braith.

She got to her feet and scouted around until she found an area easy to navigate. It led down into a small valley with trees protecting them. She hastened back and hooked her arms under his. Then, with a deep breath, she began walking backward, dragging him.

Halfway there, she looked up to find a horse following them. She recognized the dapple gray from the night before. The stallion remained with her even after they reached the valley. She stretched her back and caught her breath before she checked on Braith's wounds.

He had stopped shivering, which was a good sign. And his sweating had lessened. She sat back on her haunches and closed her eyes.

That's when she heard the trickle of water. Leoma jumped to her feet and quickly traced the source of the sound to a small stream. She bent and gathered handful after handful, drinking until her thirst had been quenched.

Then she filled her waterskin and made her way back to

Braith. She lifted his head and poured a little water on his lips, but he wouldn't drink.

With his tunic ruined, she took out her knife and cut off a few strips that weren't stained with blood. She soaked one and wiped his face to help cool him.

Unable to help herself, she smoothed aside a lock of his dark, lustrous hair, the deep chestnut brown color reflecting the light. Her finger trailed across his brow, noting the lines permanently furrowed by either worry or his constant frown.

She gazed at his face, wishing she didn't find him handsome. Now that she had touched him, she couldn't seem to stop. She enjoyed the feel of his stubble against her skin.

It wasn't long before her eyes drifted to his chest. Before, when she had been intent on healing him, she hadn't taken the time to look. She intended to do that now.

Her hands shook a little when she pushed open his sliced tunic to reveal an upper body corded with muscle and honed to utter perfection. She wanted to touch him, craved to feel his warmth against her palm, but she held back.

The smattering of dark hair across his chest did little to hide his various scars. He appeared to look at life as if it were one long battle. His body reminded her of a blade forged in fire and pounded, again and again, to take the correct shape before being thrust into cold water to harden—making Braith the perfect weapon.

She wiped his face again before trailing the cloth down his neck to his chest and then his shoulder. Gently, she cleaned off the dried blood to better see the healing wounds. All the while, her thoughts remained on him.

Who was he? What was his story? She wanted to know all there was.

She took out the leather pouch once more, thankful that it didn't look as if she needed to use more on his shoulder. That left his hand for her to tend to. She carefully gathered his hand in hers and turned it over.

The skin was blistered badly. It was time she took care of that, as well. Gently holding his fingers open, she loosened the pouch strings with her teeth just enough to pour the herbs onto his palm. He jerked against her, causing her hand to open the bag fully.

"Easy, Braith," she said. "Maybe I should call you 'my lord' since the witch said you were an earl."

She spoke slowly, making sure he was calm before she brought the pouch over his hand and began to pour. No sooner had the few herbs fell upon him than he sat up, knocking the bag from her hand and sending it flying.

Leoma stared into his deep blue eyes that were filled with rage and hate. "No one is hurting you. I'm tending to your wounds. Lie back."

"Brigitta," he ground out in a hoarse voice.

"We'll find her."

His lids lowered as he fought against sleep. "Have...to."

"I know," she assured him. "I heard. But you have to get well first. Now, lay back."

Finally, he did as she said. Once he appeared to fall asleep, she moved to where the pouch had fallen and stared aghast at the spilled contents.

"Nay," she whispered in dread.

The only way for her to get more would be to return to the abbey, and that would take time away from locating Brigitta. But fighting witches without some way to heal her wounds would be like walking into battle without a weapon.

She lifted the pouch cautiously so as not to spill any more. When she looked inside, she realized there was enough for her to heal Braith's hand. Or for her to save it for herself.

Without hesitation, she returned to Braith and tenderly

applied the last remaining herbs to his palm. She could only hope and pray that she remained unharmed. The one thing she didn't want was to suffer a wound from a witch and be far away from anyone who could help.

She tucked the empty pouch back into her bag and then took the other strip of cloth, wetting it before bringing it to Braith's mouth. After a few dribbles had made it past his parted lips, she repeated the process several more times.

Her eyes became heavy. It had been over twenty-four hours since she'd slept, and it was taking a toll on her. She checked on Braith's wounds again and then curled up on her side, using her arm as a pillow.

With her eyes closed, she went over everything she had seen and heard in the Grove. If only Helena would've stayed, Leoma could have enlisted her help. The witch's power would be useful in the fight against the Coven.

That was if Helena continued to stand against them.

Most witches didn't have the gumption to fight back. They joined the Coven out of fear, but it didn't matter why a witch joined. Each new addition brought the Coven more power.

They seemed intent on growing their numbers, but for what purpose? No matter how much Edra and everyone speculated, no one had anything solid to go on. Yet there was a mounting unease within Leoma. She felt that whatever the Coven was up to, it would be devastating to everyone.

The Coven had gone unchecked for too long. And there were so few Hunters. If only more witches would stand against them as Edra and Asa and Helena were.

Leoma sighed as her body began to relax. Helena had fought. That was something.

6

The first thing Braith thought of as he came awake was her eyes. He lifted his lids and looked at the tree limbs above him and the soft gray of a morning sky beyond, but that's not what he saw.

His mind was locked on her. The warrior with deep pools of dark cinnamon eyes seized him with the raw emotions that blazed in her beautiful orbs.

She could've left him behind, but not only did she get him out of whatever that place was, but she also tended to his wounds.

The reminder of his encounter with Brigitta made him take stock of his body. It was the lack of pain that confused him. The agony he'd endured was the worst of his life. How did he feel none of that now?

He raised his right hand to look at his burns. Shock went through him when his gaze landed on his palm—without a mark on it.

Turning his head, he looked at his left shoulder but saw only four pink lines of healed skin. He sat up and took stock of his tunic that had been cut. There were slices through the linen and the leather of his jerkin, which was proof that he hadn't dreamed his encounter with Brigitta.

He spotted two strips of material lying across sticks that had been gathered. Then his gaze caught sight of the woman.

She was on her side facing him, her arm tucked beneath her head, and her cloak over her like a blanket. Her lips were parted, her breathing that of someone deep in sleep. He couldn't tear his eyes away from her.

In the sunlight, he was able to see the full glory of her dark locks. Her hair reminded him of the rich soil of his land after a heavy rain. Strands as black as midnight fading to rich, decadent shades of brown with every hue in between.

He was so lost drinking in the contours of her face that it took a moment for his mind to register the song of birds. Braith lifted his gaze and spotted the creatures flying from branch to branch, their cries music to his ears after the silence of the day before.

So much didn't make sense. Not what he'd seen Brigitta and the other women do in the clearing, not the strange beings in the forest, and certainly not that he was healed.

His gaze scanned the area. The female had chosen a good place for them to hide. He heard something behind him and turned to find his horse staring at him with dark, soulful eyes.

Braith climbed to his feet and quietly made his way to the top of the hill. From there, he was able to find where he had stashed his saddle and bridle. He brought them back to the camp and set them aside.

His stomach rumbled, reminding him that it had been a while since he last ate. He rummaged through his pack and found what little food was left. The bread was stale, but it would fill his stomach.

He tore off a large chunk and slowly ate it while sitting

against a tree. Again and again, his eyes returned to the woman. He wasn't sure what question he wanted to ask her first since there were so many.

Halfway through eating his portion of the bread, she inhaled, signaling that she had woken. Her eyelids lifted. As soon as she saw that he wasn't where she had left him, she rose up on her elbow and turned her head until their gazes clashed.

And just like that, he sank into her eyes once more.

"How are you feeling?" she asked as she fastened her cloak into place.

"Like my palm wasn't burned and Brigitta's nails didn't slice into my shoulder."

A slight smile pulled at her. "That's good."

"Who are you?"

She crossed her legs and raked her hands through her long locks to get the hair out of her face. Gathering her mane in her hands, she pulled the thickness over one shoulder and braided it. "My name is Leoma. I'm sure you have many questions."

"I do. Tell me how you healed me. And where did you learn how to move as you do during battle?"

Leoma drew in a deep breath and placed her arms on her legs as she finished her hair. She studied him a long moment before she finally spoke. "I healed you with magic-infused herbs. As for my training, I was taught several different fighting techniques."

Those responses only raised more questions. Braith tossed her the other half of the bread as he chewed and swallowed his food.

After she had taken several bites, she said, "Let me start from the beginning."

"Please." His mind was still reeling from the mention of magic.

Then again, there were those creatures that looked to be part of the trees. And the green mist.

Leoma gave him a skeptical look, as if already determining that he wouldn't believe her. The truth was, he wasn't sure what to think about *anything* he had seen the day before.

She wiped her mouth and began. "First, you need to understand two truths. There are witches among us, and magic is real. Brigitta and her friends from yesterday are witches. They are part of a Coven that forces other witches to join them."

"Like the woman with her hands tied," he interjected. "Helena?"

Leoma nodded. "Helena is like the woman who found me on the streets and took me in. Edra is also a witch who refused to join the Coven. She and her husband, Sir Radnar, created their own coven—a Hunter's Coven—to stand against evil witches."

"You hunt witches? Yet you were raised by one?"

"You misunderstand," Leoma replied. "We Hunters are after those of the Coven. Witches like Helena, we leave alone."

He tried to remain calm at the easy talk about witches. Then again, he had experienced several things the previous day that he couldn't wrap his head around no matter how hard he tried.

Leoma's lips twisted. "By this time, most people are telling me I've gone daft."

"Aye," he murmured and rubbed his hand over his chin, feeling the stubble. He was in need of a shave. "Your words are difficult to believe."

"But you saw for yourself."

He couldn't disregard that fact. "Brigitta being a witch is why you tried to stop me from finding her?"

"It is."

His gaze lowered to the ground while his mind went back over his encounter with Brigitta. As soon as he recalled thrusting his sword into her back, he also remembered how she hadn't died.

Braith's gaze jerked to Leoma. "Brigitta should be dead. My sword went through her."

Resignation filled Leoma's face. "The witches' power makes them very difficult to kill. No matter how many times you struck her with your sword, she would not have died."

"You killed a witch. I saw it."

Leoma's hand went to the weapon lying on the ground beside her. "My sword was specially made for me. When the steel was forged, Edra added magic to it. Every Hunter has weapons with magic to kill witches."

"I want one of those."

Her answering smile made his stomach flutter. "Knowing Radnar, he would happily give you such a blade."

"You were raised to hunt witches?" he asked, still unable to fathom such a life. Then again, how different was it from his? He had been raised for battle, as well.

Both of them were trained to kill.

"It was my decision to become a Hunter," she replied.

"Can you do magic, then? You said it was magic that healed me."

Her eyes crinkled with her wide smile. "Nay, I've no power. It was Edra's magic mixed with the herbs. Had I not administered them, Brigitta could've used your wounds to track you. She wants you for something, and anything the Coven wants, we make sure they don't get."

"The pain of those wounds was...terrible."

"They could've killed you if left untreated."

He swallowed and gave a bow of his head. "Thank you for

helping me. Even if it was to keep me out of Brigitta's and the Coven's hands."

Leoma glanced at the ground and rotated what was left of the bread in her hand. "I'm sorry she hurt someone you loved. Josef?"

"My ward and heir," he replied. "I swore to get retribution for what she did. I'd set aside battle. Had intended to go to bed each night washing off dirt, not blood. Yet, she changed all that by killing Josef."

"To get you to chase after her."

He frowned as he realized Brigitta had said exactly that. His mind was still processing what had happened, the reality of it difficult to grasp through the haze of pain he'd been under. "That doesn't make sense. She could've killed me then. Or taken me, even."

"Whatever she wants you for, you cannot fall into the Coven's hands."

"Aye. I've no wish to help them, even before I knew who they were."

Leoma reached for her waterskin and drank before leaning forward to hand it to him. "This is my first time hunting alone. I'm after Brigitta for killing my best friend. Meg wasn't a Hunter. She chose another path at the abbey. She often came with me on my missions, though, more as an excuse to see some of the world than anything else."

"Did she know how to defend herself, at least?" Braith asked.

"Aye. Radnar wouldn't have allowed her to come other-wise. We came across Brigitta and another witch. I went one way, while Ravyn, another Hunter, went another. The attack was unplanned, but we saw that the witches were targeting children, so we had no choice but to intervene right then. I told Meg to go left and said I would go right to corner one of the witches. Except when I found Meg, Brigitta was standing over her. She had beheaded my best friend."

Braith knew all about guilt, and Leoma carried plenty of it. "It wasn't your fault."

"It was. Had I not made Meg separate from me, she would still be alive. She didn't want to go alone."

"You can second-guess yourself for the rest of your life, but you will never know what might have happened had the two of you remained together. You both might be dead."

Leoma nodded as she looked at the bread. "Radnar said the same thing. I thought he might stop me from hunting Brigitta, but he didn't."

"Anyone who has fought in battle has lost someone as you have. We all carry and feel the weight of regret and sorrow. As well as the need for revenge."

"It looks like we have the same goals when it comes to Brigitta," Leoma said.

Braith grinned at the thought of fighting side by side with her. "Shall we band together then?"

"Aye."

7

London

F ear. Its claws were sunk deep into Brigitta, making her heart thump in dread and turning her blood to ice.

Yet she kept it all locked behind a mask she'd perfected years ago. She stared out the second-story window of the house, her gaze drawn to the Thames and the ships arriving.

Behind her, a door opened. Brigitta steeled herself and turned to face her mentor. Eleanor's steely gray eyes held no warmth. Her long, narrow face was set in a relentless frown of disappointment.

The only time Brigitta had ever seen Eleanor's thin lips curve into what passed for a grin was when Brigitta was a young girl and some witches trapped Edra. Somehow, Edra had won against three witches that day. And Eleanor's wrath was catastrophic.

"You're alone."

Two words. That's all Eleanor said. But in them, Brigitta heard displeasure, irritation, and anger. Though she was ready to tell her side of the story, Brigitta had learned not to speak until Eleanor gave her leave.

As one of the Coven's council of elders, Eleanor chose to be stationed in London to keep an eye on the royals and anyone who arrived in the city. That meant Eleanor was invited to all the parties and social events others yearned to attend. With the elder's husband—a duke—she easily walked in the upper circles of society.

Brigitta watched as Eleanor ran her hand down her red silk gown, the sunlight coming through the windows glinting off the large ruby on her finger.

Eleanor's lips pinched in a sneer. Whatever beauty she'd held while younger fled long ago. She had the superior attitude of most of the nobility, and she wasn't afraid to let it show.

"Where is Helena? More importantly, where is Braith?" Eleanor demanded.

Still, Brigitta waited to speak. It didn't matter that her mentor posed questions. To try and reply now would mean getting struck with a rather nasty dose of magic. That had only happened once. Brigitta learned quickly to wait.

Eleanor glared at her for a long moment before she tilted her head of gray hair. "Speak."

In some ways, Brigitta would have rather remained silent. No matter what she said, there would be reprisal. Since Eleanor appeared to be in a particularly nasty mood, Brigitta would likely feel the pain of her punishment for a long time.

She took a deep breath and said, "Braith followed me just as I knew he would. I lured him into the Witch's Grove as we planned. It took him longer than expected, so he was there when Janet and Mary arrived with Helena."

"And that matters to me, why?" Eleanor demanded.

"He was not alone."

Eleanor clasped her hands before her and sighed loudly. "So?"

"It was a Hunter."

The slight tremble in Eleanor's hands was unmistakable, even if she did quickly move them behind her. Brigitta knew the Hunters were becoming a nuisance, but now she wondered just how much they had interfered with the Coven's plans.

"How did the Hunters find Braith?" Eleanor asked.

Though Brigitta was loath to correct her, she had no choice. "Hunter. Just one. And I don't know."

"One Hunter?" Eleanor asked with her lips peeled back in revulsion. "You allowed a single Hunter to get the best of you?"

"You forget, Helena was among us. The Hunter freed her, and they quickly dispatched Janet and Mary. The female Hunter was quick and very good. I wasn't able to get to Braith. I chose to return and give my report, knowing that I could find Braith again since I wounded him."

"You saved your own arse, is what you did," Eleanor stated harshly.

Brigitta didn't deny it. She didn't want to die, and between the Hunter and Helena, the possibility had been real. She'd feared for her life for the first time since she discovered her magic.

"Are we to guess that Helena is with the Hunter now?"

Brigitta refused to fidget beneath her mentor's rigid gaze. "I cannot say one way or the other."

"You should be happy you have reached the third level and have become an important part of the Coven. Otherwise, I'd kill you on the spot."

Brigitta didn't fear that threat. The Coven needed witches. At one time, a witch would have been struck down painfully for such a failure, no matter where they were in the hierarchy.

Now, with the elders having their sights set on such a grand plan, it was more important to have the numbers than to reprimand someone.

"However," Eleanor continued, pausing a moment. "You won't get by completely unscathed."

Brigitta steeled herself, preparing for whatever pain Eleanor wished to inflict. It was the sudden look of delight that narrowed Eleanor's eyes that made Brigitta tremble in trepidation.

"Ready yourself. My husband will be home soon. He's been asking for you since your last punishment."

Brigitta wanted to scream, to hurl insults and magic at Eleanor. She could handle anything but having to service Walter. He was a disgusting individual whose breath smelled as foul as his body.

"What are you waiting for?" Eleanor demanded.

Brigitta kept her head high as she walked past Eleanor. All the while, she planned how she intended to find Braith and the Hunter. Before she brought the earl to Eleanor, Brigitta planned to inflict every spell she knew on the Hunter, killing her slowly.

Eleanor waited until Brigitta ascended the stairs to the third floor of bedrooms, then she made her way back into the chamber she used for her magic.

She walked to a small, round table with a black bowl in the middle. The water lay still as glass within. She put her fore-finger in the water and moved it in a circle three times to call to the other elders.

As the ripples raced across the surface, she said, "Sisters, I have news. Unfortunately, Brigitta failed. Braith is not in my possession, and neither is Helena. She fought against our witches, so I suppose we know where we stand with her."

The water stilled, only to ripple from the middle out as the voice of Catherine came through the water. "Shall I send someone?"

"I promised to bring Braith in, and I shall do it," Eleanor announced. Even if she had to go find him herself.

No sooner had the water stilled than Eleanor heard Matilda. "We must have Braith. There is no other option. Without him, we've failed."

Eleanor gripped the edge of the table tightly. "When have I ever let any of you down?"

"Never," Angmar replied. "You have a second chance, Eleanor. Do not fail us."

Eleanor put her hands on the bowl to halt the water, ending the communication. Spinning around, she paced the length of the room as her mind raced with thoughts.

Her feet halted when she heard the stairs creak under the weight of her portly husband as he made his way up to his chamber. She could've used her magic to make herself beautiful and secure a handsome husband. She could've used her powers to make herself young and vibrant.

Instead, she used them to advance her husband in order to secure herself. But that only took a small portion of her magic. The rest she used for the Coven because they were after something much more than youth. They were after the means to pull the magic from any witch who wasn't part of the Coven.

Only those within the Coven would be allowed to pass magic on to their offspring. No one else would ever have abilities. It would ensure that the Coven became untouchable. Their power and might would be widespread.

And absolute.

But first, they needed Braith.

Eleanor was furious that the earl had gotten away from Brigitta. How had he come to know a Hunter? Brigitta had spent weeks studying Braith and his ward, Josef. She'd never mentioned any sign of Hunters.

Since Eleanor didn't believe in coincidences, she wanted to find the explanation for how Braith and this Hunter came to travel together. The sooner the Coven got him away from the Hunters, the better.

The Hunters had become increasingly problematic. If only the council could find out who was training them and how they were getting their weapons. If the Coven could discover what witches were helping them, then they could eradicate the rebellious idiots.

If the witches didn't have to worry about the Hunters, then they could succeed in their plan sooner rather than later. As it was, the infernal Hunters were sticking their noses where they didn't belong.

Eleanor waited until she heard the light steps of Brigitta coming down the stairs. Eleanor waved her hand, the magic opening the door. Brigitta paused and looked inside the room.

Eleanor motioned the witch inside. "I take it my husband is satisfied."

"Completely," Brigitta replied, stony-faced.

"Good. Now, tell me, how do you feel about finding the Hunter who caused you to fail in your mission?"

Brigitta's blue eyes lit with rage and retribution. "I was going to ask if I could go after her."

"If she and Braith are together, which I believe they are, you should be able to get both of them."

"I'll be sure to make the Hunter suffer."

Eleanor lifted a hand to halt Brigitta from turning away. "The Hunter will be brought to me. I've questions for her. And she *will* give them."

"Then I can kill her?"

"I doubt she will survive my interrogation, but if she does, the Hunter is all yours."

Brigitta's nostrils flared as she gave a curt nod. "Then I hope she withstands your torture."

"Find them. Quickly."

Brigitta nodded and turned on her heel to walk out. Eleanor followed her out of the chamber and watched the young witch descend the stairs.

"How bad is it?" Walter asked behind her.

She turned her head to look at the top of the landing. "Bad. She lost Braith and another witch."

"There's more."

"A Hunter."

Walter grunted as he moved his bulk and leaned a shoulder against the wall. "They're becoming a problem."

"You don't need to tell me what I already know."

"Then do something about it."

She glared at him. While some witches chose to keep their husbands out of their business, she had recognized Walter's shrewd, clever mind that made up for his lack of decent features.

"I intend just that. And I'm going to find out who is in charge of these Hunters."

He smiled at her, one side of his large jowls moving with his mouth. "I adore your ruthlessness, my dear."

"Because it exceeds your own?" she asked with a quirked brow.

Walter chuckled. "Exactly. Together, no one will ever get the upper hand. My family clawed our way to our dukedom. But I've my eye on the crown."

"All in good time. I'm going to keep tabs on Brigitta."

"Let me come with you. We do this together."

She stared at him, debating whether to leave him behind, but he did have his uses. "Be ready to travel. Once she finds Braith and this Hunter, I intend to bring them in myself."

"You no longer trust Brigitta?"

"The Hunter got the upper hand. Granted, Helena helped, but it was still three of our witches against them."

Walter pushed away from the wall. "I'll have the servants start packing for us immediately."

Eleanor rubbed her hands together. The Coven was so close to getting what they wanted that she could practically taste it.

8

Teaming up with the knight had never been in Leoma's plans. Then again, she knew the best way to defeat an enemy was to adjust course whenever necessary.

And having Braith fight with her was the best decision.

At least she could keep an eye on him instead of trying to fight him as well as Brigitta. Now that he knew what he would be going up against, she suspected Braith could be a good ally.

She finished her bread as she observed him. While it wasn't her first time seeing a man's bare chest since she trained with males at the abbey, this was different.

Braith was different.

No matter how much she tried to tell herself that he was only a man, just like Radnar or any of the others at the abbey, he wasn't.

Braith might look at the world like a knight at home in battle. But he also carried himself like a man who looked death in the eye. Then spat at it.

Those qualities appealed to her on a primal level. He caused her heart to thump wildly, and her blood to rush through her. She was drawn to him. Without rhyme or reason, she could feel herself gravitating toward him.

She was shocked and alarmed at the way her body reacted to him. But even she couldn't deny the exhilaration that being near him brought.

The glimpse she had of his chest made her recall how she had spread his ruined tunic to get a better look at him earlier. Even now, she wished to see the rest of him.

Her mouth went dry when his indigo eyes met hers after he inspected his hand once more. It took her two attempts to swallow. She wished she knew what he was thinking.

His chest expanded as he drew in a deep breath and released it. "What's our next move?"

"We wait."

"Wait?" A dark brow shot up in question.

She couldn't help but grin. Of course, he wouldn't agree. She expected as much, and she knew it wouldn't be the last time. "Aye."

"Why?"

"The main reason is that we know Brigitta wants you for something."

Braith crossed his arms over his chest, his lips flattening in displeasure. "I'm bait."

"Is that a problem?"

"Nay," he said tightly. Then he asked, "And the other reason?"

Leoma looked in the direction of the Witch's Grove. "I've seen witches do many things with magic, but I've never seen one use it to disappear."

"That was...shocking."

"She could've gone anywhere." And that bothered Leoma greatly. She slid her gaze back to Braith. "We have no way of tracking her."

He lifted a shoulder. "Consider me bait, then."

They shared a grin. She hadn't expected him to be so accommodating. Most men were used to being in control. The idea of a woman running things generally went against everything a man knew. Especially men like Braith.

Then again, maybe he was smart enough to know that if he wanted to stay out of the Coven's hands, he needed her. Or they needed each other since he had no experience with witches.

Leoma wasn't sure what to make of the emotions that swirled seductively within her. Having his eyes on her did strange and amazing things. Heat and...need glided through her. Slowly. Seductively.

"Tell me I don't have to return to that place again," Braith said. "What did you call it? A Witch's Grove."

His question made her inwardly shake herself to pull out of the desire consuming her. "Aye. They're not numerous, thankfully. But the larger the Coven grows, the more Groves appear. I don't like those places, so I won't be going back unless I have to."

He nodded slowly. "That's reassuring."

"How did you feel when you came upon it?"

His forehead furrowed, and his gaze narrowed as he looked at the ground. "I saw where you had stood. It wasn't until I looked up and realized how close the trees were that I recoiled. The next thing I noticed was how dark it appeared."

"You sensed the evil."

His gaze returned to her. "Aye."

"And still you walked inside."

He dropped his arms and stretched his legs out before him. Then he shifted to the side and braced himself on one elbow. "I knew if I followed your trail that you would lead me to Brigitta. And *you* went into that place. Evil or not, I had no other choice."

"There are few who would have dared as you did."

"I've nothing to live for now that Josef is gone."

She heard the truth of his words, and it made her sad. "What about your land?"

"We both know there is little hope of me surviving an encounter with the Coven. Tell me about the mist in the Grove. And what were those tree creatures?"

Leoma wasn't surprised that he changed the subject. There was too much hurt within him to think of the future. Brigitta was his enemy, and focusing on her gave him a way to shift his anger so he felt as if he were doing something.

"The tree creatures are Gira. They can be found anywhere, but they prefer a Witch's Grove."

His brows shot up. "You mean a Gira could be on my land?"

"It's unlikely, but aye. They gravitate to magic. If you find one outside of a Grove, there will be others. They travel in small packs. You're right to be wary of them. The whispers you heard in the Grove? That was them."

"I couldn't understand them."

She twisted her lips. "That's the point. They lure people in with those whispers."

"And what do they do to them?" he asked with a frown.

"The Gira push them against the tree, and the tree wraps around them so the Gira can use the person however they want."

"Are the Gira all female?"

Leoma nodded. "They have also been known to go after someone if they want them badly enough."

"I knew I felt someone behind us when we were leaving the Grove."

"That could've been the Gira, but I think it might have been something else."

His eyes widened. "Something else? What else was in there?"

"Many things you didn't see or hear. Witch's Groves call to beings with magic. The mist is controlled by witches, but I also think it is a living, breathing thing."

"How do you fight mist?"

She understood the mix of horror and doubt he was experiencing. "You really cannot."

"That does nothing to calm my growing anxiety."

"I'm giving you just the basics. There are so many things out in the world that you know nothing about. The Coven, however, should be your main concern. They're the ones changing things. Do you know why they would want you?"

He sat up and raked a hand through his long hair. "I've no idea."

"We need to figure that out to counter whatever they have planned."

"You make it sound so simple."

"It won't be."

He climbed to his feet and looked down at her with his fathomless eyes. "Thank you for saving me. And for sharing this information."

"I expected you to balk at the idea of a woman aiding you in any way."

He looked up, his eyes moving about the trees. "Aye, I've known men like that. But I've also been in battles where it wasn't another knight who helped me, but a squire. I even had a horse pull me from a pile of dead atop me. But the one instance I'll never forget was when the army I served with was overrun. We were surrounded. I took an arrow to the shoulder, and my horse was killed. I wasn't able to get free, so he fell with my leg trapped beneath him. Once again, I had been left for dead. After the battle was over, a group of women from the enemy camp found me. They freed me from the horse and also removed the arrow before patching me up and helping me get back to my men."

Leoma listened raptly. She wondered just how many times Braith had come close to dying.

His head swung her way. "The point I'm trying to make is that I've learned not to look down on anyone who gives me aid, regardless of their gender or where they are from."

"I wish more men thought like you."

"We're delicate creatures, didn't you know?" he said with a slight grin. "We have to believe we are strong and capable at all times lest the fairer sex realize they don't need us."

The longer she talked to Braith, the more she found she liked him.

He nodded at the hill. "My belly is still craving sustenance. I'm going to go out and see what I can find for us to eat."

Leoma waited until he walked away before she got to her feet and stretched her back. She patted the stallion and made her way to the stream.

There, she removed her clothes and took out a small cream, oval object. She held the soap in hand as she stepped into the icy water. Leoma longed for a hot bath that she could soak in at her leisure. Though that was unlikely to happen anytime soon, so she would have to make do with what she had.

She moved out into the middle of the brook and discovered that the water only reached her knees at the deepest part. Lowering herself down between the rocks, she let the water rush around and over her as she unbraided her hair.

Then she leaned back until she was semi-floating. She remained that way for several minutes until the cold became too much. Then she lathered the soap and washed her hair and body twice before rinsing off.

Finally, she stood and walked from the stream. She wrung out her hair and let the sun and air dry her as she sat naked on a rock and finger-combed her locks.

Her thoughts turned to Braith, but she wasn't surprised. The man intrigued her. He was at once stubborn and amenable. He appeared unrelenting, yet she was discovering that while he stood as strong as an oak, he could bend when needed.

With her hair combed, she dressed and returned to camp by another direction to see if she could find any indication of witches. She wished she had magic to put up wards so they'd be alerted if a witch was close, but all she could do was stay vigilant.

Leoma gathered some wood and started a fire. It wasn't long after that Braith returned with a pheasant dangling from his hand.

"There is little game in these woods," he grumbled.

She jerked her chin toward the Witch's Grove. "We're still too close. The farther out you go from the Grove, the more normal things will get. This was as far as I could drag you, and the location seemed suitable for us to hide."

"It is. Though we could return to the cave." He glanced at the sky. "At least we'd be dry while we wait for the witches."

"It's also much farther from the Grove, which I like."

He gave a nod. "Then it's settled. We'll head that way after we eat."

Leoma held out her hand. "Give me the bird. I'll get it ready to cook. There's a stream to the east if you want to take advantage."

"Aye," he replied.

She took the pheasant and moved away from the fire to

pluck the dead bird. A glance showed Braith rummaging through a bag on his saddle before he headed off toward the water.

In no time, the bird was cooking on a spit over the fire. Her mouth watered at the thought of the meat. She was starving, but she was used to eating very little when she was on a hunt. The food she had brought with her lasted longer than expected, and she got more whenever she was in a village.

But to have a warm meal was something she hadn't had in a few months.

Her head snapped up when she heard someone approach. Braith's hair hung wet about his face as he strolled into camp with a new tunic on that stuck to his damp skin and outlined his wide shoulders and muscular chest.

It was almost impossible to tear her gaze from him.

9

Braith dropped his jerkin on the ground at his feet and squatted near the fire. He looked across the flames to Leoma, desire tightening his gut. Her dark eyes studied him. He could see her mind working, and he wished he could discern what she was thinking.

He took a long stick and stirred the fire before turning the pheasant over. "About this abbey you speak of, do you have a man waiting for you there?"

"If you had a woman who hunted, would you let her go alone?"

"Never," he stated.

She raised a brow in reply. "Since you've said you don't care about your lands or home, I take that to mean you don't have a wife."

"All I know is battle," he said. "My life is too rough for women."

"For *some* women," she corrected.

He grinned at her. "There are few like you."

"I'm not talking about Hunters like me. While I admit,

there are some women who faint at anything, for the most part, we females are sturdy. We do bring life into the world."

"Perhaps I've not found a woman who fit into my life. Though, I wasn't looking for one either. I knew too many of my friends who married and then left for years at a time while off at war. I didn't want my focus split."

Leoma braced her hands behind her as she leaned back. "That makes sense. I tried to tell Meg something similar, but she kept insisting I should find someone."

"Did your friend have someone?"

Leoma's lips curved into a smile as she gazed at the flames. "She fancied someone at the abbey, though she wouldn't let him know. Or allow me to tell him." Leoma's eyes lifted to Braith. "Meg would've liked you. She had a way with people. She could get a sense of them quickly, sometimes without even having a conversation."

"What do you think she would've said about me?" he asked curiously.

"That you were strong, determined, and honest. And that I should trust you."

Her words affected him deeply. With the red-orange glow of the flames rippling over her face, he found himself sinking in to her eyes.

"Do you?" he asked, needing to know. "Do you trust me?"

Her voice was barely a whisper as she replied, "Aye."

This woman affected him on a primal level. He recognized her strength and her cunning. Her beauty was just an added bonus. But all of it made him burn with need. It was fiery and brilliant.

And felt damn good.

He fought with every fiber of his being to keep from going to her and taking her face in his hands so he could feel her skin beneath his palms. But that wasn't all he yearned for. No, he hungered to plunder her lips, to taste her on his tongue so she would forever be part of him.

But he couldn't do any of that. Couldn't...and wouldn't. They were partners with a common enemy. To give her any indication that he physically craved her touch would destroy what they had tentatively built between them.

The fact was, he needed her to help him navigate all the beings and magic he was learning. Not to mention, the witches. Maybe if they both survived, then he would think about kissing her. It would give him something to look forward to.

If he didn't want to make a complete fool of himself now, he needed to turn his mind to other things. He looked at the roasting pheasant.

"It's done," she said.

It was her husky tone that had his gaze jerking to her. Except she had turned her head away so he couldn't see her face. Perhaps that was for the best, because if he saw even a hint of interest on her part, he would go to her.

Without a word, he took the bird from the fire and drew his knife to begin slicing the meat. When he handed her the blade, their fingers touched. He saw her hand tremble in response.

He studied her face, but she kept it averted as if she knew he observed her. What was she hiding? What was it that she didn't want him to see?

Excitement stirred his blood at the thought that she felt the same attraction he did, suffered the same longing.

Bore the same hunger.

They ate in silence, and it wasn't long before they picked the bird clean. When he caught sight of her licking her fingers, his balls tightened with a need that surged almost painfully through him.

"It'll be dark soon," she replied and got to her feet. "We should relocate."

He rose quickly and moved to stand before her, so she had no choice but to face him. "Look at me," he urged.

She kept her eyes down. "Why?"

"Why not?"

Silent moments passed before she lifted her face and raised her gaze. The moment he stared into her eyes, the passion reflected in her dark orbs made his knees weak.

He was so shocked that all he could think about was closing the few inches that separated them. Braith tried to remember the last time he had touched a woman other than a barmaid.

At the snapping of a branch, they both swiveled toward the sound. Even his stallion was staring off in that direction. Every instinct within Braith told him that danger was upon them. He grabbed his sword, saddle, and bag while Leoma put out the fire and got her weapon.

"We need to go. Now," Leoma whispered.

He gave a soft whistle to the horse, who trotted off. Then he and Leoma began to slowly back up the slope of the hill. They stayed low, using cover as much as they could.

No sooner had they reached the top than he looked down to find Brigitta strolling into their camp and stopping next to the extinguished fire.

"Go," Leoma whispered and pushed him away.

He reluctantly moved, still in a crouch until they were far enough away to stand upright. Leoma kept up with him as they ran through the forest. Every once in a while, they looked back to see if the witch followed.

"Why didn't we fight her?" he asked when they paused next to a giant oak.

Leoma cut her eyes to him. "We want her to think we're

afraid of her. She'll get overconfident and not be prepared for what I have planned."

"And you decided not to share this plan with me?" he questioned. "We are partners."

Her chest heaved from their run. She licked her lips, her gaze on the trees behind them. "I did tell you. You're the bait, remember?"

He ground his teeth together as she pushed away from the tree and started running again. Braith was quick to follow, but they didn't get very far before Brigitta appeared before them, her blue eyes filled with fury.

Leoma tried to stop but slid on the thick carpet of leaves on the ground. Still, the Hunter managed to free her sword by the time she got to her feet.

Braith halted and slowly lowered his saddle to the ground. He kept his gaze on the witch. She glanced his way, but her attention was directed at Leoma.

"You made a mistake, Hunter," Brigitta said. "The Coven wants to have a word with you. Once the council is finished with you, the real fun will begin when they hand you over to me."

"My knees are knocking in terror," Leoma quipped.

He grinned despite the situation. Few, no matter their training, would've stood against someone like Brigitta with as much pluck and courage as Leoma. And it made him crave her all the more.

Leoma looked around. "You came alone? For both of us?"

Brigitta cocked her head to the side. "Are you trying to rile me? It won't work. All I have to do is knock your sword away, and you'll both be at my mercy."

Braith pulled his blade from its sheath. He was the bait, after all. "I will not come easily."

"I'm not going to give you a choice," Brigitta said, then turned her head to him.

He looked at Leoma, who met his gaze. With a slight nod of agreement, they attacked the witch simultaneously. Brigitta was so worried about Leoma's blade that she left herself exposed, which allowed Braith to sink his sword into her side.

Brigitta screamed in fury and swung her arm to him.

"Duck!" Leoma bellowed.

Braith dropped to his knees and shoved his weapon further into Brigitta. He yanked his sword free and swung it with all of his might at her leg. Just as he was about to chop it off, the witch said something. Suddenly, his blade went flying from his grip, even as his body turned with the momentum of the swing.

He landed on his back and rolled to come to his feet. Leoma moved closer to him and thrust a dagger into his hand. No longer weaponless, Braith attacked again, with Leoma coming at Brigitta from the other side.

The witch was quickly losing the battle. Braith knew his opponent's defeat when he saw it. He inwardly smiled and renewed his assault.

With his first cut weakening her, she was using all of her skills to keep Leoma's sword from making contact as her skirts and cloak tangled about her legs. All the while, she had no idea that the dagger in his hand was one of Leoma's.

Every time he made a cut, Brigitta weakened more. It was when smoke began to waft from the wounds that Leoma shoved the witch to the ground. They stood over Brigitta while the lifeblood drained from her.

"The Coven will fail," Leoma said.

Braith knelt beside the witch and held the dagger over her. "This is for Josef and Meg and all the other innocents you've killed," he said before plunging the blade into her heart.

Brigitta gasped, and the light faded from her eyes. Braith yanked the dagger free and stood as her body began to burn.

"Well, that wasn't really my plan," Leoma said with a smile.

He looked at her, grinning. "We survived."

"This day. They won't stop coming for you," she warned.

Braith realized her words were correct, and it left an unsettled feeling within him. Damn. Just when he thought he was free of the witch. "Then we rest tonight. I think I'd like to visit the abbey and learn more. I want to be prepared for when they do come for me."

"That's a good idea."

He frowned when Leoma swayed slightly. Then he noticed that her face looked pale. And sweaty.

In two steps, Braith was before her, catching her in his arms as she fell sideways. "Where are you hurt?"

"I thought I evaded her nails," Leoma said.

"Tell me what to do."

She nodded.

Braith gathered her in his arms and hurried toward the cave. He could return later for everything else. First, he had to get Leoma healed.

Her eyes were closed by the time he reached the cave. After gently lowering her down, he patted her cheeks to wake her. "Open your eyes, Leoma. You need to tell me what to do to heal you. Look at me."

Braith removed her cloak and searched for the wound. He found it on her right side near her stomach. Blood flowed through the thin gash.

"Leoma, wake up!"

Her eyelids fluttered a few times until she lifted her lids to look at him.

"What do I do?" he asked.

"Pouch."

He looked around. "Where?"

"On. Me."

He found the purse attached to her hip and opened it. A smile was on his lips when he located the pouch. "I've got it."

But when he opened it to pour the herbs, nothing came out.

He tossed it aside and cupped her face in his hands, feeling her damp skin on his palms. "It's gone."

"I know," she murmured, her eyes drifting closed.

So she knew she was going to die? No. He wouldn't let her go out this way. "Nay. You need to fight this. Fight!"

"Keep...the...wound...."

He waited, hoping she would finish. "Aye? Keep the wound, what? Tell me."

But there would be no answer because she lost consciousness.

10

Helplessness. The emotion twisted and coiled through Braith until he wanted to bellow in frustration. While Leoma's wound didn't seem to be serious, he knew what it felt like to have a witch's lethal magic within him.

He left Leoma long enough to return for his saddle, bridle, sword, and bag. Then he tore a strip from his damaged tunic. She had wiped him down, and he would do the same for her.

His fingers fumbled and refused to work properly as he attempted to remove her cloak. Finally, he got it off. Next, he worked on the four buckles of her black leather vest. He tenderly lifted her upper body and removed the item.

Moving as quickly as he could, he took off her gauntlets, briefly looking at the Celtic knotwork carved into the leather with meticulous precision. His fingers slipped beneath the hem of the black tunic that curved along her body, showing off her shapely figure.

He pushed the cloth upwards to reveal her stomach. It was the dark ink he saw on her left side that caught his attention. He followed the delicate curving design that also had knotwork from her waist and moved upward to disappear onto her back.

While Braith knew some women got tattoos, he was surprised to see Leoma marked in such a way. Surprised and intrigued. No doubt the design meant something, and he was curious to know what it was.

Putting aside those thoughts, he used both hands to maneuver the tunic over the swell of her breasts. He allowed himself a brief peek at the pert globes with dusky pink nipples before yanking his gaze away.

Once her tunic was off, he laid her back and stared in awe. The slice from Brigitta's nail wasn't Leoma's first wound. She had various scars over her upper body, some large, some small.

Yet, once again, it was the sight of her tattoos that made him speechless. On her right inside wrist was a Celtic design that looked like a fingernail moon. The ink on the inside of her left forearm looked fairly new.

While Braith didn't know what it was, it had a Norse feel to it with the runes, but it was the eight points of the design that made him think of a compass. When he flipped over her left hand, he was shocked to see an image of a snake eating its tail atop her wrist. His gaze moved on to Leoma's right side where two birds were beak to beak, their feathers transforming into more knotwork that moved to their intertwined tails.

He lifted his eyes to her face. "You're not going to die. There's no way you'll allow Brigitta to end you with one small swipe of her nails. You're going to fight, Leoma. Do you hear me? Fight."

Braith sat back on his haunches and stared at the injury. Leoma's skin glistened with sweat as her body shook almost as if she had a fever. Did he bind up the wound to stop the flow of blood? Or did he allow it to continue to seep out? If he made the wrong choice, he could hasten her death.

With a loud sigh, he covered her breasts with what was left of his ruined shirt. Then he soaked a strip of the tunic with water and began wiping her down again and again.

The sun sank into the horizon, taking away his light. He paused in tending to Leoma long enough to build a fire so he could see. Then he was back to wiping her down.

Hours drifted by with no change. Braith had no idea if she was getting better or worse. It made him second-guess every decision he made in regards to taking care of the wound.

When he ran out of water and had to search out the stream, he returned to the cave to find his stallion there. He gave the animal a pat and continued in to Leoma. If he knew the location of the abbey, he would take her there so someone could help her. He couldn't believe she had used all of her herbs on him.

He didn't think things could get any worse, but he should've known better. Leoma's body cooled, and she lay still, but she didn't wake.

"You have witches to hunt. The Coven has plans, remember?" he said, needing something to break the silence other than the pop of the wood as it burned. "I'll be happy to fight the Coven on my own and take all the credit, but you should be there."

He threaded his fingers through her hair, letting the strands glide along his palm. He should've kissed her when he had the chance. There were so many regrets in his life, and not kissing Leoma was close to the top.

Such thoughts did him no good. Braith untangled his fingers from the dark mahogany strands and checked her wound. Blood no longer seeped from the injury. Now, a milky substance tinted a sickly yellow trickled out.

Braith ran a hand down his face, despair riding him hard. He pushed it away and began to tenderly wipe away any of the liquid that showed. He then dribbled water into the wound in an attempt to flush out the poison of the magic.

He had no idea how much time passed before the injury stopped producing the cloudy fluid. There was a smile on his lips when he lay down beside Leoma. He'd give himself a moment to rest.

—————

Leoma opened her eyes to the dark rock of the cave ceiling. Fatigue pulled at her limbs—after effects of the witch's poison. It would be another day before it was completely out of her system.

She turned her head to the side and smiled when she spotted Braith with a cloth clutched in the hand that was thrown over his stomach. His other hand rested atop hers.

Though she had gazed at him while he was ill, she found she quite enjoyed looking at him. His whiskers were forming a beard, not that she minded. He was one of those rare men who looked good with or without facial hair.

His chest expanded as he drew in a deep breath. His lids opened, his fingers tightening around hers. She waited for his head to turn to her, and when he finally did, his deep blue eyes widened.

She turned her hand over to interlock their fingers. "I heard your voice telling me to fight. Every time I thought the magic was taking me, your words broke through and pulled me back."

He turned onto his side, propping himself up on his elbow, but never letting go of her hand. "You passed out before you told me what to do with the wound. I took a guess and left it open."

"I'm glad."

"Why did you use all the herbs on me? Why not save some for yourself?"

She rolled toward him. "The magic Brigitta poured into you was severe. It was taking the herbs a long time to work, so I went to add more to your palm. Only you knocked the pouch from my hand. Unfortunately, they spilled."

"Then you need to return to the abbey for more. We can't chance going up against the witches without it."

"I wish we had time to do that, but we don't."

His brows snapped together. "We killed Brigitta."

"She is just one within the Coven. No doubt someone from the council sent her."

"Which means when she doesn't return, they will send more witches," Braith said and rolled to his back.

Leoma sat up, holding the cloth at her breast. She quite liked having his hand with hers. "The Coven doesn't know where the abbey is, and it needs to stay that way. I can't take the chance of returning for more herbs and end up leading the Coven right to the Hunters' door."

His indigo eyes met hers.

"They can defend themselves," she said before he could ask the question. "But the abbey is a sanctuary. Edra and Radnar know that one day the battle might come to them. They've made provisions for that, but there aren't enough witches willing to stand against the Coven yet."

He nodded and sat up to face her, their hands between them. "You don't need to explain further. I understand. I just don't think I can see you suffer again as you did last night."

"If the wound Brigitta inflicted had been more serious, I'm not sure I would've made it."

One side of his lips lifted in a grin. "You're a fighter. You won't go easily."

"Neither will you."

His eyes lowered to their hands. She waited for him to pull away, but he didn't. The longer they sat there in silence, touching, the more aware she was of her lack of clothing. She contemplated letting the tunic that she held against her drop.

What would he do?

What would *she* do?

"What happens now?" Braith asked.

She wasn't sure if he was talking about them. Her lack of knowledge when it came to these situations was never more evident.

His gaze met hers. "Do we wait for more witches to find us?"

Leoma was more than a little disappointed that Braith's mind was on their common enemy and not passion. Then again, she should be thankful. If she didn't stop thinking about touching him, kissing him, then she could get them both killed.

"The witches will attack us wherever we are. I tend to stay away from villages if I know there might be a confrontation to make sure that no innocents are caught in the crossfire."

He turned their hands over. "We could keep moving in the forest, but I believe remaining here and preparing would be the better course of action."

"Agreed." She could barely think with the way his other hand moved to cover the back of the one he held. He slid his hand up her arm like a caress.

He glanced out the cave to the new morning. "When should we expect them?"

"Soon. Brigitta was given a second chance to bring us in. She was counting on you being under the effects of magic and only having to fight me," Leoma explained.

"In other words, more witches could show up anytime."

"I'm afraid so."

He frowned while continuing to stroke her wrist. "How do you know who is a witch and who isn't?"

"You have to wait for them to reveal themselves."

"There has to be another way."

She shrugged, shaking her head. "We've yet to find it, but I agree. If we had a way to know who was a witch, then it would save us time waiting to hear about magic being used and then hunting those responsible."

"If your operation expanded to have a Hunter in every large city and a few scattered through England, it would save even more time."

"I've mentioned the same to Edra. The problem is getting enough Hunters and training them properly."

Braith's fingers tightened on her. "You need to grow faster than the Coven."

"They force witches to join. I wanted to tell Helena about us, but she ran off before I could."

"You need people out there looking for witches, willing to stand against the Coven. As well as individuals who will fight for the cause."

She grinned as she stared at him. "You talk like a man used to leading an army."

"An army is exactly what you need," he stated. "I might have begun this journey for revenge, but I've found a cause I can fully support. And one that needs me."

Elation unfurled like the petals of a flower within her. "Aye. We do need you."

They stared at each other for a long moment. Leoma kept wondering what his reaction would be if she leaned up and kissed him. She had never been one to wait around for something to come to her.

But Braith was different. The magnitude of the desire she

felt made her question her thoughts and actions when it came to him.

"Forgive me," Braith said. "I imagine you want to get ready for the day."

She watched as he slowly withdrew his hands. The tips of their fingers were the last things to touch. As soon as he was gone, she missed his warmth, his strength.

She missed him.

11

Walking out of the cave without giving in to the desire to kiss him was one of the hardest things Leoma had ever done. She knew very little about relationships. What she did know, she learned from observing those at the abbey—but from afar.

She knew from the moment Radnar first began training her that she wanted to be a Hunter. At first, he told her it was so she could defend herself against anyone, but it soon became apparent that she had the skills to do everything he asked and more.

Within a few years, more knights came. Each one taught her all they knew, and every time, she hungered for more. It became easy for her to realize that she was meant to be a Hunter.

So while Meg and the others were wooed by suitors, Leoma was happy to continue on the path that had been set before her.

That is, until today.

Her feet felt weighted down in mud as she made her way

to the stream, still holding Braith's tunic against her. If only she knew how to flirt. If only she knew how to be seductive and make a man fall at her feet. If only....

But she had no such ability. So, she would either have to ignore the longing within her or attempt to seduce Braith. The mere thought made her slightly nauseous.

With her tunic, gauntlets, and vest in one hand, she walked to the edge of the creek. She stared at the water that rushed over and around the various rocks for several moments, thinking about Braith touching her.

The longer she stood there, the more irritated at the water she became. She wanted a pool to swim in, to immerse herself fully. To be able to sink beneath the surface and pretend the world she didn't fit into didn't exist.

Leoma turned her head upstream. She touched the sword hanging at her waist before she followed the bank to see if she could find a deeper section.

The brook meandered through the forest, and just as she had hoped, she found a large pool being fed by water coming through a wall of rocks on a hill.

She dropped her clothes and Braith's tunic, unbuckled her sword, and removed her bag, boots, and trousers. Then she walked into the water.

It was deep and dark, but she wasn't afraid. The trees hung over the water, blocking out the sunlight for the moment. Leoma swam out to the middle and treaded water before she took a deep breath and let herself slip beneath.

The soft humming noise as the water filled her ears soothed her. It calmed her mind and allowed her to think more clearly. She stayed under until her lungs began to burn, then she surged upward, gasping for air when she broke the surface.

Her wound pulled slightly, reminding her that she wasn't

fully healed yet. She swam back to the edge and fished out her bar of soap from her bag. After washing off the sweat and magic, Leoma found she wasn't ready to leave.

She dove under again to swim out to the middle and back again. Though she longed for a third run, she was in pain from her wound.

Leoma walked from the water and stood at the edge, then gathered her hair over her shoulder to wring it out. She stilled, her heart dropping to her feet when she heard Braith whisper her name.

She couldn't breathe as he moved up behind her. Chills raced over her damp skin as he ran a finger from the base of her neck to where her tattoo began down her spine, following the intricate design to the top of her bum.

Her hands went numb when his finger slowly traced back up her spine to the swirls that branched off toward her left side. He leisurely, tenderly sketched every swirl, as if putting the design to memory.

"Why have you marked your body so?" he whispered just behind her right ear.

The heat from his body surrounded her like a blanket, cocooning her in erotic thoughts. His hand splayed upon her back as he moved closer.

"Tell me what they mean," he urged in a tight voice, as if he were pained. "I find they...rouse my blood."

Incapable of controlling her body, she leaned back against him. No man had ever seen her body. The only person who'd seen all the tattoos was Asa. Leoma wasn't sure how she felt about Braith seeing her, but she didn't have the desire to cover herself either.

"Tell me," he repeated in a husky whisper.

She was powerless to resist his plea. "I mark my body for

protection, for strength, and to stay on the path I was set on long ago."

He moved his face to her other ear and put his hand on the double raven tattoo on her right side. "Their meaning?"

"I was raised with magic, power that has both Celtic and Norse roots. The raven is important to both cultures."

"The Celts believed ravens were linked to death and darkness, especially for warriors who die in battle."

She turned her head to the side, shocked that he knew that. "Aye. In Norse myths, Odin, the All-Father, uses two ravens for his eyes and ears."

Her stomach quivered when Braith's lips lightly brushed her cheek before he shifted to the other side. He took her right arm in his hand and turned it over to show the Celtic moon tat. "This one?"

"The knotwork fashioned in the shape of a crescent moon denotes femininity, women, growth, and creativity. The Celts prized their goddesses, making them strong and fiercely protective, but also feminine. It's a reminder that I am all of those things."

She felt his gaze on her. He brought his lips to her ear. "Aye. That you are."

Next, his hand touched her right shoulder. No longer did he have to say the words. She knew the tattoos by heart. Not only had she picked them, she had chosen the placement as well.

"Triple horn of Odin," she said. "For Hunters, it symbolizes strength and wisdom."

With a slow, seductive caress, his hand traveled from her back and down her left arm where a snake was eating its tail.

"The Ouroboros. It is one of the oldest symbols on earth. It represents rebirth and transformation. It's also the emblem Edra chose to signify her coven."

He then turned her left hand over and pointed to the Vegvisir on her forearm.

"It's a Norse stave that helps the bearer find their way."

Her eyes slid shut when his hand rested on her left thigh and he tapped a finger, indicating the tat on her calf.

"Shield knot," she whispered, trying not to think of his hand on her leg. "Distinct by the four corners to make a square within a circle. The Celts put them on battle shields to ward off evil."

"Fascinating," he said. He ran his finger along her spine again. "And this one?"

She shivered at his touch, craving more. Her nipples puckered, and her breasts swelled. "It's my journey. The start at my neck and the end—"

"Here," he murmured as he skimmed the backs of his fingers over her bottom.

Leoma nodded, unable to find her voice.

"These?" he asked and once more traced the swirls that started at her spine and curved down over her side, one going all the way to her hip.

It took her two tries before she could speak. "My training. Hunting. And my journey to try and stop the Coven."

"Why no swirls on the right side?"

Her eyes opened to look out over the water. "That side is for family. And love."

When he didn't reply, she wondered if she had been mistaken about the meaning of his interest in her body and her tattoos. Did she know so little of men that while her body had been burning with longing, he felt nothing?

"I've never seen anything more beautiful," Braith whispered.

She was too afraid to move, even to speak. It might shatter whatever was happening.

"I've lived a hard life, Leoma," he said. "I know there are ways I should talk to you, actions I should take to make my interest known, but I know little of those things. Death has come for me many times, and so far, I've eluded him. But he could catch up tomorrow. So I will tell you that I desire you. Greatly," he replied in a hoarse whisper. "I...hunger for a taste of you. If you don't feel the same, then walk away now, and I will never speak of this again."

Leoma straightened, and she heard him sigh in disappointment. She faced him, gazing into his liquid, indigo gaze as the wind ruffled his dark locks. "And if I do feel the same?"

His eyes blazed with desire as his arms came up to rest on her hips. "Then we'll be talking, but with our bodies."

The idea of giving herself to him, of feeling him within her was exhilarating. Her heart thumped so loudly against her ribs, she thought it might burst from her body.

Her gaze dropped to his chest. It didn't bother her that she stood naked while he was still fully clothed. Her hands itched to remove every garment until she could see all of him, every muscle, every scar.

While she knew what happened between a man and a woman, she had never experienced it herself.

"Have you changed your mind?" Braith whispered.

Leoma lifted her gaze to his face. "I've not."

"Your eyes say otherwise."

She should just tell him. The faster she got it out, the quicker they could get past it. "I.... That is to say, I've never lain with a man."

For a moment, Braith merely looked at her. Then his lips curled into a delighted smile. "Fortune smiles upon me then that you would choose me to give your maidenhead to."

"You're...happy about it?"

His fingers tightened on her hips. "Oh, aye. Very much. Why does that surprise you?"

"I heard that men don't like it when women aren't experienced."

"If this is coming from Radnar or those at the abbey, I think I need to have words with them," Braith stated, anger tingeing his words.

She shook her head. "I've heard this a few times in pubs. Radnar and the other men would never speak such a way."

"Then let me dispel any fears you might have. You have a gift, and you get to choose who to give it to."

Without a doubt, she knew she wanted it to go to Braith. No other had ever made her feel so needy. No one had ever made her long for their touch before.

"Then I give it to you," she replied.

He gently placed his hands on either side of her face, his blue eyes burning with undisguised hunger. "I've never been given anything so special before."

Whatever fears she had about being inexperienced fell away at his words. He gazed at her as if she were the most precious thing he had ever beheld.

And through it all was the palpable longing, the profound yearning.

The tangible desire.

Breathing became difficult as a strange, astonishing feeling slid through her veins, heating her from the inside out before curling low in her belly.

Braith's ragged breaths comforted her. His pupils dilated, and his hands shook slightly. She needed to have him against her. It was a demand that roared louder with each second their bodies remained apart.

His head lowered slowly. The closer his face got, the faster her heart pounded. Her lips parted in expectation. When he whispered her name in a voice laden with longing and delight, her eyes fell shut.

The moment his mouth touched hers, her body became liquid. She sank against him. He had one hand tangled in her wet hair, and the other wrapped around her tightly while his lips moved over hers slowly, seductively, teasing and tempting her.

Each kiss lasted longer, sending her already heated body to scorched heights.

Then his tongue skimmed along her lips.

Her taste was sweeter than any wine. And Braith knew that with one sip, he was lost forever.

Leoma kissed as she did everything—wholeheartedly. She didn't pull away when he licked her lips. Instead, she did the same to him.

He had been unable to hold back the groan that rumbled through him the first time their tongues tangled together. The fire that was between them grew quickly and turned into an inferno, scorching everything around them.

Braith flattened his hand on her back, taking in her soft skin beneath his palm. He had looked over her breathtaking body when she stood from the water and had been awed by her.

The story of her tattoos gave him a deeper understanding of her. He found the marks beautiful and alluring, just as she was.

Lust burned through his veins, but he held himself in check. Leoma's first time would be full of pleasure. He would spend however long it took until she was a shivering mess, crying out from her climax. Only then would he allow himself to see to his own gratification.

He jerked back at the unexpected touch of Leoma's hand beneath his tunic. He stared down at her and saw the passion blaze in her dark eyes. It made his knees weak. While he didn't know why she wanted him, he wasn't going to question it.

Never had he disrobed so quickly in his life. As soon as the last garment was tossed aside, he yanked her against him as the water lapped at their feet.

He wanted to keep kissing her, but she had other thoughts. Her hands flattened on his chest and leisurely roamed over his shoulders, arms, and abdomen. She paused when she came to each of his scars.

Then she walked around to stand behind him.

Beautiful. That's what kept running through Leoma's head as she gazed in wonderment at Braith's magnificent body. His muscles were honed to utter perfection. Her favorite part had to be his back with the corded muscles that shifted each time he breathed.

"I could stare at you all day," she said as she let her fingers run over his tight behind.

He whirled around to face her, his face tense with some unnamed emotion that seemed to make his eyes glow brighter. That's when she realized it was her touch that brought him to such a point.

She let her hand run down his side to his trim hips and the slight indent from his muscles there. His arousal, thick and long, jutted between them.

It called to her, urging her to touch it. She kept her gaze on Braith's face as she wrapped her fingers around him. He released a low moan as his eyes closed. Veins protruded from his neck and temples when she slowly ran her hand up and down his hard length.

While she had seen a man's rod before, she had never held one. She looked down at his cock. The hardness was in direct contrast to the soft skin.

Suddenly, Braith's hand locked around her wrist, halting her. Her eyes snapped to his face, his expression tight as if he were in pain.

"You have to stop," he stated in a harsh voice. "It feels too good."

She reluctantly released him only to have him grab her about the waist and lift her. Leoma smiled down at him as he held her against him and walked into the water. The deeper he went, the more his arms loosened so she slid down his body.

The need that pounded through him was a dangerous thing. Yet Braith didn't stop—because he couldn't. Witches could come upon them right now, and he'd never know it. Because he was lost in Leoma.

But he had lived on the knife's edge of death for many years. He was all too aware of how suddenly and quickly life could be taken. When one courted death as he did, they learned to take what pleasures they could whenever they came upon them.

"Stop thinking about the witches," Leoma said and pulled his head down for a kiss.

He smiled as he kept his mouth just out of reach. "How do you know what I'm thinking?"

"It's the same thing I'm thinking about, but I don't want to consider them. I want to concentrate on us, right now, in this moment."

"The danger be damned?"

Her arms wound around his neck as the water moved around them sensuously. "Aye."

He didn't need to be told twice.

Braith took her mouth in a fiery kiss. Her fingers slipped into his hair as he deepened the embrace. With her arms holding her in place, he had both hands free to run over her amazing body.

While she had the curves of a woman, there were firm muscles instead of the usual softness—and he found it most pleasing.

He loved that she could hold her own, that she was strong enough to stand against even him. She wasn't a woman who needed a man. She was a woman who *wanted* a man, and the difference was startling.

And intoxicating.

Once more, he lifted her so that her lovely, pert breasts were even with his face. He glanced up at her to see her biting her lip as she waited to see what he would do. When he looked at a dusky nipple, he saw a drop of water beading on it.

Braith leaned in and wrapped his lips around the turgid peak and flicked his tongue over it. Then he suckled the nub, softly at first before tugging harder.

Leoma's fingers tightened in his hair, half pulling him away, and half holding him to her. All the while, her hips were slowly rocking against him. Her deep-throated moan made his cock jump.

He was ready to spill his seed right then. How in the world was he going to last? Braith steeled himself and moved to her other breast.

But it wasn't enough. He wanted more, he needed more of her.

When he lowered her back into the water, her face was flushed with desire. He moved them closer to shore until her feet could touch, then he turned her so that her back was to him. Her hands immediately reached around and grabbed him.

He bent and nipped at her earlobe. "Hold on to me," he whispered.

Her breath hitched when he cupped her breasts and fondled her nipples for several long moments. Then he moved his hands gradually down her front and over her flat belly before he reached the juncture of her thighs and the curls that hid her most precious part from him.

Without touching her sex, he held his fingers at the edge of her curls as his feet widened her legs. Her breathing was ragged, her chest heaving with expectation.

"Can you feel the water move over your sex?" he asked.

She nodded.

He smiled and shifted his hand so that he cupped her.

"Braith," she said in a hoarse whisper.

Even in the water, he could feel her wetness. He had to get control of himself before he proceeded, lest he take her as savagely as he yearned to do.

"Aye?" he asked. "Do you like this?"

In reply, she ground herself against his hand.

He shut his eyes and clenched his teeth together. Damn, but she was pushing him closer and closer to losing control.

"Please, touch me," she begged. "I need more."

He kissed the side of her neck. "Then let me give it to you."

The moment he slipped a finger inside her, she sucked in a breath, her body stiffening. Undaunted, he moved his finger in and out of her, feeling her relaxing with each thrust. Then he circled his thumb over her clit.

Her breath left her in a loud moan as her head fell back against him and her nails dug into his legs. He continued to tease her, plunging his finger deeper and deeper before he added a second.

His other hand returned to her breast to roll a nipple between his fingers while he brought her closer and closer to her orgasm.

All the while, he rocked against her, doing all he could to stave off his own needs.

Though he had only taken a couple of virgins, he had learned during his many travels how to minimize their pain—and he intended to do just that with Leoma. If only he could get control of himself.

Nothing had ever felt so good. Pleasure engulfed Leoma, moving over her as erotically as the water. And she never wanted it to end.

The feeling of his fingers inside her made her want to take him deeper, to feel his body sliding against hers as he thrust inside her.

It was the onslaught of the water, his hand at her breast, his fingers inside her and teasing her clit that had her body trembling with something she couldn't explain. She felt as if she were moving toward something, but she didn't know what it was—only that she had to get there.

"Give in to the pleasure. It'll take you," Braith murmured against her neck.

His hand quickened in tempo, causing his fingers to go deeper. Then he lightly bit her neck.

Her eyes flew open as pure ecstasy poured hotly through her. She was powerless to do anything but experience the incredible sensations as her body convulsed with the force of her climax.

It took her a while to realize that Braith halted all movement. His rough breaths caught her attention. She lifted her head from his shoulder, intending to ask him if he was all right.

"Don't. Move," he ground out.

Her gaze scanned the area, thinking there were enemies approaching. "What's wrong?"

"I need to be inside you. If you move, the last of my control will shatter. I want to take you gently, and that's not what this will be."

As he spoke, his words sent chills of excitement through her. "I want you inside me."

"I...need time," he stated gruffly. "So I don't hurt you."

"You won't hurt me."

"Le—" he began as she shoved his hands from her and turned to him.

The sight of his face lined with strain concerned her. Until she saw the hunger blazing in his eyes. But she wasn't scared when his hands pulled her against him, or even when he wrapped her legs around his waist.

She wound her arms around his neck and stared into his eyes. The one thing that couldn't be stopped was the pain of pushing through a maidenhead, and Leoma wasn't afraid of that. She was more terrified of not feeling any passion.

His large hands rested beneath her bum and lifted her slightly. The scrape of her breasts on his chest made the walls of her sex clench.

Then she felt the blunt head of his arousal against her. As he slowly lowered her down upon his length, she could feel her body stretching. His thrusts were shallow, but her desire grew anyway.

When he stopped, she frowned in question.

"Your barrier," he said through clenched teeth.

She didn't look away from him. "Don't hold back."

No sooner had she spoke the words than he pulled out of her, hesitating but a moment before he plunged back in, breaking through her maidenhead.

13

Heaven. Being inside Leoma was heaven, and now that Braith had found it, he was never leaving.

He was conscious of the slight stiffening of her body when he broke through her hymen. Instantly, he stopped moving. He opened his eyes and saw that her head was dropped back as she gripped his shoulders and leaned away before rocking her hips.

The erotic sight of her pushed aside all his fears. He braced his hands on her back and bent forward to tease her nipples once more.

Leoma sat up, her lips parted and her eyes heavy-lidded. He drove inside her, building in force as she moved with him, pushing him onward. Each time he tried to rein in his passions, she would easily break through his control.

He walked them to the edge of the water and dropped to his knees. Setting her on her back, Braith gave in to the hunger that rode him, the longing that demanded he claim Leoma as his own.

Her soft moans turned to cries of pleasure that only

spurred him onward. He pounded into her body, taking everything she offered.

When the orgasm came, it barreled through him. His hands sank into the wet earth as he gave a final thrust, and his seed poured into her body. The intensity of the climax left him shaking and gasping for breath.

Then he looked down at her. She was smiling up at him with such adoration and delight that his heart skipped a beat. Always he'd had to hold back with other women. This was the first time he had ever given in, and it was the first time he truly felt complete after lovemaking.

He stared at her in wonder. Now that he'd found her, Braith didn't think he could ever let Leoma go. She was a treasure in all ways. And he would fight to the death for her.

She raised a hand, touching his face. He leaned down and kissed her softly.

"Did I hurt you?" he asked.

A quick frown furrowed her brow. "Nay. Why did you think you needed to hold back?"

"For fear of injuring you. I've been told I can get rough."

"I don't want you to ever hold back with me."

He drew in a breath. "I can only do that if you vow to tell me if I ever hurt you."

"I promise."

She pulled his head down for another kiss before they rose and washed off. As they dressed, he kept looking at her and finding her staring at him. He wasn't sure what was happening between them, but he quite liked it.

There was a smile on his face as they walked back to the cave. And if the grin Leoma wore was any indication, she was happy, as well.

He saw to his horse and got the fire going while Leoma hunted. She returned a short time later with two hares. While the animals roasted on the flames, Braith reclined on his elbow, his legs stretched out to the side.

"If I were the Coven, I'd come for us tonight," he said.

Leoma looked up from sharpening her sword. "By now, they will know that Brigitta has failed. They probably already had a plan in place for just such an event."

"Coming at night would hinder our sight. They could hide in the shadows."

She returned the whetstone to her bag, her lips flattening briefly. "Brigitta made it sound as if they needed you to do something now, which means they don't want to wait. And that means they'll come tonight, probably around dusk."

"That gives us time to set some traps," he replied.

She raised her brows and smiled. "I do like how you think."

He inwardly beamed at her words. "How many do you think will come?"

"I'd say at least four."

"What about any of the council?"

Leoma shook her head as she stirred the fire with a stick. "From what little we know of the council, they leave such work to those below them. The Coven is very protective of the councilmembers, and they go to great lengths to make sure no one outside the Coven knows who they are."

Braith sat up and turned the hares. "Have you tried to get that information from a witch before?"

"Edra wants to know the names, but we've never gotten to that point. Mostly, we react to something the Coven has done. We Hunters are sent to dispatch the witches making a nuisance of themselves. Besides, you need a witch to catch a witch. I have nothing that would stop any magic they would use to break free."

He kept forgetting about the magic. "I'm used to fighting

enemies who don't have magic. I only need to worry about spies or betrayal, not a witch with powers."

"I think, in some ways, your way of fighting is harder." Leoma sheathed her sword and set it beside her. "We trust everyone at the abbey because each of us has a reason to fight the Coven."

"Then you're very lucky. Discovering that someone you trusted has betrayed you is one of the worst things that can happen to anyone."

Her dark hair fell to the side as she regarded him. "Was it a close friend?"

"A knight I trained under." Braith shook his head. "I've not thought of him in years. He was a hard man, but he was good to me...in his own way. I soaked up all the knowledge he shared, and it saved my life. But while I was getting stronger, he was getting older. And weaker.

"I was too busy winning battles to take much notice of how quiet he had become. Or that his ailments were getting worse. I assumed he would let me know if he needed anything. While we were after a particularly malicious enemy that I was running to ground, that same adversary found my mentor and offered him riches beyond his wildest dreams if he led me into a trap."

Leoma brow was furrowed. "And did he?"

"Aye. It was only my quick thinking that saved my hide. I lost nearly half my men that day."

"And your mentor?"

"He didn't try to run. I found him back at camp. He told me everything while sitting among the gold and jewels promised to him. Then he plunged a dagger into his own heart."

She glanced at the ground. "I'm sorry that happened."

"It was a hard lesson learned. In the end, I followed the

trail left by my enemy after he delivered the gold and attacked his camp. I let the men divide the riches, and I brought the man to the king for execution."

Leoma was silent for a long while. "If we're going to set traps, we need to make sure they slow the witches down enough so they can't do magic."

"Can nothing but a blade such as yours kill them?"

She hesitated before she said, "There are other things that can kill witches, but its different for every witch. By the time you figured out what might work, you'd be dead."

"Like what things?" he pressed.

"Certain woods, some metals, and even specific flowers. But like I said, it's different for every witch. The more powerful a witch, the less likely it is that one of those random things will be enough to kill her."

He'd really been hoping for some better news. While he was happy he had Leoma's dagger to fight with, it wasn't a sword or axe, or even a bow.

Braith stood and walked to the cave entrance. He looked at the various trees and rocks around him. While a boulder might not kill a witch, it would certainly slow them down.

He turned to look over his shoulder at Leoma who watched him. "They'll be after me."

"Meaning?" she asked.

"You need to stay hidden." He walked back to the fire and removed the rabbits.

Leoma sat forward, a grin curving her lips. "You have a plan."

He glanced at her and shrugged while grinning. "I have the beginning of a plan. We'll need to act fast, though."

"Talk as we eat," she said.

They stood at the entrance and ate as he explained his

ideas. Leoma added some of hers. By the time they finished eating, they were ready to get started.

Braith used some rope from his things to gather as many large rocks as he could move to the edge of the cliff above them. He fashioned the cord to hold them back and let the rest of the rope dangle down to the cave entrance, hidden from view.

Meanwhile, Leoma shaped spears out of thick branches that were attached to another log and strung up into a nearby tree with a rope she'd fashioned from vines. Braith then set a vine across the path that, once tripped, would set the spikes into motion.

A matching set of spears were set on the other side of the cave, as well.

Using more vines, they hoisted up a large piece of a fallen tree that would swing down and smash into the back of anyone who approached the cave and didn't see the vines across the path.

While none of the traps would kill a witch, it would give Leoma time to get to them and use her sword before the others realized what was happening.

When he next looked up, Braith saw that the sun was nearly to the horizon. He turned his head to Leoma, who stood near his stallion.

"Are you sure about this?" she asked.

He knew she was asking about her hiding as he faced the witches alone. "It gives us an element of surprise."

"As soon as they see that you're healed, they'll know I helped you."

"I'm sure they will."

"As a Hunter, I would remain with you."

He lifted a shoulder. "Maybe you went to get help."

"Why wouldn't you come with me?"

"Why would I?" he countered.

She crossed her arms over her chest. "If they get to you, they'll take you, and I won't be able to follow."

"I'm not going to let them take me."

"You may not have a choice," she argued.

Though he hated to admit it, Leoma was right. If the witches threatened Leoma, he'd do whatever they wanted as long as they left her alone.

Leoma sighed loudly. "No matter what they threaten to do to you or anyone else, you can't agree to do whatever it is they want of you. You have to resist."

As he did before any battle, he thought of the worst-case scenario. His stomach soured when his mind pictured a witch with a blade to Leoma's neck.

"Did you hear me?" Leoma demanded as she stalked to him. "Whatever the Coven has planned will be more terrible than you can imagine. Anyone you care about will most likely be obliterated. You are the only one who can stand against them and refuse."

He touched a lock of her hair and put it behind her shoulder. "I hear you."

"Clear your mind of any thoughts, especially your fears," she warned. "I've known some witches who were able to read minds and bring your greatest fear to life."

Braith glanced at his horse. "Maybe we make a run for it. I'll go one way while you go to the abbey. We'll meet up somewhere, but the extra Hunters, and even Edra can help."

Leoma stared at him for a long time, her gaze searching his face. "I would gladly sacrifice my life if it meant stopping the Coven."

"Aye, but maybe I don't want that."

Her chest expanded as she took a breath. "You've fought many men, right?"

"I have."

"And during those battles, you've come across true evil, haven't you?"

He gave a nod, wondering what she was getting at.

"That's one man leading an army. Or maybe one man *in* the army. That's not an entire coven of witches. We don't know their plans or what their ultimate goal is, and it doesn't matter. Stopping them is what we have to do."

He took her hand in his. "I'll do as you ask, but know that it'll kill me to do it."

14

Northern Scotland
Blackglade

Malene stood at the top of the tower and looked out over the ocean as the waves rose violently before crashing into the cliffs below. The wind was fierce as it whistled around her, tangling her skirts and hair.

She'd never wanted her position. In fact, she had fought against it, but there was no running from being a Varroki. The ancient order was kept secret from others, but their reach extended everywhere.

"My lady."

She drew in a breath and turned to face her second in command. Armir stood tall and straight, his pale green eyes penetrating as his black cloak billowed around him from the wind. His long, golden blond hair was pulled back at the top of his head in a queue, bound with strips of leather every three inches as it fell past his shoulders. He kept the hair on the sides of his head shaved so others could see the intricate tattoos.

Armir had the kind of face that stopped people in their tracks. A strong, defined countenance with prominent cheekbones and a square jaw. His bottom lip was fuller than the top while his strength could be seen in even his neck from the twining cords of sinew that shaped his entire body.

Though Armir's standing within the Varroki made him wealthy, he chose to wear plain leather breeches and a jerkin. The Varroki knew him by his reputation and the tattoos, but no one else would think him anything other than a peasant.

He watched Malene silently, waiting for her. While she wouldn't say that she and Armir were friends, they were friendly. He was the one who had looked for her and then convinced her to take the role she was destined for.

She walked toward him. As she neared, he turned to the side to allow her to pass to the stairs. Once inside the tower with the sound of the wind dimmed, she walked to the hearth and waited.

"Eleanor has left London," Armir stated.

Malene had known this day would come, but she'd hoped it wouldn't be during her lifetime. She turned her head to find Armir with his arms folded over his chest.

"Do we know where she went?" Malene asked.

He gave a shake of his head. "You might be the youngest to ever helm the Varroki, but that doesn't mean you cannot handle what is to come."

She turned her hands over to find the bright blue light shining from the palm of her left hand that had signaled her as the Lady of the Varroki. "No matter how many of our people we send out, we've not been able to stop the Coven from growing their ranks. More and more children around England are being taken, and we've yet to figure out where the Coven is bringing them. If you ask me, I'm failing in my role."

"You doubt your power. Still."

Malene dropped her hands and returned her gaze to the flames. "I doubt my ability to stop the Coven."

"We don't know what they're after yet."

But she did. It haunted her dreams, making her wake with the screams of the dying ringing in her ears. No amount of research in all the scrolls and books of the Varroki could give her an answer to what was coming.

How much longer did the Varroki have before the Coven discovered them? How much longer before there was a war between the two? How much longer before she would have to face the Coven's council of elders?

"You're fighting your gifts," Armir said into the silence.

That was a truth she couldn't refute. She had been wrangling them since they came upon her thirteen years ago.

Out of the corner of her eye, she saw Armir drop his arms and walk closer, stopping a few feet away. His piercing gaze was too much for her to handle right now, so she kept her face averted. Armir was intense on a calm day, and today was anything but.

"You've been in your role for five years now, and you've still not accepted who you are."

She cut her eyes to him. "I'm here. I've accepted who I am."

"That's shite. If you truly recognized who you were, there would be no doubts plaguing you. I wouldn't hear you crying in the middle of the night from whatever bad dreams visited you."

Malene faced him as anger sizzled just beneath her skin. "We both know you should've been given my position. You were born at Blackglade and raised to be a Varroki. You're the strongest, the most cunning. You should be leading them."

His enigmatic green eyes narrowed as his head cocked to the side. "You think all of that makes me better than you?"

"Aye!"

His wide lips flattened in irritation. In two strides, he closed the distance between them and grabbed her left wrist, holding it up between them. "*This* makes you the strongest of us! You could obliterate me with a thought."

"I never wanted this."

Armir blew out a breath. "I'm here to help, but I cannot do that if you don't let me."

She couldn't look away from his green gaze. Nor did she remind him that he was still holding her arm. It was taboo for anyone to touch the Lady of the Varroki.

His touch was the first she had experienced since she took the role as head of the Varroki. And she wasn't ready for it to end.

"I don't want to fail," she said. "I fear that above all else. All the Varroki are depending on me."

"Stop thinking of them. Focus on the Coven. Let me and the other warriors worry about our people."

The blue light of her palm began to grow brighter. Malene fisted her hand, but it was too late. Armir released her and took a step back.

"Forgive me," he said with a bow of his fair head.

She spun around and strode to the window to gaze out at the storm through the cracks in the shutters. "We need to know where Eleanor has gone. No one in the council leaves their post without reason."

"One of our best warriors has been watching her for months. He's the one who alerted me of her departure, and he'll follow her. I'll report as soon as I know something."

The sound of the door closing behind him was loud. Malene walked to the wooden tub near the fire and held her hand above it. Water began to fill it as steam spiraled upwards.

She leaned over the tub and looked at her reflection. Her flaxen hair and soft gray eyes stared back at her, announcing her Norse heritage. She slapped at the water, making her image distort and vanish. Straightening, she removed her clothes when the room began to spin.

Malene stumbled back a step, her hands reaching for something to hold onto. Her knees buckled, and she hit the stone floor hard. She fell forward onto her hands as the first of the images assaulted her.

They flashed in her mind so quickly that she only saw hints of each one. Her left palm grew warm as the light from within her flared and lit up the room as if it were daylight.

"Armir," she whispered, knowing that he would hear his name when he felt her magic.

Her stomach rolled as the snippets continued to pour through her, all of them showing the same thing: slaughter. Her nightmares were now visiting her while she was awake. And that couldn't be a good sign.

Then something strange began to occur. Within the flashes, she saw others alive and then those same people fighting the Coven.

As quickly as the images began, they halted. The light from her palm decreased to resume its gentle glow. However, it took longer for her body to adjust.

"Breathe," Armir said from beside her. "Just breathe."

She didn't know how long she remained on her hands and knees before her stomach settled and the room stopped spinning. Malene pushed back onto her haunches and wiped the perspiration from her brow.

"That's never happened before," she murmured. She

glanced down at her hands and realized she was only in her chemise, but she didn't reach for her gown.

Armir squatted before her, his brows furrowed deeply. "What happened?"

"I'm not sure. Perhaps a vision, but it came in waves of hundreds of images. All showing the same thing. Death. I've seen this in my dreams, but this time was different."

His face hardened. "You were shown what could happen."

"I also saw a small group standing against the Coven."

"You mean our people?"

She shook her head as she got to her feet. Armir straightened, as well, his gaze watching her like a hawk. "The group wasn't ours. We should find out who they are."

"It shouldn't be too difficult to discover them since so few will fight the Coven."

"Good. We might need them."

"They've magic, then?"

She held his gaze. "Actually, I don't know."

"How can anyone who doesn't have magic be of use to us?"

"I cannot answer that any more than I can say why I was chosen for this position or why I was shown the images tonight. That group stood out. Regardless, we need to know who they are and what their plans are. They, along with our spy in the Coven, could be what we need to win."

Armir remained in place as she walked to a nearby chair and grabbed the back. She wasn't sure if she liked that he didn't make a comment about how weak she was. Or her lack of dress.

"I will make sure they are found. Did you see an approximate location?" he asked.

"Track those of the Coven. Our warriors will be able to find this group of women."

Armir's eyes widened as his brows rose. "Women?"

She didn't hide her smile. "That surprises you?"

"If they do not have magic, aye," he replied.

Malene closed her eyes and tried to recall some of the images that included the women. Though she remembered them easily, it was putting them into focus that took the most time.

She concentrated, tuning out everything else. Little by little, one of the images began to sharpen. While she couldn't see faces because of the hoods pulled forward, she was able to pick out a few distinctions.

"There are a couple of men in the group," she said. "They also favor a symbol. An Ouroboros. They're heavily armed, and they look as if they know how to fight."

"Warriors then," Armir said.

Her eyes opened to him. "It looks that way."

"If they had magic, the Varroki would know of them."

"We don't know everyone in the world with magic. They could have been overlooked somehow."

The downturn of Armir's lips displayed his displeasure. "While that may be true, my lady, I put my faith in the Varroki."

"So you believe this group to be without magic."

He gave a single nod. "I do."

"Fighting the Coven."

A muscle bulged in his jaw. "Aye."

"Then they are allies we not only want to have, but we may need, as well."

"As you wish."

When he didn't go, she raised a brow. "Is there something else?"

"You're not alone in this."

His words caused her to frown. "I know that."

"Do you?" he asked softly. "I heard the pain in your voice

when you called out for me."

She couldn't hold his gaze, nor did she want him to continue down that path. "I'm an outsider, Armir. While my palm signals me as the chosen leader of the Varroki, I know there are those who believe I will fail. They're waiting for exactly that to happen so I can be replaced by a Varroki raised in the Blackglade."

"I'm not one of them."

Her gaze jerked to him. She searched his face, trying to decipher if his words were true or not.

He walked to stand before her and held her gaze. "I am not one of them," he repeated. "I'm the one who sought you out. I'm the one who convinced you to take your place here. I'm the one who stands beside you through all of this. If you cannot trust me, then you cannot trust anyone."

Somehow, as incredulous as it was, she had hurt his feelings. And she hated that. Armir was right, he'd been with her from the beginning, lending her his strength and wisdom whenever she needed it.

"I do trust you," she said.

His green eyes seemed to burn from within. "Then tell me what's truly troubling you."

"I'm scared. Terrified, actually."

"Of?"

"Of facing the Coven. Of making the wrong choice. Of not knowing how to control the magic within me. Of having to watch you and the others die."

His lips curved slightly. "I don't die easily. As for the rest, if you weren't frightened, I'd be worried. I've faith in you, my lady."

And, somehow, that relieved the growing anxiety inside her.

For now.

15

Leoma huddled behind a tree against the chill in the night. Braith's traps were all set and waiting for the witches. She couldn't help but smile since he was the bait. It was something he'd accepted with enthusiasm, as if he were looking forward to encountering others from the Coven.

She put her hand on the hilt of her sword at her hip. If Braith's sword were magically forged as hers was, she might feel better about the trap, but all he had was her dagger.

The two of them against...she had no idea how many would be coming, but it wouldn't be just one witch. The desperation in Brigitta's voice could have been partly due to the fact that she'd failed to bring Braith in the first time.

But Leoma suspected it might have to do with the Coven needing Braith in a timely manner. The question was, what for? What could they need him to get that they couldn't?

Then it hit her. The Coven couldn't use magic to obtain whatever it was they were after. It was also obviously something that not just any man, woman, or child could acquire. It had to be Braith. But why?

When they'd spoken of it earlier, he didn't seem to have any inclination what the item could be. If it were something of great importance, surely Braith would remember it.

What disturbed Leoma the most was that the Coven was after whatever it was to begin with. As if it weren't enough that the Coven wreaked havoc around England and even Scotland, now this unknown had to be added into the mix.

Her attention moved to the stallion when he raised his head and stared off into the darkness. Leoma followed the animal's gaze, but she didn't hear or see anything.

Tense moments slowly went by as she waited for an attack. The longer it went on without the Coven showing themselves, the more worried she became.

Why weren't they attacking? Why did they wait?

After a little while, the horse went back to grazing. Yet that didn't calm Leoma's fears. In fact, it raised them. With Braith in the cave, she had no way of alerting him to her worries. Then again, he was skilled in battle. He would be aware of everything, just as she was.

As she waited in the dark, her thoughts inevitably turned to making love to Braith. They hadn't discussed it since it happened, but then again, she wasn't sure what to say.

It had been an incredible experience that she certainly wanted to repeat. She was uncertain how to proceed, though. Luckily, they had the Coven coming for them, which put off any conversation for the moment.

Leoma had been happy about that fact at the time, but the more she thought about it, the more she wished they had spoken. Now, it hung between them like a giant wall.

As soon as she began to recall how good it felt to be in Braith's arms, how he had brought her pleasure so easily, she turned her mind to other things. If she allowed herself to remain on that path, she might very well go into the cave and have her way with him again.

She looked for Asa's owl. The bird should have gotten to the abbey and returned by now.

It was just something else for her to worry about.

———

"What are we waiting on?" Walter asked.

Eleanor looked from the vine hidden beneath the leaves to the cave. She almost hadn't used her magic to detect any snares as they approached Braith, but since Brigitta had underestimated the lord already, Eleanor wasn't going to, as well.

It was a good thing she had used her magic. Four traps were set for anyone who walked toward the cave. While none of them would kill her, it would certainly hinder her. What did the lord then intend to do once she was impaled upon one of the spikes?

She waved Walter to follow as she backed up. "He's expecting us."

Walter snorted. "So? He's one man."

"One man who fought—and apparently won—against Brigitta."

"The witch did say he had a Hunter with him."

Eleanor jerked her chin to the cave. "If there were a Hunter with him, they would have already attacked. Braith is alone."

"You're sure?"

She turned her gaze to him and glowered. Even in the darkness where he couldn't see her clearly, he knew enough to be afraid. "Do not question me."

"My love, I'm simply curious as to how you know the Hunter isn't here," he hurried to say.

Eleanor turned on her heel and made her way toward the Witch's Grove. "Because Hunters do not stand down when they know a witch is coming. They are ruled by the need to assault us at every turn."

"Could this Hunter be different?" Walter asked, breathing heavily and loudly as he attempted to keep up with her long strides.

"The Hunter isn't there."

"All right." He huffed and jogged to catch up to her. "What do you propose we do then?"

Eleanor strode into the Witch's Grove, feeling at home as soon as she was within its dark wickedness. "Either Brigitta lied about inflicting Braith with magic, or the Hunter healed him."

"That shouldn't be possible."

She halted and turned to face her rotund husband who was now sweating profusely. "It is if there is a witch helping them."

"Ah. I see."

Eleanor looked back in the direction they had come. "Braith wouldn't have been able to set those traps if he had magic in his veins."

"Could the Hunter have set them before she left him behind?"

"That is a possibility," she conceded. "But why leave Braith here."

Walter shrugged, still huffing. "Perhaps she went to get more Hunters."

"Leaving the lord behind, knowing we were coming is too stupid a move on the Hunter's part. My guess is that Braith refused to go with her, and she knew she would be outnumbered. Killing a single witch is one thing, but more?"

"Then why did Braith remain behind?"

Eleanor wanted to throttle Walter, but he brought up a valid point. "Why indeed?"

Did the earl believe he could take on more witches? Or perhaps he didn't yet believe what he had seen with his own eyes.

If that were the case, then he was going to be so very easy to capture. And once in their grasp, he would do whatever they asked of him.

First, they had to have Braith in hand. That should've been the easy part. She had wanted the earl taken at his keep, but Brigitta encountered a problem with Josef. Every time Brigitta thought she had Josef under her control, he always managed to come out of it.

Eleanor suspected that the lad had a witch somewhere in his family tree. He had just enough magic in him to push through the web of lies Brigitta weaved. It was by Eleanor's command that Brigitta killed Josef because Eleanor had known Braith would follow Brigitta to exact his brand of justice.

Away from the keep and all the servants, it should've been easy to capture Braith.

Instead, a Hunter had shown up, and Brigitta was killed. If that weren't enough to go after the Hunter, the girl's interference in their mission was.

The whispers of the Gira grew louder. Eleanor silenced them with a look. There were few things a Gira was frightened of, but a member of the Coven's council was one of them.

"We need to throw Braith off our trail," Eleanor said. "He expected us tonight, and while he might not have known who was coming, he knew we would be here."

Walter wiped the sweat from his bald head. "We can get through those traps."

She raised a brow as she looked at him.

"You," he corrected. "*You* can get through those measly traps. He's right there. You're so close to getting what you've been after for years."

"Brigitta underestimated the earl, not once, but twice. I'm not going to do the same. Right now, the board is set for him to win. I'm going to rearrange the pieces so the game falls in my favor."

Walter chuckled. "I do love how your mind works, my love. What's your plan?"

"I'm still working that out," Eleanor said and made her way to the center of the Grove to rest.

Leoma watched the rising of the sun, unsure how she felt about the witches not attacking. She quietly moved from her hiding place and checked the area in case witches were lying in wait.

When she circled back around to the cave, she found Braith standing near one of the traps, staring at the ground.

"What is it?" she asked as she walked up.

He pointed. "Someone was here last night."

Leoma squatted down and looked at the two sets of tracks. "A woman and a man."

"The man is large by how deep his imprint on the soil is."

"Aye. They turned and went toward the Witch's Grove."

Braith scratched his whiskered cheek. "Why didn't they strike?"

"I have no idea, but I don't like it. I also don't like that they're so close."

"Or that we don't know how many there are."

Leoma stood and met his gaze. "We should go. The traps

were a good plan, but they somehow saw them. They'll do us no good now."

"I agree. I'll not leave them to hurt some unsuspecting fool, though."

She glanced at the spikes. "I'll get your horse ready and clean out the cave."

"It won't take me long to cut the vines that would trigger the traps."

They separated to carry out their tasks. She was finishing saddling the stallion when Braith returned. He mounted and held out his hand.

Leoma's heart quickened at the thought of riding with him. She took his hand and swung up behind him, wrapping her arms around his waist.

"Where to?" he asked.

"Southwest. I know a place where we might be able to stay and get word to the abbey."

He turned the horse to the left and nudged it into a cantor. Leoma glanced behind her, hoping they were making the right decision. She hated leaving witches behind, but that came second to keeping Braith out of their hands.

"Are you sure you cannot think of why the Coven would want you?" she asked.

Braith shook his head and maneuvered the horse through the dense trees and rolling terrain. "Nay."

"Perhaps something for the king?"

"I only ever handed the king enemies I was sent to bring him. Dead or alive, I handed them over to the king's men."

Leoma held on tighter as the stallion slipped on an incline before gaining his footing. "No items or anything."

"Only people."

"And the Coven wouldn't need you to get someone out, would they?"

He turned his head and gave a bark of laughter. "I'd have to have the king with me to get anyone out of prison."

"If only we knew what the Coven wants you for."

"I can ask them," he teased.

She lightly punched him in the arm. "I'd rather you didn't."

"I was hoping you'd say that."

16

Braith had been in charge of many things, but watching over a woman the likes of Leoma was a first. She had grown quiet several leagues back. It wasn't long after that her head rested on his back and her arms around him went slack.

The fact that she knew he would look out for her while she slept made him grin.

In many ways, she was nearly his equal. Not once did that call into question her femininity. In fact, to him, it made her even more beautiful.

"Whoa," he whispered to the stallion, pulling back on the reins.

The sight of the village ahead made him wary. Of course, the witches following them did nothing to calm his nerves. If he and Leoma were going to come out of this alive—and remain out of the Coven's reach—they needed to be smart.

While Braith was well versed in battle and how men thought, the witches were another matter entirely. There were rules on the battlefield that the Coven disregarded. Which meant that Braith needed to forget most everything he knew.

He recalled the way Leoma had first attacked him. Her actions had not only been quick, but no movement was wasted. She used every part of her body to attack and defend. All his years of training with sword and shield would need to be disregarded. He would have to quickly relearn how to think when it came to fighting witches.

Leoma took a deep breath and lifted her head. He immediately missed her against him, but he was looking forward to actually holding her as they slept. Not that either of them had mentioned their encounter.

"Where are we?" she asked sleepily before yawning.

He bit back a yawn of his own after not getting sleep the night before and very little the night before that. "I've already skirted around another village."

She leaned to the side and looked around him. "We could use provisions. And information."

"On?"

"Anything out of the ordinary occurring around the village. There's always talk in a tavern."

Braith looked over his shoulder at her. "You want to find a witch despite the fact that we have some chasing us."

"Nay," she said with a grin. "I want to see if a witch has been around here. If so, we leave. But with information that can then be given to Edra. If not, then we can linger for a short while."

"I'm not sure that's a good idea either way. We need to keep distance between the Coven and us."

She looped her arm with his and slid from the horse. "They're all around us. They're everywhere. We'll only be able to run for so long."

"Then why did we leave the forest?" he asked, irritation filling him.

Leoma pulled up the hood of her cloak and winked at him. "Because we would've been overwhelmed."

"And we won't be here?"

"Oh, we'll definitely be here," she said as she began to walk backward.

Braith was praying for patience. "You're making no sense."

"We're going to the village separately. We'll meet at the tavern. Get us some food."

"And what will you be doing?"

"Getting a message to Edra and the other Hunters," she replied with a grin before turning and sauntering away.

Braith looked to the sky. If she had only stated that to begin with, he wouldn't have gotten riled. Then again, he supposed that's exactly what she wanted.

His gaze lowered to find her heading toward one of the two rivers the village was built around. He turned the stallion in the other direction to take the path leading into the small community.

As he rode into the town, he spotted the tavern near the entrance. Braith stopped his horse before the structure and dismounted, looping the reins around a wooden post.

He looked up and down the street, noting the new buildings. The location of the town next to the two rivers allowed everyone to thrive. The wealth brought in many different travelers, which meant it would be a good place to gather information from many regions around.

Braith merely had to follow his nose to the market. The main item for sale was fish, which wouldn't last more than a day while traveling. He skipped those booths and bought bread, cheese, and dried meat.

With the bags in hand, he returned to the tavern. He looked at every female face, wondering if any of them were witches. It's not as if their magic could be seen. That allowed them to blend in with others easily. Too easily for his peace of mind.

He strode into the tavern and halted at the door. His gaze scanned the occupants looking for Leoma, but she was nowhere to be seen.

"Good afternoon," a buxom barmaid with curly blond hair said as she passed him carrying mugs of ale.

Braith gave her a nod and made his way to a table. He sat with his back to the wall and set the bags of food at his feet. While the village appeared to be a decent place, he didn't want to remain.

"Thirsty?" the barmaid asked as she stopped at his table.

He looked up into her dark eyes. While she wasn't a great beauty, she was comely. No doubt that, along with her flirting, helped her earn extra coin.

"Ale," he replied.

"Right away. How about something to eat, milord? We've the best catch of the day."

He gave a nod, knowing he should eat while he could.

"I'll see to it," she said and walked away, hips swaying.

Within moments, she returned with a large mug and a plate of smoked fish. She set it down, and he handed her a few coins. He began eating while listening to the conversations around him.

He ignored the loud, boisterous groups and focused on a table to his left where three men sat looking as if they had seen the Devil himself. Their faces were pinched as they huddled over their ales while talking low and looking around nervously.

Traveling with thousands of men, Braith had learned to tune out things he didn't want to hear. He did that now, mentally silencing table by table until the only one left was the one on his left.

He concentrated on their words, straining to hear their

whispers. Little by little, he understood more and more of what the three men said.

"...we have to tell someone."

"Nay. No one will believe us."

"Or she'll kill us."

A mug was lowered to the table. "I cannot remain here then."

"Ye're scared."

"Of course he is, ye dimwit. We all are."

"She will come for us. I know it."

There was a loud snort. "She could've killed us on the spot, but she turned away. I don't think she means us harm."

"Speak for yourself, Bill. I'm with Robin. We should either leave or tell someone."

"They'll burn her at the stake," Bill said.

Robin shrugged. "So? Not our problem."

"She saved a boy's life. Does that count for nothing?"

The sound of the tavern door opening jerked his attention away. As soon as he spotted Leoma, he wanted to go to her, to yank her against him and kiss her until they were both senseless with desire.

Her gaze landed on him briefly before she looked around the tavern only to hesitate at the table with the three men whose conversation he'd been listening to.

She walked to the bar and ordered some food before making her way to a table on his right. She sat with her back to him and faced the hearth where a fire roared.

"I was unable to send a message," she whispered.

He sat forward, placing his arms on the table as he began to eat. "There might be someone you want to talk to."

She waited until the bowl of stew was placed before her to say, "The men beside you?"

"By their talk, I'm thinking they encountered someone like Helena."

"We'll go looking after the meal."

He downed the fish, which was excellent, as well as some bread. While his food settled, he finished the ale and tried to hear more of what the three men were saying. Unfortunately, they had stopped talking, preferring to glare at each other instead.

Two of them rose and walked from the tavern, leaving Bill, the man who was the least frightened of the trio. Braith grabbed his bags of food and ale and pushed back his chair as he stood.

Bill was staring at the table, seemingly lost in thought. Braith had to clear his throat twice before the man heard him. Bill's stringy brown hair was in need of combing.

"May I sit?" Braith asked.

The man frowned and gave a curt nod. "If ye wish."

Once seated, Braith held Bill's gaze. "Tell me what occurred."

"I'm not sure what ye mean."

Braith knew men like Bill. While the man wasn't exactly a coward, the few times he did find his backbone, it was broken easily. And that meant it would be easy for Braith to get the information he needed.

He stretched out his legs and put his hand on the hilt of his sword. Bill's gaze followed his movements, his eyes widening when he saw the weapon.

"Apologies, milord. I didn't see yer sword," Bill hastened to say.

"Nor am I dressed of my station, but there's a reason for that. Now, tell me what you and your comrades were discussing."

Bill swallowed loudly. His gaze darted around before he leaned close. "I saw a witch."

"Where?"

"Up the south river."

"What happened?" Braith pressed.

Bill's hand shook as he raised his mug to his lips and drained the last of his ale. "She saved a little boy's life who drowned."

"And?"

"That's it," Bill insisted. "She saw us, but she did nothing. And she could have. I'm sure of it."

Braith pulled out several coins and set them on the table before pushing them toward the man. "Forget what you saw at the river. Forget me. Otherwise, I'll have to come back. And trust me, Bill, you don't want me to return."

"Aye, milord," he said, his voice trembling.

Braith held his gaze for a moment longer. Then he gathered the bags and stood. He strode from the tavern without looking at Leoma. He knew she had heard their conversation.

Within minutes, he was mounted on his horse and leaving the village behind. He rode to the south river and directed the stallion upstream.

While he wasn't exactly in a hurry to talk to a witch, the idea that it might be Helena was too tempting to pass up. Especially since they were in need of more people to stand against the Coven.

However, he did have to reconcile the fact that just because the witch didn't kill Bill and his friends didn't mean that she wasn't part of the Coven.

Braith couldn't believe he was riding toward a witch when all he wanted to do was get far away from anything having to do with the Coven.

"Not going to wait for me?"

He yanked on the reins, causing his horse to jerk his head up and down and dance to the side. Braith put a hand on the animal's neck, calming him as he looked at Leoma, who stood smiling atop an outcropping of rocks.

"I knew you'd catch up," he replied.

Her smile faded as she looked in the direction he was headed. "This could be a trap."

"I know."

"It could also be someone who will help us."

Braith shrugged. "Or someone who wants nothing to do with us or the Coven."

"All witches are going to have to take a stand. Pick a side. The sooner they realize that, the better." Leoma adjusted the hood of her cloak. "I'm ready whenever you are."

He watched as she jumped from the rocks and started walking. How he wished they could have a day or two for themselves without having to worry about the Coven capturing him.

At least, it gave him something to look forward to.

17

A wrong choice could end her life and put Braith in the hands of the Coven. Leoma had never been in such a situation before. There were no good choices. It was simply a matter of finding the one that hurt the least.

"Are you sure?" Braith asked from beside her after he dismounted.

Leoma stared at the smoke from the fire. The witch was hiding. Because of fear or a trap, Leoma didn't yet know. But she was about to find out.

She pushed back the hood of her cloak as her gaze found three different places where the witch could be hiding among the rocks and trees.

"Stand at the water's edge. It's the most advantageous for you if she's hiding there, there, or there," he said, pointing out the places Leoma had already sighted.

She turned her head to him. He gripped the hilt of his sword repeatedly, as if he were imagining meeting the witch himself. The only reason he wasn't already out there was because his blade couldn't kill witches.

His indigo gaze swung to her. His face was lined with annoyance at not being able to take action. She understood that emotion. It had plagued her for years until she was able to finally hunt herself.

"If something should go wrong—"

"It won't," he said over her.

She smiled. "If it should, remember to head south toward the great forest. Once there, just say Edra's name over and over until one of them finds you and takes you to the abbey. Don't stop for anything or anyone."

"I didn't think you wanted this brought to the abbey."

"I don't, but you need to stay far from the Coven."

He raised a dark brow. "You mean until I can get a weapon of my own."

The thought of him standing against witches wielding a sword filled with magic made her stomach flutter in excitement. She wanted to stand beside him to fight the Coven.

His fingers slipped into her hair, and he cupped the side of her head as he faced her. "I don't like running from my enemies, but I'm also not a fool. I know that, right now, the Coven has the upper hand. I'll lead them on a merry chase until that advantage turns my way."

"I know. I like that about you. Probably too much," she confessed.

"Forget this witch. Let's go."

She smiled sadly and put her hand over his. "It was you who said we needed to build up our army to stand against the Coven."

"Aye, I did. I don't like that you're putting your life on the line for something that can wait."

"But it can't," she argued. "If this witch is with the Coven, then she already knows we're here. The sooner I dispatch her, the better."

His faced hardened as his dark hair blew in the wind. "I'll be helping you with that. Even if it is just with a dagger."

Gazing into his stunning eyes, she continued. "If the witch is also on the run from the Coven, then I need to get her on our side. She can help."

A muscle jumped in his jaw as he glanced at the fire.

"What is it?" Leoma asked.

"I don't like waiting behind. I'm a warrior, dammit."

She turned and kissed his palm. "We work together. This time, I'm the one going out there. You can go next time."

"Don't get hurt," he demanded.

"Aye, my lord," she replied and rose up to give him a quick kiss.

He tried to hold her, but Leoma quickly stepped away. She knew if she allowed the kiss to continue, she would forget about the witch and give in to her desires. That wasn't wise at present.

Leoma hopped onto a rock in the river. She spread her arms to keep her balance and then rapidly jumped onto the next four rocks until she was across. Only then did she look back at Braith.

His hand was once more on the hilt of his sword, his grip tight. She gave a nod and waited for him to return it before she faced the camp. And the waiting witch.

As Braith suggested, Leoma kept to the edge of the river as she made her way toward the fire. The birds sang, filling the silence along with the noises of the burning wood. There was no evil vibe that Leoma sometimes felt when hunting witches, but that didn't mean she was going to let her guard down.

She kept her sword sheathed as she came to a halt. Her gaze went to all three hiding places, but something kept drawing her back to the fire and the two trees about ten paces behind it.

"I know you're here. Come out," Leoma called.

There was a rush of wind as a feminine voice said, "I know what you are. Hunter."

"You need not worry about that unless you are part of the Coven."

Laughter floated on the wind. "I would sooner slit my own throat than become part of them."

"Then show yourself." Leoma looked around while trying to determine where the witch was. Her voice was coming from every direction.

"The Coven grows closer with each passing moment. Why linger here?"

"Because we need witches who will rise up against them."

More laughter, this time tinged with sadness. "I cannot and will not help you, Hunter. I've remained hidden from the Coven for over twenty years, and I'll continue doing that."

"You wouldn't have to hide anymore."

"Is that not what you and your companion are doing?" the witch asked.

Leoma was tired of talking to a disembodied voice. "They want him for something, and we're going to make sure they don't catch him."

"Then you should run. I'll slow them for you, but that is all I will do, Hunter. Ask no more of me."

The wind died, as did the fire. Leoma blew out a frustrated breath and turned on her heel to make her way back to Braith. It infuriated her that she hadn't had the words to convince the witch to join them.

Someone as powerful as she, who could disguise herself and use the wind as her voice was someone the Hunters needed on their side. Unfortunately, Leoma had failed to secure her.

"I gather things didn't go well," Braith said when she returned.

Leoma stretched her neck first one way and then the other. "I never saw her. She remained hidden, but she told me she wouldn't join us."

"So she knew who you were?"

"She knows I'm a Hunter, aye." Leoma looked at him. "She also said the Coven was close, and that she would slow them down for us to leave."

Braith gave her a flat look. "Then what are we waiting for?"

He vaulted onto the stallion's back and held out his hand. She grasped it and threw a leg over the animal as Braith pulled her up. Leoma glanced over her shoulder at the camp as he spun the horse around and nudged it into a gallop.

It was some time later once they had put a good distance between them and the village that Braith slowed the horse to a walk.

She grinned as she glimpsed the frown he had worn for several leagues. "You've been mulling over something for a while now. What's bothering you?"

"The witch," he replied. "Why wouldn't she fight?"

Leoma adjusted her grip on his waist and rested her chin against his back. "She said she has been hiding from them for over two decades."

"That's a long time."

"I suppose. Then again, Edra hid from them for seven years before she made a stand. Some would say she's still hiding."

Braith covered her hands with one of his. "Edra isn't concealing herself. She's being strategic in her warfare. I'm sure when the time comes, she will step out and stand alongside you to fight the Coven."

"All these years, as I've trained and hunted, I always believed we would defeat the Coven."

His head snapped to the side to look back at her. "You no longer feel that way?"

"I still have hope, but something has changed. I've been trying to determine what it is that made me shift my thinking. It took me a while, but I have it figured out."

"And?" he asked, looking forward.

She looked up at the profile of his face. "It's you."

Braith stopped the horse. He was silent for several moments. "Me?"

Before she could reply, he lifted his leg over the horse's head and slid to the ground. He gazed up at her in confusion and anger. "Because you gave yourself to me."

"Nay," she said and dismounted to stand beside him. "This has nothing to do with us. I've been going over everything Brigitta said, and I keep coming back to why they want you."

He grabbed the stallion's reins and drew them over the animal's head as they began walking. "I've told you I have no idea what they want me for."

"What puzzles me most is that witches can use magic to get anything they want. Their relentless pursuit of you concerns me."

"Because you believe they may have a grander plan that the Hunters have overlooked."

She nodded, her stomach souring as he put her thoughts into words. "If that is indeed what is happening, then the army you spoke of needs to be brought together now."

"That's going to be difficult if the witches won't come out of hiding."

When his hand brushed her fingers before linking with hers, she smiled. But it quickly faded as she recalled their topic of conversation.

"My fear is that it is going to take the Coven gaining power for the witches to realize they need to do something."

Braith glanced at her. "You cannot force anyone to do what they aren't ready to face. Trust me, I know. That which you fear will most likely come to pass."

"It may be too late by then."

He halted and turned to her. "Regardless, if I have a weapon to fight the Coven or not, I will stand with you. Not because the witches want me for some nefarious purpose. And not because we made love. Because it's the right thing to do. Because to stand idle is to allow a group of reprehensible witches to gain power. Once they have a taste of it, they'll crave more."

"You speak as if you've seen this happen."

"I have," he said in a low voice. "Too many times. The only difference is the men I fought didn't have magic."

Leoma drew in a deep breath and slowly released it as she looked off into the distance. "I have to get a message to the abbey. They need to know what's coming."

"You're once again of the mind to not go there?"

She shot him a quick grin. "If I'm killed, the abbey is the best place for you to get prepared for the war."

"The same could be said now, with you alive."

He had a point, and a part of her wanted nothing more than to run as fast as she could to the abbey. Not to mention, Edra and the others needed to know what she had discovered. Besides, Radnar and his knights were prepared for an attack.

"I'm split," she said, turning to him. "I do want to go home. Yet, another part of me, a louder part, cautions against heading to the abbey. The Coven has no idea who is training us, or who is in charge. If I lead the Coven there, they would not only get their hands on you, but they could also wipe out everything Edra and Radnar have worked so hard to create."

Braith ran a hand over his jaw. "Those are valid points. Do you really believe the Coven could wipe out the abbey so easily?"

"They have the advantage of greater numbers," she pointed out.

He nodded and began walking. "Then the decision has been made. We're on our own."

18

There was something familiar about the area. Braith stood at the fork in the road with Leoma and his horse behind him. He had been here before, he was sure of it. But he couldn't remember when or why.

He rubbed his tired eyes and looked again at each direction the road veered. His attention kept returning to the right.

"Why don't we rest here for a bit," Leoma suggested. "The horse could have a respite, and you could get some sleep."

Braith shook his head. "I'm fine."

"You've not slept in nearly two days."

Though she didn't finish her sentence, he understood her meaning. The lack of rest was affecting his body as well as his mind.

"I've been here before." He lifted his hands and pointed in either direction. "I just cannot recall if it was for battle or something else."

The bridle jingled as the horse shook its head and side-stepped. Braith closed his eyes as his mind was suddenly filled with the sounds of war. The screams of the dying, the bellows of foes attacking, the clashing of steel meeting steel.

His hands fisted at his sides as the memory remained just out of reach. The harder he fought for it, the further it moved.

Suddenly, soft hands were on either side of his face. Leoma's voice reached him, soft and even. "Take a breath. Now, stop fighting."

He did as she bade, but when he began to open his eyes, she quickly said, "Leave them closed. I want you to forget about everything around you. Me, your horse, the Coven. All of it. Let it go."

It took a few tries because of his exhaustion, but he was able to clear his mind of everything except for Leoma. Her, he held onto tightly, refusing to ever let go.

"Let your mind wander," she whispered.

It felt so good to have his eyes shut. They no longer burned as if someone had poured sand into them. Sleep pulled at him incessantly, and he wanted nothing more than to give in. But first, he needed to find a safe place for them.

That's why the fork was familiar. It led to Falk Castle, renamed after his friend Roger Falk had taken it for the king. In exchange, the king gave the castle, lands, and title to Roger.

Braith's eyes opened, and he smiled down at Leoma. "To the right is Falk Castle, which belongs to a good friend. We will find shelter and food."

"You remembered, good," she said as her hands fell away.

It was the frown he saw on her face that confused him. "What is it?"

"Should we venture to the castle? The Coven will follow us wherever we go."

He pointed to the fork. "We'll cover our tracks so they won't be able to determine which direction we went. And

Roger will keep us hidden. I know the back entrance. No one will see us other than those Roger trusts."

"Do you think I could get a hot bath?"

"Aye," he replied with a grin. "Let's go. I want to reach the castle before dark."

With Leoma leading the horse, Braith covered their tracks. When they were a safe distance away, they mounted the stallion and began the ride to the castle.

Braith grinned at the idea of having a bed in which to hold Leoma. It would be nice to catch up with Roger, as well. It had been nearly six years since they last spoke.

"Tell me about your friend," Leoma urged.

"He was one of the best fighters I've ever stood with," Braith said. "He was fearless, if a bit reckless at times. Yet, he never lost a battle. We watched each other's backs on multiple occasions. And when the king sent him to dispatch a disloyal duke, Roger asked for my help."

She shifted behind him. "Which you gave."

"Without hesitation. I was in charge of a significant number of knights by that time, and I gave them the option to accompany me. They all joined in. The duke, who had been planning an assassination of the king, didn't stand a chance against both Roger's army and mine. Still, His Grace refused to give up. He sent his men into battle."

"Needless deaths," she murmured.

Braith drew in a breath, recalling the horror of that day. "Roger spared many of the knights when we overran them and captured the duke."

"Many?"

Braith didn't wish to drudge up such horrible memories. "War is a bloody business."

Her arms tightened around him, giving him quiet comfort that he hadn't realized he needed until then.

"Roger is a good man," he said.

"Then I cannot wait to meet him."

Braith nudged his mount into a gallop. He didn't question his desire to get to the castle quickly. There was a very good chance the witches following them would choose the other path.

But there was also a chance they would come to the castle.

While he didn't wish to put anyone at the castle in danger, he knew that Roger wouldn't allow anyone he didn't know inside after dark. That meant he and Leoma would have at least one night to sleep and prepare for their next move.

The castle towers came into view. He halted the stallion atop a hill in order to take in the sight. There was a thread of wariness, but that had been with Braith since Josef was murdered.

"It's a beautiful castle," Leoma said.

"One of the largest around. I wish I had remembered Roger earlier. We could've been here hours ago."

She gave a tug on his hair. "We could go there now instead of staring at it."

He was smiling when he clicked to the horse.

Braith rode around to the west side of the castle, keeping to the tree line as he noted the men stationed around the battlements.

"It looks as if your friend is expecting trouble," Leoma said.

"He doesn't wait for it to find him. Roger likes to head it off before trouble ever comes calling."

Leoma cut her eyes to him and grinned. "And the occasional reckless nature you described?"

"That comes in the heat of battle."

"Are you also as rash?"

His smile widened. "More so."

"Good to know," she said. "So how do we get in?"

Braith dismounted, and Leoma followed closely behind. He loosely tied the horse so the animal could graze. Then he waited until the guards were turned away before sprinting toward the castle. Leoma was right on his heels. They plastered themselves against the stone.

"I would greet anyone sneaking into my castle with a blade," she said.

He grinned at her. "Aye, but there was only a handful of us that knew of this secret entrance. It leads into the master chamber."

"This could get us killed."

"Mayhap. We would no longer need to worry about the Coven then."

She rolled her eyes, but there was a smile on her lips.

"Ready?" he asked.

As soon as Leoma gave a nod, he maneuvered along the castle wall until he found the hidden door.

"This was how the duke tried to escape," Braith whispered. "The castle architect designed the wall in such a way that the door is tucked so you would walk past it without seeing it unless you knew of its existence."

Leoma leaned forward to look at the castle wall. "All I see is stone."

"It's an illusion. Watch."

He stood before the wall and winked at her. Then he stepped forward. Braith heard her gasp. Within seconds, Leoma was standing where he had been, smiling at him.

"This is amazing," she said.

He motioned her forward to the door. "It was a brilliant design. I've always wondered what other little surprises Roger found within the castle."

Leoma glanced at the door. "There's no handle on the door. Or a lock."

"Another trick."

He counted the slats of wood, choosing the third from the right and pushed against it toward the top. There was a slight popping noise as dust puffed out. Braith squatted down and repeated the same thing on the lower part of the slat.

There was another loud pop.

A glance at Leoma showed she was studying the door carefully. Braith straightened and put both hands on the wood. One palm on the third slat, the other on the seventh. Then he gave another push.

The door opened a crack without a sound.

"I'm duly impressed," she said with a grin.

They pushed the portal open and slipped inside the narrow tunnel. Braith closed the door behind them before squeezing past Leoma and leading her through the darkened corridor.

Neither said a word as they made their slow progress. Leoma had her hand on his back as they walked. It had been years since he'd been in the passageway, and even then, he'd had a torch to light his way.

With little flow, the air was stale and hot. He ignored the sweat running down his brow as they continued climbing the stairs that rose ever upward.

They came to a bend in the tunnel where the soft flow of air met him, cooling them enough to breathe easier. Braith didn't pause. He kept moving even if his steps were shortened as he felt his way through the dark.

Finally, his outstretched hands met wood. A door. If Roger had left everything as it was, a tapestry hid the entrance from view.

Braith slowly opened the door and took in a deep breath of fresh air. Light from the candles about the master chamber came under the massive tapestry that fell to the floor and along the sides, allowing him to make out that little bit.

Once Leoma gave him a pat that she was ready, he moved between the tapestry and the wall. She waited at the door of the passageway.

Braith reached the edge of the tapestry and gradually peeked out. There were no sounds of anyone within the chamber, but he wasn't going to take a chance of startling a servant.

When he realized there was no one inside the room, he walked from the tapestry and wiped his brow with the back of his arm. "You can come out now," he told Leoma.

"I'd rather wait," came her reply.

Braith lowered himself onto a chair and propped his forearms on his thighs. He needed to sleep. If anyone attacked him now, they would likely get the upper hand, and that didn't sit well with him at all.

The sound of a voice reached him from the hallway. Braith sat up as the door opened and a man walked inside. Roger's black hair was cut short now, but he still held himself like a warrior.

Roger's hazel eyes landed on Braith as his hand went to the dagger at his waist. But he paused, frowning. "Braith?"

"I'm very sorry for the intrusion, old friend, but events have left me little choice," Braith said as he got to his feet.

Roger dropped his hand from the weapon and smiled as he approached, arms open. "It's good to see you."

Braith clasped his friend against him briefly before stepping back. "I do apologize for coming in through the secret tunnel."

"I told you to use it if you were ever in need. I'm just sorry that you actually had to utilize it. Can you tell me what's going on?"

Braith glanced at the tapestry. "First, I should say that I'm not alone. Leoma," he called.

She walked from behind the tapestry and faced Roger.

"My heavens," Roger whispered, astonishment filling his voice. "She is a magnificent sight to behold."

Braith moved to stand beside Leoma, their eyes meeting briefly before he returned his gaze to Roger. "We ask only for this one night. We'll be gone at dawn."

"What kind of friend would I be to refuse?" Roger asked with a smile.

19

Leoma sat back in the hot water of the wooden tub and sighed. She had been cautious of Roger since entering the castle. It was a habit long honed from her training. She did her best to put it aside and trust in Braith.

The ease in which Roger greeted them relieved some of her concerns. It also helped that he kept their arrival quiet from all. Not even the servants who came to fill the tub or bring platters of food to the tower knew of her and Braith.

And that's how Leoma wanted to keep it.

She looked around the tower room while letting the heat of the water soak into her sore, tired muscles. Braith was sequestered in the master chamber with Roger. Leoma had no idea how much Braith was telling his friend, if anything, but Roger did deserve some kind of explanation for their unexpected arrival.

There was nothing in the tower that gave her pause. It was bare except for the bed and the tub, which the servants had brought in. Why then couldn't she rid herself of the warning that churned her gut?

She slipped beneath the water to wet her hair, remaining until her lungs began to burn. After rising and wiping the water from her face, she admitted, at least to herself, that her problem was that she didn't trust anyone.

As a Hunter, she was trained to rely solely on herself or other Hunters. The only reason she'd trusted Braith so quickly was because they had a common enemy. She knew nothing of Roger, other than what Braith told her.

Of course, she would immediately think the worst of Roger. It's what she was tutored to do. It was something she would keep to herself, however. The strain that had lined Braith's face lessened considerably when Roger welcomed them.

She couldn't imagine what Braith was going through, knowing the Coven was after him—without knowing what the witches wanted him for.

With her thoughts now on Braith, a flutter of excitement ran through her at the prospect of the night ahead. Her lips ached to feel his mouth again, just as her body hungered to have him inside her.

She was suddenly eager to see him again. Instead of lingering in the bath as she intended, Leoma hurriedly washed her hair and body before rinsing. She rose and dried off, only to stand at the foot of the bed where her clothes were.

A tray of food awaited her since Braith was eating with Roger. It was the first time she had been alone since she and Braith fought Brigitta.

How quickly she'd gotten used to Braith's nearness. So much so that she missed him now—like a hollow ache inside her. She also didn't particularly like how she was left out of his discussions with Roger.

Although, to be fair, Braith was giving her some privacy, as well. In her world, she was used to being treated equally.

Radnar told each of them—boys and girls—that if they picked up a weapon, he would train them the same. There was no quarter given simply because she was female.

Braith, for his part, treated her fairly. He accepted her skills and didn't look down upon her for them. Except he'd acted differently since arriving at the castle.

Which was why she was up in the tower, and he was with Roger.

She hated that it aggravated her. Roger had been shocked to see her in breeches at first, and then lust had filled his gaze. That was the moment Braith grew protective and found a way to get her away.

Braith should know she could take care of herself.

Her thoughts ground to a halt as she heard Meg's voice in her mind, telling her that perhaps Braith was protective because he didn't like the way Roger looked at her.

Leoma grinned at the idea of Braith being jealous. If he was, that meant he must have some feelings for her. She inwardly berated herself. Of course, he had feelings. She'd felt them as they made love. Because no man could touch someone as Braith had with her and not feel something.

He had been gentle but possessive, tender but merciless in his goal of giving pleasure as well as taking it. Her first encounter with a man had been wonderful, and she knew from Meg that that wasn't always the case.

With her arms wrapped around herself, she debated whether to get dressed and go down to find Braith. It was the threat of someone seeing her that kept her in the tower with only a single candle to light the round chamber.

She eventually walked to the bed and dropped the towel before blowing out the candle and climbing beneath the covers to face the door. Her eyes closed, and she hovered on the edge of sleep, drifting in and out of consciousness as every noise woke her.

Her eyes snapped open when the door creaked as it swung inward.

"Leoma."

She rolled onto her back and looked at Braith. His hair was wet, signaling that he too had taken a bath. With his jerkin, boots, and sword in hand and his shirt untucked, he shouldered the door shut and set the items down beside the bed.

Braith sank onto the bed with his back to her. He looked at the ceiling and sighed loudly. "Roger believes I'm sleeping in another chamber."

"And why aren't you?"

He turned his head to look at her. "You really want me to say?"

She nodded.

"Because the thought of sleeping with you in my arms is something I've craved since we made love."

Leoma moved aside the covers. "What are you waiting for?"

He yanked off his tunic and trousers before slipping beneath the covers beside her. She closed her eyes in contentment as he brought her against his hard body.

"I heard that sigh," he said, a smile in his voice.

"Aye. Your shoulder makes a good pillow."

With one arm holding her against him, he put his other beneath his head. She opened her eyes to find him staring at the ceiling.

"Did you tell Roger about the Coven?" she asked.

"I told him that a woman killed Josef and that I was after her. That's how I stumbled upon you. In the mix, we discovered Brigitta was part of a larger group that is now after both of us. I decided it was better to leave off all mention of magic. I wasn't sure if he would think you bewitched me."

She swallowed and let her fingers run through his chest hair. "That was probably wise."

"Roger had many questions about you. Specifically why you were dressed as you were."

"Is that so?" Somehow, she wasn't surprised.

Braith's chest rose as it expanded with air. "I told him it was my idea to help you hide from the group."

"And he believed you?"

"I'm not sure. He wanted me to bring you down so he could pose his questions directly to you."

She wrinkled her nose. "I'd rather not."

"You don't like him."

She didn't bother to rebuff his statement. "I have a difficult time trusting anyone."

"I know the feeling well."

"We should've seen to your horse."

He kissed the top of her head. "Roger had a stable boy bring him some oats and water."

"There will be questions. Who was the tower prepared for? Whose horse is it?"

"And we'll be gone before anyone even starts looking."

She heard the fatigue in his words. While she hoped they might make love again, she knew that, above all, Braith needed sleep. There had been three occasions where she'd gone without sleep for a day or more, and the toll it took on her was swift and severe.

If they were to have a chance of outmaneuvering the Coven, then both of them needed to be at their best.

"Tell me how you came to be with Edra," he asked.

Leoma rested her palm flat against his chest. "I've not thought about that day in a long time. I remember it was raining. There was mud everywhere. I couldn't find a dry place. And I was hungry. The kind of hungry where you're weak and nauseous, where you can feel your belly rubbing against itself."

"How long had you been on your own?"

"I don't know. A long time. I begged for what food I could, and I occasionally stole some. It was a horrible life. I kept out of sight because some men tried to take me. I'm not even sure how Edra saw me that day. I watched everyone from my hiding spot while trying not to think about food. I saw her ride into town with Radnar. And then she stopped and got off her horse to walk to me."

Braith's head moved toward her. "You didn't run?"

"Nay, and I don't know why. Maybe I was too weak. Maybe it was because of the food she gave me. I'm not sure why I trusted her immediately. Then she offered me a home, and since my situation wasn't getting any better, I went with her. She and Radnar became my parents, I suppose you could say."

"It's fortunate that they found you."

She knew that all too well, having brought in homeless children to the abbey herself. "I remember when Edra brought Radnar and me to the abbey. It was nothing but ruins then, hidden mostly by the forest that had grown up around it. But it was a stunning sight. Right there in the abbey, I watched Radnar and Edra exchange their vows to become man and wife."

"You love them very much," he said sleepily.

"Aye."

He grunted softly. "My mother died giving birth to me. My sire used to tell me often how I was born in battle and blood. That wasn't exactly the case, but he had to cut open my mother so I could be born. I suppose, in my father's eyes, that was battle."

"At least you knew him. I recall nothing of my parents."

"For as far back as I can remember, blood and death have been my life. My father brought me to every skirmish he led. He employed a wet nurse at first, and then an older woman. By the time I could crawl, I was passed around in the camp, knights taking turns watching me as my father trained or went to war."

Her heart broke for him. "That couldn't have been an easy way to grow up."

"I learned how to wield a sword earlier than most. I earned my meals by completing whatever training my father had for me or fighting others for it. It continued that way until I was twelve summers and my father was killed. A spear right to his heart."

"What did you do then?"

Braith moved his hand from behind his head and lightly touched her face. "I was given a choice. Become the squire of the lord my father served, or get kicked out of camp. The idea of leaving what I knew terrified me, so I remained. My training continued, and it wasn't long before I earned my spurs and was knighted. From then on, I used my skills to win at tournaments as well as battles."

"How did the king find you?"

"He was at a tournament and saw me. It just so happened the lord I was in service to—an earl—sang my praises to the king, who then sought me out."

Leoma lifted her head and placed a soft kiss on his lips. She smiled to see that he had been talking with his eyes closed. "You sure made something of yourself."

"You, as well," he said, his eyes opening a fraction to look at her.

"You'll fit in nicely at the abbey."

Braith chuckled. "You mean after we get the pesky Coven off my arse, right?"

"We will. Somehow, we will."

His arms tightened around her. "We'd better because there are lots of things I'd like to do with you. I certainly don't want this to be our only night in a bed together."

She grinned as his words trailed off and he began to snore softly.

20

The softness of her skin lulled him, but it was the warmth of her body that tugged him from the arms of sleep. Braith opened his eyes, staring in wonderment at the woman lying beside him on her back.

He wound a long, dark lock of her hair around his finger, mesmerized by the silken texture. He found everything about Leoma utterly fascinating, and completely beguiling.

His cock hardened when her leg slid against his. How he craved this woman, hungered for her with such profound intensity that he was shaken by it.

But that didn't make him withdrawn.

Instead, he found himself wanting to be closer to her. He longed to know every thought in that amazing head of hers, to have her dark, enthralling eyes directed at him with desire and...love.

Braith knew it was foolish for someone such as he to want love. He understood very little of it. It wasn't as if his father had given him much, but he had witnessed the act despite living with a sword in his hand and death beside him.

Not once had he sought out a woman to be his wife. He had neither the patience to deal with a bride nor the mindset to worry about a household.

At least, that's what he'd once thought.

Everything had changed when Leoma walked into his life that night and knocked him out. Ever since, he hadn't been able to get the burning, consuming need for her out of his system. And the longer he was with her, the more he craved her.

He released her hair and skimmed the backs of his fingers along her jaw. Long, black lashes fell against her cheek, her lips parted in sleep.

There were so many things he had wanted to do to her—with her—last night. Having her naked against him had been heaven. And then he'd fallen asleep.

He grinned as he pushed the covers down to reveal her breasts. Her nipples puckered beneath his gaze. With his mouth watering, he leaned over and wrapped his lips around a turgid peak. He swirled his tongue around the tip before suckling it.

But that wasn't enough. He wanted so much more.

Braith slowly removed the covers from both of them and nudged her knees apart. With his eyes on her face, he cautiously settled between her long legs.

His gaze lowered to the patch of dark hair at the juncture of her thighs. He gently ran his fingers through the curls a couple of times. Then he bent and put his mouth to her. He ran his tongue softly against her all the way up to her clit. Then he swirled his tongue around the sensitive nub, gradually moving faster with each swipe.

A glance up showed her breath deepening as her hips began to rock. Braith doubled his efforts, tonguing her, licking her. Her chest rose and fell rapidly, and her head began to roll on the pillow.

Suddenly, her eyes flew open, meeting his. Her dark gaze widened as a soft cry of pleasure fell from her lips. With her hands fisted in the linens, her back arched as her body stiffened with her climax.

The sight of her body flushed with pleasure, and the taste of her desire was too much. He rose up over her, his cock straining with need.

Her eyes opened after she collapsed onto the bed. She reached for him, rising up as she did. With a hook of her leg against his and her momentum, she flipped him onto his back and straddled him.

Braith smiled up at her. "My wild woman."

With her dark hair flowing around her, she leaned forward and braced her hands on his chest. "I like being woken like that."

"Then I'll do it every morning."

She reached between them and wrapped her fingers around him. Rising up on her knees, she moved him to her entrance and slowly lowered herself onto him. "Aye," she whispered.

He grasped her breasts and massaged them, thumbing her nipples as she began to rock her hips. Desire, lust, and need surged through him, gathering in his balls as he watched her head drop back while she moved faster and faster.

It never entered his mind to try and control his needs. Not with her. With his orgasm growing closer, he sat up and clasped her to him.

Her head lifted as she looked down at him. With her hands running over his face, he watched as pleasure pulled her closer and closer to the edge once again.

"Braith," she murmured.

He fisted her hair in his hands. "Not yet. Wait for me. We'll go together."

"I...can't," she replied breathlessly.

With her body moving sensuously against him and the tight walls of her sheath stroking his arousal, he was hurled to the edge, knowing that she was waiting for him.

"Now," he ground out as he grasped her hips and slammed her down on him.

Her nails dug into his arms as her walls began to milk him. As soon as the first cries of ecstasy fell from her lips, he flipped her onto her back and covered her mouth with his hand. He continued to thrust into her, drawing out their shared climax until both were spent and slick with sweat.

He moved his hand away when she grew silent. With her dark brown eyes looking up at him, he lowered his forehead to hers. They remained with their bodies joined and their limbs tangled for several moments.

This was the kind of morning he longed for. Perhaps he had always wanted it but never understood the hollow ache in his chest.

"You look sad," Leoma said as she touched his face.

He lifted his head. "I like...us."

"As do I."

"I want more mornings like this."

Her lips lifted in a soft smile. "And nights. And days."

"Aye. Do you th..." His words trailed off as his hearing picked up something.

"I heard it, as well," she whispered.

Without a word, they rose and hurriedly dressed. He was sheathing his sword when Leoma looked through the slats of the window. "It's nearly dawn. We should go."

"We'll head back out the passageway that we came in."

"I don't think we'll have time."

He frowned at her words and walked to the window to see what caught her attention. As soon as he saw the women approaching the castle, he knew it was going to be a fight for them to get out before the witches found them.

His head turned to Leoma. "The gate is closed, so the witches cannot get inside the castle. Few are up at his hour. We can sneak out."

Her gaze turned back to look outside briefly. "We should hurry."

"They shouldn't have found us," he said as they strode to the door.

"It does no good to try and determine how they found us."

Braith opened the portal, and they started down the tower stairs. They reached the bottom, and he halted at the sight of Roger, who was leaning against the wall casually eating an apple.

"We need to leave now," he told his friend. "The group we're running from has found us."

Roger bit loudly into the apple and chewed a few times before he lifted his gaze to them. "I know, though I'm afraid you won't have time to get out. I let the Coven know you were here last night."

Braith couldn't have heard him right. "Why?"

"Why?" Roger asked as he pushed away from the wall and tossed aside the fruit. "How do you think I came to have this castle, Braith? How do you think I got the title? How do you think I was able to outmaneuver the duke that once owned this place? With all the hidden passageways and tunnels running through this castle, he could've easily gotten away. And he would have, had the Coven not helped me."

Braith shook his head. "Nay."

"All I had to do in exchange for them creating the lie that the duke planned to assassinate the king was serve them. The more I served them, the more they gave me." Roger shrugged, his lips turning down in a frown. "Sorry, old friend, but they have need of you." His gaze moved up to where Leoma stood on the stairs behind Braith. "And your companion."

"I was with you when we fought the duke's men for this castle. There was no magic involved."

"Of course, there was. You just didn't see it."

Braith withdrew his sword from its sheath. "You were a good, honorable man. What happened to you?"

"I got tired of battle, of being covered in blood all the time. I grew weary of fighting for the rich and getting little in return. I had no idea I was bedding a witch until I told her what I wished for. When she told me I could get everything I wanted and more if I served her, I happily agreed."

Braith held his sword, the blade lowered to the ground. He didn't know what to make of his friend. He never would have believed Roger could be swayed by the Coven.

"Make it easy on yourself," Roger said. "Give me your sword. I'll walk the two of you out to the Coven."

Although Leoma hadn't uttered a single sound, Braith didn't need to look at her to know what she wanted to do. Fight. And he was in complete agreement.

There was no way he would so casually give up his sword. He was a warrior, a knight of the realm, who vowed to fight against evil. Unfortunately, that turned his sights on Roger.

"Nay," Braith stated.

Roger let out a loud sigh. "I'd hoped you would see sense, but if you want to do this the hard way, I'm happy to oblige."

As soon as he finished speaking, a dozen armed men filled the area. Roger gave him a smile and stepped aside.

Braith lifted his sword to block the downward swing of a blade. He dropped onto one knee and yanked Leoma's dagger from his boot to stick in the man's side. His attacker stumbled away, holding his bleeding wound.

Out of the corner of his eye, he saw Leoma put a hand to the wall and launch herself over him, her feet connecting with the opposite wall to propel her forward. He watched as she twisted in midair and came down in the middle of the men, landing on one knee.

She raised her head and slowly stood, unsheathing her sword as she did. The men were so taken aback by her moves, that they didn't know what to do.

Braith smiled as he let out a bellow and advanced on the man closest to him. As their swords connected, he got a glimpse of Leoma as she used her blade, hands, feet, and body to launch her attack.

Then he was mired in blood once more. The familiar sounds of swords clanging, bellows of pain, and shouts of attack settled over him.

He grabbed one man by the hair and slammed him, face-first, into the stone. Braith then punched another in the nose, using the pommel of his sword before swinging his blade to the side and slicing a man through the middle.

Braith ducked a fist and straightened before turning slightly to slam his elbow into an opponent's throat. There was little room to maneuver in the tower, and with every man that fell dead at his feet, he tried not to trip over them. Thankfully, the disadvantage affected everyone in the space.

He took a deep breath as the final man gurgled his last. He yanked his sword from the knight and raised his head to look for Leoma.

Braith heard the clanging of swords and jumped over the dead bodies to follow. His heart hammered against his ribs at the idea that Leoma had left the tower and he hadn't even known.

Was it Roger who led her out? Or was it the Coven. Braith was more concerned about Roger because he knew how treacherous the bastard could be. His treason had always been against others in the past, but Braith now knew the sting of that betrayal, as well.

He rushed toward the sounds of battle and slid to a halt when he spotted Leoma fighting four knights in the hall below.

Just as he was about to jump down to help her, more men poured out from either side of him.

21

S he was going to kill him. Leoma cut through the men as
she fought her way to Roger. The bastard had betrayed
Braith, and she wouldn't stand for that.

After Braith had sung his praises, she watched her lover's
face as shock and anger contorted his features. The fury that
swallowed her had been thick and cloying. Her hand had
immediately gone to her weapon while she locked her focus on
the traitor.

The moment Braith drew his weapon, she was ready for
combat, ready to sink her blade into Roger.

While their host had taken Braith's stillness as one of
defeat, she saw the way Braith's knuckles whitened from his
tight grip. She noticed the hunching of his shoulders. She
glimpsed the vein on the side of his neck that bulged from
anger.

And she knew that battle was coming.

She could taste it in the air, feel it in the tension that
filled the tower. Though she was trained for such clashes, this
was the first time her skills would be pitted against men. She

wasn't averse to stopping anyone trying to kill her, but it took a little adjustment since she was used to battling witches.

The knights were ill prepared for her. At first, they weren't sure what to do, but that didn't last long. Still, they seemed hesitant to actually hurt her, which gave her a major advantage that she eagerly and willingly took.

After cutting down two men, the knights changed their tactics and went after her full force. Their training hindered them. Her quick movements confused them.

She zigzagged in and around them so that some of their swings landed on the man next to them instead of her. Despite their multiple clashes with her sword, her arm withstood their onslaught thanks to years of instruction from Radnar.

Leoma quickly took care of the men in the tower and went after Roger. She vaulted over the last of the stairs leading down to the great hall to land in front of him. In one glance, she took in the rows of tables and benches as well as the four exits and two sets of stairs.

Roger's smile was more of a leering sneer. "I should've known Braith lied when he said you were dressed like a warrior to hide that you're a woman. He was protecting you."

Leoma shook her head. "He was shielding you."

"I don't need protecting," he stated and stepped to the side.

He was entirely too confident for her liking. There was something about his attitude and his lack of a weapon that made her take note. They circled each other, their gazes locked.

"Pick up a weapon," she demanded.

He snorted contemptuously. "I'm not afraid of you."

"I never said that you were. I told you to pick up a weapon. Unless you don't want to fight me."

"Sweetheart, if I fought you, there would be nothing left for the Coven. And they're very keen on getting you."

She bristled at his tone and the mocking endearment. "I know one thing for a fact. You're going to die today. Whether I kill you, or Braith does, your life ends. And there's nothing the Coven can do to stop it."

"You obviously know very little about them," he replied with a grin.

Leoma lifted her sword before her. "And you know so very little about me."

She lunged at him, but it wasn't his body her blade connected with, but that of another knight. Roger's cackle made her seethe, but she kept her rage under control. For the moment.

Four men surrounded her. She eyed them, noting they were much bigger than any of the other knights she had found at the castle. Their swords were twice the length of hers and much weightier.

She would have to move fast because if one of them connected with her, she would have a tough time recovering. Standing still, she moved her head to look at each man.

"Put your sword down," Roger called from behind the biggest of the knights. "If you keep this up, I cannot promise your life."

Leoma smiled. "Sure you can. The Coven wants me, and that means you have to deliver me alive. It also means that you've told your men not to kill me."

"They can still hurt you."

She leaned to the side to avoid a punch to her head. Leoma dropped down onto one foot, extending her other leg and turning, sweeping her attacker's legs out from under him.

As soon as he landed on his back, she straightened and

somersaulted over him, thrusting her sword into his heart before landing on her feet.

Her gaze locked with Roger to find a woman beside him. Leoma had never seen her before, but she put the blonde's face to memory as the woman cupped her hands before her and blew. Sparks flew, flickering in the air before thickening into a black smoke with fire sparking on the edges.

The smoke went over Leoma, gathering like clouds. She hoped the witch would get in the fray because Leoma's sword yearned to taste witch blood again.

Apprehension slithered its cold fingers around her when the witch stood with Roger to watch. There was a play going on here, and Leoma didn't have time to figure it out as she prepared to fight the three men walking toward her.

No longer could she hear Braith battling above her, and with the smoke, she couldn't see him either. That's when she knew it had been a mistake to leave him. They should have remained together.

But she had to let her anger of Roger get to her. That might very well cause her death. Or worse, allow the Coven to capture Braith.

"I think she finally sees the big picture," Roger said to the witch.

The woman's smile confirmed Leoma's suspicions.

―――

Braith ignored the cut on his right thigh and the throbbing of his left arm. He had his back to the balcony and fought man after man. They kept coming, and he kept slashing his sword.

He kicked one in the balls and shoved another over the balcony to the great hall below. A sword tip sliced through the shoulder of his jerkin. He bellowed his rage and thrust his sword upward into the gut of a knight.

Blood. So much blood. He was soaked in it, drowning in it. But he didn't let it take him. Not this time. Leoma needed him, and he had need of her. The thought of her was what kept him from sinking beneath the tide of red that he saw everywhere.

He blinked through the blood that dripped down his face to look at the five remaining men. His breathing was loud, even to his own ears. The men backed away slowly before they turned and ran.

Braith took a moment to close his eyes. Then he snapped them open and whirled around to look below where he last saw Leoma.

The four dead men made him smile until he saw the big knight fighting. He had Leoma retreating toward another set of stairs that led upward.

Braith stepped over the men at his feet and rushed to help her.

Leoma swallowed and gripped her sword with both hands. This was the fight of her life. Not only would she need to keep her eyes on the three hulking knights, but also the witch.

She debated whether to call out to Braith, but she didn't want Roger to know how worried she was about being separated from him. So she kept quiet and hoped that somehow Braith could see the smoke between them.

One thing she never liked was being on the defensive. The tides of fate could change in a heartbeat, but she wasn't going to wait for such luck. She was going to make her own.

Leoma set her sights on the biggest of the knights, the one

who stood directly in front of her. The one on her left favored one of his knees. It was barely discernable, but it was a weakness she planned to exploit. The man on her right didn't take her seriously, and that's what would get him killed.

She took a deep breath and calmed her racing heart as the men kept advancing on her. Then she moved to her left, slamming her foot into the knight's injured knee.

He went down with a scream. She palmed his dagger and slit his throat before spinning and facing the man on the right. She leaned back to miss the swipe of his sword at her head.

While Roger shouted at the knight, she straightened and slipped the blade between his ribs, right into his heart. She began to turn when something knocked into her from her back left side. Pain exploded near her kidney. Before she knew it, her feet were swept out from under her. She went down hard on the stones, knocking the breath from her.

Leoma immediately rolled away and came up on her feet as air finally filled her lungs. The knight smiled as he came at her.

Once he was within distance, she jumped on the bench and then the table. She ran a few steps and vaulted into the air, sending her legs over her head to land on his back.

She thrust her sword into his neck where it met his shoulder and twisted. Blood flowed in thick rivulets from the wound as he staggered.

Leoma yanked her blade free and pushed off him to flip backward. She landed on her feet as he crashed into the table, unmoving. Her head swiveled to Roger and the witch.

She wasn't surprised when the woman stepped forward. In fact, she was quite happy about it. With the witch dead, the smoke would vanish, and she could then find Braith.

"How's Brigitta?" Leoma asked the witch. "That's right. She's dead. I killed her."

The witch's steps faltered slightly. "You lie."

Leoma laughed. "They didn't tell you who I was, did they? The Coven sent you inside to fight me without informing you that I'm a Hunter."

"I've faced your kind before," the witch stated.

It was the slight shaking of her hands that told Leoma the woman was lying. Not that she minded. Leoma liked the idea that she and the other Hunters instilled fear in the witches. It was just a taste of what the Coven dished out to others.

"You won't live to tell about your encounter with me," Leoma declared.

The witch cupped her hands again and took a breath. Leoma ran toward her, dropping down to slide along the floor. She lifted her sword as she neared the witch and impaled her in the stomach before the woman could release her breath.

Leoma stood and pulled out her sword. Her eyes cut to Roger as the witch dropped to her knees, wailing. Within minutes, she was on her back and beginning to burn from the inside out.

Blood dripped from the end of Leoma's blade. She strode to Roger and pinned him against the wall with the tip of her blade to his throat.

"You won't kill an unarmed man," he said as he stretched his neck to keep away from her sword.

"Are you so sure about that?"

His lips trembled, and his hazel eyes clouded with fear. She couldn't see the legendary knight that Braith had spoken so highly of. All she saw was a traitorous coward.

But he was right. She couldn't kill an unarmed man.

She lowered her weapon and turned away to find Braith. He could decide what to do with his friend. Except she didn't get three steps away before she heard the whistle of a blade.

Leoma turned away, but not quickly enough. The dagger

sank into her left shoulder. She looked at the protruding hilt and then at Roger.

Without hesitation, she pulled the blade from her shoulder and threw it at him, watching it sink into his eye. Roger screamed in pain before he began to twitch, and then he fell dead.

Leoma put a hand on her wound to slow the bleeding and turned on her heel to find Braith, only to be met by silence throughout the castle.

Panic and dread churned within her gut. She raced up the stairs to find the numerous bodies. But no sign of Braith. Leoma kept her sword at the ready as she ran through the castle, searching for Braith.

Her exploration led her to the master chamber. She shoved aside the tapestry to find the door to the passageway ajar. The fluttering of wings drew her gaze to the open window.

She watched the piercing eyes of a falcon land on her before it flew away as she hesitantly made her way to the window. Her eyes locked on the older couple that stood outside the castle gates while another witch led Braith to them.

Leoma knew Braith wouldn't leave her. She was too far away to even call out to him. But she could follow.

22

Something was wrong. Braith kept shaking his head, but he couldn't make the fog within go away.

"Leoma," he called, seeking her hand.

He knew magic was being used on him, but he didn't know how to combat it. Or even what it was doing exactly.

Her arm came around him. "Everything is all right. You're going to be fine."

Braith stared into her face. There was something off, but again, he couldn't pinpoint what it was. She looked the same, spoke the same. It wasn't until he stared into her brown eyes that he realized what was off.

She no longer looked at him as if she cared, as if they had shared their bodies—and their hearts. Her gaze was...dead.

He pulled away from her and got to his feet. His limbs didn't move as if he had complete control. He felt disconnected from his body, his mind floating as if upon a mountain of mist, shrouded and suppressed.

Now that he was beginning to grasp the truth, the fog surrounding him fell away little by little.

"Braith?"

He didn't want to look at Leoma because he knew in his heart that it wasn't really her. The witches had tricked him.

Did he play along with them? Did he fight?

If they could alter his mind in such a way, how could he fight them? He had no weapons with which to either defend himself or hurt them. And it infuriated him.

He held onto that rage and let it build inside him to help him continue acting the fool. It was a new role for him, but it was the only thing he could do until he broke free of whatever spell they used. Then he would find a way to get the upper hand.

Somehow. Someway.

He wasn't going to be a willing pawn for the Coven. Their guard would be down as long as he played along with the scenario they created. That gave him the advantage, and that was all he needed to win the war.

So many times, his opponents believed he was beaten. They grew cocky instead of being smart and getting the win. The Coven was the same, and it would be their downfall.

All the while, he wondered where Leoma was. Did the Coven have her? Was she still at the castle? Or was she...dead?

Nay. He refused to believe that her life had been taken. She was too smart, too well trained to allow Roger or even the Coven to kill her. But there were very good odds that the witches had her.

He would need to be vigilant and gather all the information he could. It's what Leoma would do in his place. He would find out what the Coven wanted him for. He would get free. He would find Leoma.

And they would make it to the abbey. Together.

"Braith?"

He jerked away from the woman who was supposed to be Leoma. "My head aches."

"Sit," she urged. "Rest. We survived a betrayal by your friend."

"And killed dozens of men."

The woman shrugged as she came to stand before him. Leoma's face distorted as he stared. "It's kill or be killed in those situations."

He lowered himself back to the ground when she sat and tugged on his arm. Braith didn't want to be anywhere near the witch when he kept seeing Leoma's face. He stared into the fire, wondering how many more witches were around him. No doubt they were watching him carefully.

They had no idea that he and Leoma were lovers, and he was going to keep it that way.

"Where are we headed now?" he asked.

She turned her head to him, her beautiful dark locks shifting to gray. "I know of a place where we can rest for a few days. The witches won't be able to venture within."

"Why didn't we go there before?"

Her gaze stared at him a long moment. "It's a secret the Hunters don't share with others. I was hoping we wouldn't have need to go there, but the Coven isn't letting up."

"Have you figured out what they want with me?" he pressed.

The longer Braith stared at the woman, the more the vision of Leoma fell away to reveal that of an older woman with a long face and a sour expression.

"It doesn't matter," the woman said. "We need to make sure you don't fall into their hands."

"Aye," he agreed, trying not to pull away when she handed him the waterskin.

Her gaze watched him closely. "Do you wish to wash the blood away?"

He lowered the waterskin and looked down at his hands. How could he have forgotten the blood? As much as he wanted to leave that life behind, he seemed to constantly be pulled back into battle. Worse was the fact that he was good at it.

Braith lowered the waterskin to the ground and rose to walk to the river. With every step, he realized that he couldn't escape his past, couldn't shake off the blood and death that clung to him like a heavy mantle.

He was death.

Leoma squatted down to look at the tracks on the ground after following the Coven for hours. Behind her, Braith's horse neighed softly. She looked back at the animal.

"I know. We're going to get him back," she promised.

The stallion snorted and stared at her with its large, soulful eyes. She rose and walked to the horse to stroke its neck. The animal had tried to follow Braith when he left. Thankfully, the mount stopped for her.

Leoma gazed into the distance. She wanted nothing more than to get closer to the witches, but she suspected the older woman leading them was a councilmember.

While Leoma had a sword spelled to kill witches, getting close to the elder was going to be an issue. No witch became a councilmember unless they had the magic to back it. Which meant, the woman would be a formidable foe.

One Leoma wasn't so keen to go up against by herself.

"Come," she said to the stallion as she took the reins and led him to a copse of trees that would shield them.

There would be no fire for her this night. She didn't bother to tie the stallion. The horse only wanted to find his owner, and he seemed to understand that Leoma was trying to do just that. She gave the animal a scratch behind his ears, grateful that the stable lad had left the bridle on.

Leoma grabbed some of the food they had gotten at the village and ate it while trying not to move her wounded shoulder. She'd tied a bandage around the injury to stop the bleeding, but it was seriously going to hinder her in any upcoming battles.

She lowered herself to lean against a tree and unsheathed her sword. She attempted to close her eyes, but she kept seeing Braith running straight toward the Coven.

With a sigh, Leoma opened her eyes and looked into the distance, but she didn't see the trees or plants. Her thoughts turned inward as she thought of waking up to feel Braith's tongue on her, sending waves of unimaginable pleasure through her.

He'd said he wanted many such mornings. She grinned thinking about it because it was something she wished for herself.

How she longed to talk to Meg about Braith and the feelings she didn't quite understand. Thanks to the Coven, Leoma had lost her best friend. She wouldn't lose Braith, as well.

The night deepened as the moon rose higher in the sky. No matter how many times she tried, sleep evaded her. Leoma's mind kept turning over everything in her head to see if she had missed something when they arrived at the castle.

Nothing had set Braith off. Roger had been the perfect friend and host. Yet there had to be something she should've picked up on, some word or action that would've alerted her that Roger was in league with the Coven.

The stallion blew out a breath, his big head swinging to the side as its tail swished in agitation. Leoma kept still as she listened. The sounds of the night masked any movement she might hear, but she wasn't fooled. Something was out there.

Man, witch, or beast had found her.

The shadows parted, and a form took shape. The wolf was huge as it unhurriedly walked toward her, ears pricked forward as its yellow eyes locked on her. Directly behind it, the darkness shifted to reveal a person cloaked so that she couldn't see a face.

She grabbed her sword and rose to her feet to face the duo. The person walked to the wolf and laid a hand upon the beast's head. The wolf sat, never taking its eyes from her.

Not even being exhausted from battle and hurting from her wound would stop her from defending herself. Leoma was prepared for anything. Or at least she thought so until the individual pushed back the hood of the cloak to reveal a portion of his chiseled face showing a square jaw and wide, thin lips.

"Good eve, Hunter," he said in a deep voice.

Leoma was instantly on guard. "You know me?"

"Aye. The Varroki know of you."

"Varroki?"

His head bowed as he clasped his hands together on the staff he held before him. "I was sent to learn more about you, but after what I saw at the castle, I believe you could use my help."

She raised her blade and took a step toward him, even as the wolf stood, a low growl rumbling from the beast. She glanced at the animal to find its teeth bared. "You were at the castle and didn't lend me aid?"

"You had things well in hand for a while. While you are

skilled in combat, you can do nothing about the magic used on your friend."

Leoma studied him. "How do I know you aren't part of the Coven?"

"You cannot," the man stated. He then lowered the hood of his cloak to reveal long, pale blonde hair that fell past his shoulders with the top portion bound behind his head with a leather strip. "You will need to take my word for it."

"Why would I do that?" She tried to see the color of his eyes, but the darkness kept that from her.

He glanced down at the blade of her sword. Then he lifted his hand and raised a finger before moving it to the right.

To her shock, her blade began to follow his hand. The more she fought it, the more her sword pushed against her. Leoma gasped as she realized the man was using magic.

He lowered his hand, the enchantment used on her sword halting immediately. "Did you really believe magic was only for women? Witches and warlocks go hand in hand."

"Warlock?" she repeated, shocked to her very bones.

He took a deep breath and said, "My ancestors welcomed the magic that found the females. Those women were revered and worshipped. Magic has always come more easily to women, and they can have a wide range of magical strengths within them."

"And warlocks?" she asked.

"Warlocks are rarer. When magic comes to us, it is strong. There is much more I can tell you, but you need to invite me into your camp."

Leoma raised a brow. "I don't even know your name."

"I do not know yours either."

She really didn't know whether to like or hate the warlock. After Roger's betrayal, she was loath to trust again. But he was right. She knew how to kill witches, not stop their magic.

"I'm Leoma."

A slight grin tilted his lips. "Jarin, at your service."

She sheathed her sword and said, "Welcome to my camp, Jarin."

23

Blackglade

The drumbeat was steady, hypnotic as it reached up to the top of her tower. If Malene looked down, she would see the massive fires and the Varroki dancing around them. Their songs of battle rose up from below.

Because everyone knew she'd had Armir send out more warriors.

Malene looked down from her vantage point on the roof of the tower to see the powerful display of lightning that spread like fingers across the sky from cloud to cloud.

The sizzling on her left arm made her look down to find the blue light from her palm running up her arm much like the lightning she had been watching outside.

There was a fair amount she had yet to understand about the powers within her. For years, she'd fought against them while Armir guided her—not always patiently.

They butted heads often, but the one thing she could

count on was his loyalty. It wasn't that he cared about her. He cared about the Varroki.

She fell to her knees as the tingling in her arm spread to the other. It grew with each beat of her heart, becoming so painful that she shook with the need to be rid of it. It gathered, becoming stronger and brighter the longer it remained within.

Malene hunched over, the thunder drowning out her scream of pain. And fear.

"Why?" she demanded as she looked at the sky. "Why did you pick me?"

Armir knocked on the door on the top floor of the tower to check on Malene. She had been more reclusive of late, and he feared that she was keeping her worries to herself.

It could mean she was beginning to accept her role as leader of the Varroki. Or she was turning away from all that she was.

He cracked open the door and looked inside to see if she was asleep. One glance showed that she wasn't there. And he didn't have to look far to find her.

Armir flattened his lips as he closed the door and looked to the stairs leading to the roof of the tower. For some reason, Malene was drawn to the place time and again.

When she'd first taken her place as Lady, he feared she might throw herself off. But he soon learned she was a fighter. Malene didn't want her role, but she accepted it until the time came that she could pass it on.

Unfortunately, the only way she could transfer it was through death.

And he wasn't ready for that.

He took the stairs three at a time and found her on her knees, her head lifted to the sky as she shouted something that the wind carried away from him.

Armir started toward her when she raised her arms over her head, and blue light shot out of both hands. He stared dumbfounded at what he saw—because it was a prophecy come to life right before his eyes.

Every leader of the Varroki had the blue radiance on their left hand, but for ages, there had been one foretold who would have the glow in both hands.

That person was said to be the one who would usher in a new era for the Varroki. The prophecy never said what the new age would be, however. There was no distinction between good or bad. The Varroki could be destroyed for all anyone knew.

When the blue light faded, and Malene fell to her side unconscious, Armir hurried to her. He knelt beside her and moved a lock of her flaxen hair from her face.

He knew in his gut that he couldn't tell her about the prophecy. She already balked at her role. If he told her the rest, it might be the very thing that finally broke her.

Malene was one of the strongest women he knew—and he had known several—but she was frightened of the power within her, and she was vulnerable.

Why did it have to be her that was meant to fulfill the prophecy?

He took her hands in his and turned them over to see faint blue radiance running from the center of her palms, up her wrists, and into her forearms before fading. His gaze lifted to her face, but she remained asleep.

Armir gathered her in his arms and stood. Her hands flashed a bright blue before dimming. Even unconscious, her power was formidable.

Any enemy of the Varroki should beware of what was coming for them. If Malene acknowledged who she was, then she could leave destruction in her wake with merely a thought.

The wind shifted, and he heard the numerous drums from below. The beats were even and calm, while the people sang loudly, offering up their voices and magic.

It was Malene who inspired such songs. He allowed her to believe that their people didn't accept her, but that wasn't the whole truth. The Varroki trusted in the magic to bring them their rightful leader, but anyone who fought against the title led the people into disasters that had nearly wiped them out. So Armir pushed Malene in another direction.

For his people. For her.

And for himself.

He had watched two other leaders die, and he didn't want to lose another on his watch.

The wind stirred around them, lifting her hair to dance about his face, tickling his cheek with a faint brush of the fair locks before falling away.

He began to turn when his gaze landed on one of the six stone pillars stationed around the roof of the tower that stretched toward the sky. Before, they stood straight. Now, each was curved inward as if they were reaching for something.

Malene had done that. But for what purpose? And had she even known what she was doing?

Armir turned and carried her down the stairs and into her rooms. Inside the tower, he walked to a bed she had ordered set up. Her sleeping quarters were a floor below, but she preferred this room. Almost as if she couldn't get close enough to the sky.

He gently laid her down and covered her with a blanket before turning to the hearth. Holding out his hand, he let a ball of fire swirl in his palm before he shot it to the dying embers. Flames erupted, causing light to flare in the chamber for a moment.

Turning, he walked to the table with one of the opened books Malene had pulled from the shelves. He stared at the pages, but he didn't see the words. His thoughts were on Malene and what he had witnessed above.

With the Varroki involved in their songs, there was a good chance few of them saw the blue lights. Without a doubt, there would be those who kept their eyes on the tower and saw the display, though.

Malene, like most Varroki leaders, kept to herself. There wasn't a reason to protect her from the knowledge of the prophecy, but he would. He wanted no talk of it to cross anyone's lips—not even his own. He would keep that well hidden.

With the threat of the Coven and their growing power, as well as Malene's hesitant rule and doubting her own confidence, he didn't want to add anything else to her burden. So he would shoulder the worry alone.

He braced his hands on the table and dropped his chin to his chest. Hopefully, the warriors he'd sent out would find those Malene had seen in her vision and report back. Uneasiness sat heavily upon his chest after her predictions of slaughter, now compounded by the rise of the prophecy and the Coven's growth in power.

None of it was a good sign.

"You should let me see to that wound."

Leoma untied the bloodied bandage around her left shoulder and glanced at him. As soon as it was safe for her to build a fire, she planned to put a dagger in the coals to heat a blade and cauterize the wound.

"You need to stop the bleeding," Jarin said as he came down on his haunches next to her.

She looked up at him. "I plan on taking care of it as soon as I can."

"We'll do it now." He stamped the end of his staff on the ground and a small fire formed before her.

She jerked her focus from the fire to him. "How did you do that?"

The light shed on his face allowed her to see what the shadows withheld—his eyes. They were the palest blue she had ever seen. They were so fair they were nearly colorless. Only the bright cerulean outlining his irises allowed her to see the hue within.

"You know how I did it."

She shook her head, coming to terms with knowing there were warlocks out there.

Jarin set down his staff and dropped to his knees. He went to reach for her, but Leoma leaned away. His lips compressed as something wild and angry flashed in his eyes. "If I wanted you dead, I could've killed you at the castle or anytime while I followed you here," he said.

The truth of his words upset her the most. She had been so intent on pursuing the Coven that she'd forgotten to look behind her. "You could be taking me to them."

"Then why have they not already surrounded you?" he asked with the quirk of a brow.

She licked her lips, nodding in agreement. "Tell me why you're here."

This time when he reached for her, she held still. With his help, she removed her cloak and vest. He looked at her wound for a long moment.

"I'm here because I was told to find you."

"Me specifically?" she asked.

He gave a shake of his head. "Our leader had a vision of slaughter. In the aftermath stood the Coven and a small group. It's your people Malene saw."

"She saw Hunters?"

He gave a quick shake of his head. "I heard the term while at the castle."

"And what do you want with us?"

Jarin stood and shoved his cloak over his shoulders as he walked a few paces from her, inspecting different plants. "An enemy of the Coven is our friend. We fight the Coven and everything they stand for."

"That's good to know." Leoma bit back a wince when she moved her shoulder, causing more blood to flow. Fighting was going to be painful.

He picked a few leaves from a plant and returned to kneel beside her. Except he didn't touch her. He doused the leaves with water before handing the waterskin to her. Leoma drank deeply while watching him gather soil in his hands and roll it into a ball around the wet leaves.

"Why do you fight the Coven?" he asked as he flattened the ball into a thick disk before placing it on her wound.

Leoma was about to balk, but almost immediately, she felt warmth and then a slight tingling seep into her injury that minimized the ache so that she could breathe easier.

"Thank you," she said. After he bowed his head and sat back, she thought over his question. "Long ago, the Coven hunted a witch to bring her into the fold. She eluded them for years before she decided to take a stand. She ended up killing four of them. She and her knight found me, a starving, homeless kid on the streets. They brought me with them and set up a place to teach others to fight against the Coven."

"Witch Hunter," he replied staring into her eyes.

"Just those of the Coven. I know the difference between those who do evil with their magic and those who do not."

Jarin patted the ground, and the wolf that had stood silently the entire time padded forward and lay down next to him. "Without magic, you cannot kill a witch."

"I may be without magic, but my blade isn't," she said, nodding to her sword.

He grinned. "I like you, Leoma."

"You like that I can fight and that I'm standing against the Coven."

"Aye, there is that. I also like your courage. I've not seen it in one such as you before."

She raised a brow. "You mean a woman?"

He sank his hands into the wolf's fur and petted the large animal. "Our leader is a woman. Your sex is not what I speak of."

"What do you mean then?"

"You're a warrior. You call yourself Hunter, but there is little difference in us. There are those who say they are warriors, and then there are those like you."

She stretched out her feet toward the warmth of the fire. "You're not so bad yourself, warlock."

His answering chuckle made her smile.

Trust wasn't exactly something she gave the warlock, but Leoma wasn't too prideful to know when she needed help. If Jarin were going to heal her injury, she would accept that and all the information he shared.

"I've never heard of the Varroki," she said.

He clicked to the wolf that rose and trotted off into the night. Jarin then dug into a bag hidden beneath his cloak and produced a loaf of breath. Without hesitation, the warlock handed it to her. She met his gaze before accepting it.

"You need this more than I do. Eat," he urged.

She didn't need to be told twice. Leoma took the bread and tore off a chunk before stuffing it into her mouth.

Jarin shifted so that his back leaned against a tree and his face was averted from the fire. "I've been tracking the Coven for some time. Specifically Eleanor."

"Who's she?" Leoma asked around a mouthful of food.

"One of the Coven's councilmembers."

Leoma swallowed and blew out a breath. "I knew it as soon as I saw her. She has to be the one with Braith."

"She rarely leaves London," Jarin continued. "I've been trying to get close to her for months. As soon as Eleanor left the city, I let my commander know."

"And where are the Varroki located?"

He grinned, telling her he wasn't going to share that information. Just as she wouldn't tell him where the abbey was.

So she tried a different question. "How do you communicate with the Varroki?"

"Ravens mostly," he replied. "They carry messages back and forth for us, but I prefer Andi."

Leoma frowned at the name. "That means spirit."

"You know Norse?"

"Aye. Who is Andi?"

Jarin grinned as he said, "My falcon. She's fast."

Impressed, Leoma then asked, "How does the Coven not know you're following them?"

"The same way you didn't see me in the great hall as you fought the witch and the others."

He had been in the hall and she hadn't seen him? That left Leoma reeling. "I notice everything."

"Magic is easily overlooked," he stated in a soft voice. He turned his head to the darkness. "The Coven doesn't know of us because we don't wish them to. Much as you and yours have kept to the shadows."

"If you can get that close to me, why not get to Eleanor and kill her."

Jarin shot her a flat look. "If any of us were able to, we would have."

"So you're just going to follow them around?"

"We know more about what's going on within the Coven than you do. You chase your tail, trying to figure out what the witches plan to do next."

Leoma sat forward. "What are they doing?"

Jarin stared at her a long moment before he said, "They're after an object."

"What object?"

"The Blood Skull."

She slowly sat back. "That doesn't sound good."

"It's not. It's a relic from the first witch to ever have magic. It is said that her power was so strong that it's even in her bones."

Leoma sat down the remaining bread. "I hope your people are guarding the witch's tomb then."

"If only it were that easy. You see, the witch's bones were scattered across multiple countries."

"Tell me you at least know where the skull is?" The more the warlock spoke, the more anxious Leoma became.

He shook his head. "We do not. However, the Coven somehow discovered it."

"Why does this involve Braith?"

"I do not know."

Leoma let the news digest as she tried to determine her next move.

Jarin spoke, breaking into her thoughts. "Finish the bread, and then rest, Hunter. We start before dawn."

She ate because she was still hungry, but there was no sleep for her. Though she closed her eyes, she didn't allow herself to drift off. Not even when Jarin rolled onto his side and promptly fell asleep, or when the wolf returned and lay at the warlock's back.

All Leoma could think about was Braith, the Blood Skull, and how they might be connected. She pulled her cloak over her to ward off the chill. How she missed Braith's warmth and his arms around her.

When the sky turned a pale blue as night receded, she sat up and stretched her neck. She looked over at Jarin to find his unusual eyes locked on her. He rolled into a sitting position, and the wolf trotted off to do who knew what.

"Is he your traveling companion?"

Jarin stood and glanced at the wolf before the animal disappeared into the copse of trees. "I found him when he was a pup and raised him. I belong to Valdr as much as he belongs to me."

"He's quite intimidating," she admitted.

The warlock walked to her and squatted down beside her. "I'll be sure to let him know you think that. Now, let's check this wound."

She had forgotten about her injury since it no longer pained her. When he removed the disc of dirt and leaves, she waited to feel a twinge, but there was nothing.

"Ah," he said with a grin. "Perfect."

Leoma looked at her shoulder to see the wound healed except for a pink scar puckered where her skin had melded back together. Her head snapped to him. "You used magic?"

"Herbs," he replied as he tossed aside the remnants of the disc. "And magic. Magic can only do so much."

Edra had once said much the same thing to her. Leoma tested her shoulder to find that it was almost good as new, as if a dagger hadn't embedded in her shoulder. "Thank you."

He bowed his head. "I hope this goes a long way to proving that you can trust me."

"Do you trust me?"

His lips twisted in a half-smile. "As much as I can."

"I feel the same."

Jarin stood and held out his hand. "Shall we?"

She took his hand as he pulled her to her feet. Leoma put on her vest and cloak again while Jarin doused the fire with more magic, then she went to the horse.

"Valdr will not bother the stallion," Jarin said as he walked up beside her.

She smiled as the horse nudged her. "He's Braith's. He tried to follow his master. I think he stays with me because he knows I'm going after Braith."

"And because he trusts you."

Her head swiveled to Jarin. "You can speak to animals?"

"Sadly, I do not have such a gift. I just understand animals better than most."

"Are there more Varroki out there waiting to attack the Coven?"

He leaned upon his staff that he put before him, clasping both hands on the wood. "It's just me. For now."

"I'm ready to fight them before they reach wherever they're going for the skull."

"It may come to that," Jarin said. "Until then, we track them."

———

Braith woke to find the gray-haired woman smiling at him. He looked around and saw no one else. But he knew they were out there.

"Did you sleep well?"

It irritated him that he still heard Leoma's voice when the woman spoke. He made himself grin as he faced her. "Aye. I did some thinking last night. I'm tired of running from the Coven."

Her eyes widened. "You want to fight them? Even knowing you cannot kill a witch?"

"I'm a knight. Running from a foe isn't something I do. I hate looking over my shoulder."

She shifted, her face falling and settling into the lines of a frown. "We don't know what the Coven wants with you. It's better that we keep moving until we can meet up with other Hunters."

If there had been any doubt in him that he wasn't with Leoma, the woman's words sealed it for him. While he was in the Coven's hold, he was going to make things difficult for them.

"You sent word to them two days ago. They'll be looking for us," he lied.

The woman didn't bat an eyelash as she replied, "I'll let them know where we're at so as not to worry them."

"Wouldn't it be more prudent to go to them so the Coven and however many of those evil witches are following us can face off?"

The woman slowly smiled. "You are ready for battle, aren't you?"

"I was born into it."

"It makes you a formidable adversary."

He got to his feet. "We're wasting daylight."

The woman was slower to rise. No longer did he see Leoma's svelte figure with black leather molded to her body. Instead, he saw a red gown and a wrinkled hand.

"Lead the way," he told her.

Braith fell into step behind her. He looked over his shoulder, hoping for some sight of Leoma. His mind refused to believe that she wasn't out there following them.

When he turned around, he squared his shoulders and put one foot in front of the other. It felt as if he were being led to his death, and in fact, that's probably exactly what was happening.

Though he wouldn't go down without a fight.

He touched the hilt of his sword, not at all surprised that he still had it since it couldn't kill a witch. As he walked, he glanced down at his boot, looking for Leoma's dagger that he kept there, but it was gone.

With no blade to kill a witch, Braith would have to bide his time until he could get his hands on another weapon. Or Leoma could catch up with him.

"How far is this secret place?" he asked.

"We should reach it by tonight."

The news soured his already hostile disposition. He had only a few hours to get away from the Coven. Until he knew how many witches surrounded him, he couldn't accurately come up with a plan.

They walked in silence until they stopped midday to rest and eat. The woman left to hunt, and he didn't argue with her. He used the time to walk around the area, looking for signs of anyone else.

He caught a whiff of body odor that left him nauseous. It would be easy to know when that person tried to sneak up on him. He also made out half a footprint. It was smaller than his, most likely a woman's.

Despite his search, he found no other evidence. Either there wasn't anyone else out there, or they were very good at hiding themselves.

When he returned to their resting place, the woman was already there with a fire going. He came to stand across the flames from her. "That was quick hunting."

"You know how good I am."

"I do, but that was quick. Even for you."

The woman held his gaze as she stood. After a moment, the fuzziness around her that kept trying to put Leoma's face on hers stopped. "What a surprise you are. How long have you known?"

He didn't bother to act as if he didn't know what she meant. "Since last night."

The woman lifted a hand, and eight witches along with a portly man came into sight. "Just so you know, it's pointless to attempt an escape."

He glared at her. "Just so *you* know, you're going to lose."

25

Whether she wanted to admit it or not, Leoma was glad to have Jarin with her. Though she could track, he had a gift for it that left her amazed. Of course, it helped to have a wolf as a friend.

Valdr rarely strayed far from Jarin. There were times while observing them that Leoma saw the pair move as one as if they could read each other's thoughts.

Just as Jarin had said, the wolf didn't bother the stallion. But as a precaution, she made sure to keep the horse and Valdr as far from each other as possible. So far, they were all getting along fine.

Jarin led their small group, often stopping to survey the land before setting off again. She remained on the stallion and kept an eye behind her for any other surprises.

Mid-morning, they reached the spot where it was obvious the Coven and Braith had bedded down for the night. She dismounted and studied the ground around the cold remains of a fire.

"There were only two of them here," she said.

Jarin's face was lined with unease. "The rest were spread out and hidden. Until this morning. Their tracks led to you."

Leoma looked to where he pointed and found evidence of others on either side of her and behind her. "I don't understand."

"How do you think they convinced Braith to leave the castle without restraints?"

She swallowed and looked away. "You saw the same thing I did. He ran right to them."

"But why didn't he fight them? Why didn't he return for you?"

Her head swiveled back to Jarin, hating that he was making her say aloud the very thoughts that had plagued her since the castle. "He wouldn't have left me. Which means he thought he was running toward me."

Jarin nodded slowly, compassion softening his lips. "There were only two sets of tracks at the fire. The deeper set was Braith's."

"And the other is Eleanor," Leoma said. "Posing as me."

"There are no signs of a struggle. Either Eleanor is using magic to convince Braith to stay with her, or he's united with the Coven."

Leoma took a step toward the warlock, anger making her voice come out harsh. "He wouldn't do that."

"I do not believe he would," Jarin replied calmly. "I'm stating our options."

"What changed this morning, then?"

The warlock's gaze went to his wolf, who was sniffing at the ground where the Coven had set off. "How much does Braith know of magic?"

"Not a lot. He was only recently acquainted with it when

we ended up tracking the same witch. I was hunting Brigitta because she killed a friend. He was after her because she murdered his ward. I attempted to ensure that he couldn't find us, but he was better than I expected."

Jarin leaned against his staff with a grin. "He's resourceful. That's good to know. What happened?"

"He tracked Brigitta and me into a Witch's Grove."

The warlock's smile faded as shock filled his face. "Braith willingly walked into a Grove? Alone?"

Her brows rose as she nodded. "He was that bent on revenge. I was waiting for the right time to attack Brigitta, but he came at her from behind. He discovered his sword couldn't harm her, and she cut him."

"Magic in the blood," Jarin said, distaste filling his visage.

"There was a skirmish, and I managed to get Braith out. I had herbs given to me for just such an encounter with a witch. I used them on Braith."

Jarin straightened as he said, "Ah. That's it, then."

"What?"

"Once someone's blood is poisoned with magic and then they are healed with it, that person can push through the veil of any powers used on them if they're strong enough mentally."

Leoma glanced at the ground. "Braith is strong enough."

"So, he saw through Eleanor's magic. That is quite a feat," Jarin stated, impressed. "I cannot imagine that Eleanor would have dropped her disguise already."

Leoma followed the trail of footprints away. "Then why is he still with them? Why isn't he fighting to get away?"

"Because he's smart. He knows there is nowhere he can go while surrounded by witches. He has no desire to have magic used on him again either. To keep his head clear and focused, he's going along with what they want for the time being."

"Then we need to get to him."

Jarin began to turn when the shrill cry of a falcon stopped him in his tracks. His face turned upward as a smile curved his lips.

She followed his gaze and spotted a dark shape circling above them. The bird gave another cry before diving straight for Jarin. Suddenly, the falcon spread its wings and reached its talons out as Jarin held up his arm.

Leoma watched in utter amazement as the bird perched. A moment later, the falcon's penetrating gaze turned on her.

"She's magnificent," Leoma said.

Jarin ran his hand down the bird's feathers. "That she is. We have a message."

Leoma watched while Jarin freed the small roll of paper from the falcon's leg while Valdr came to sit beside Jarin. As the warlock read the message, something butted Leoma from behind. She turned to find the stallion.

"We're getting close," she whispered to the horse while stroking his nose. "Soon, you'll be reunited with Braith."

"I'm to stop the Coven."

She lifted her head to look at Jarin. "It's a good thing we already decided to do that."

There was a slight grin on his lips when he said, "I didn't need to be told to attack. Armir, the second in command of the Varroki, wants me to know that he guessed my intentions. Because they would have been his, as well."

"Any chance we'll get Armir to help?"

Jarin rolled the message back up and dropped it in the bag slung across is chest. "He will never leave Blackglade and our Lady. Only if Malene ventures out will he join her."

"Perhaps we need to get Malene here."

He simply grunted in response. "My people remain hidden

for a reason. None of the leaders have ventured from our land. Our Lady protects our people."

Jarin whispered something to the falcon who flew off before he knelt to look at the footprints leading away. Without a word, he jogged away with the wolf at his side.

Leoma vaulted up on the horse and set out after them. They moved quickly over the terrain, and with each hour that passed, Jarin's face grew tighter and tighter.

She couldn't dispel the notion that they were headed to something she wanted no part of. Hunting down rogue witches of the Coven had been her objective from the beginning, but now she was on a path to something much grander.

Something she wasn't prepared for.

Something she feared.

But she wouldn't stop. She had a target to take out—and her man to find.

When Jarin halted, she drew the stallion up beside him. The warlock was breathing heavily as he gazed ahead of them over the rolling landscape. He pushed the hood of his cloak back and pointed with the tip of his staff.

"They've increased their speed of travel."

Leoma frowned, not sure she'd heard him right. "How? They're on foot?"

He shot her a flat look and lowered his weapon. "You were raised with magic. Why do you forget it?"

"Do *you* forget that I don't have it?"

"Nay, but you overlook the fact that you're dealing with the Coven, who uses it for their gain. I gather your teacher did not?"

Leoma shoved aside the hair that lifted in the wind and blew over her face. "Rarely."

"If you're going to win, you need to remember that magic

rules the Coven. They use it for anything and everything. Don't trust your eyes or your ears."

She shifted atop the horse. "Then how am I to fight them?"

"With your heart."

"I was trained with a blindfold before. I know to open my senses."

Jarin stuck the end of his staff into the ground and faced her. "Your senses can be deceived."

"So can the heart."

"Not with magic."

She stared at him a moment before shaking her head in confusion. "You talk as if it will be just the two of us going in after the Coven."

"Because it will be."

Leoma lifted her gaze but saw nothing in the distance that suggested the Coven's destination. "Do you know where they're going?"

"I have a suspicion," he replied cryptically.

She slid her gaze to his. "Which is?"

"A place no one wants to be."

"A Witch's Grove?"

He gave a shake of his blond head. "Worse. An Altar."

Her stomach knotted at the word, even though she had no context to go along with it. It was the way Jarin said it. As if it were the worst place he had ever been.

"What is it?"

His brow furrowed. "I wonder if your teacher knows so little or if she has kept things from you in an attempt to shield you."

"I cannot answer that. Though I intend to find out later. Right now, I'd like to know why the Altar bothers you."

Jarin sunk his hands into the fur at the wolf's neck. "It was a place used thousands of years ago for punishments and sacri-fices. It's a place drenched in blood."

Leoma's heart missed a beat as Jarin's words made her think of Braith.

"Though the history of the place has been forgotten, the feeling of death and despair around it keeps others away. I suspect that's why the Blood Skull was most likely brought there."

"An attempt to keep it hidden," Leoma said.

Jarin glanced her way. "Unfortunately, it's a place that draws witches like those in the Coven."

"Is the skull displayed for all to see?"

"Legend tells that it was buried."

She absently stroked the horse's neck. "The Coven must have found it."

"Possibly."

"But you believe we're going to the place where the Blood Skull is buried?"

Jarin inhaled deeply before releasing the breath. "It's a guess, and right now, that's all I have."

"It's more than I had. It doesn't matter what the place is or why they want Braith. I'm going after him."

"You must love him very much."

Her mind went black as she thought over Jarin's statement. She thought of Braith, of his beautiful eyes and strong arms. Her body grew warm just thinking about the passion that had erupted between them.

When she looked at Jarin, he gave her a half-smile. "Ah, I see you have yet to realize the depths of your feelings."

"Why do you say I love him?"

Jarin shrugged and tilted his head. "I saw the way you fought by his side. I watched as you realized what the witch at the castle intended, and I saw your determination to reach

Braith. You were ruthless in your endeavor to find him. Such passion and motivation develop deep within a person who already has a strong, solid connection to another."

"I'm going to find him," she stated.

"You're going to do more than that, Hunter."

26

Cold. It surrounded Braith, battering him on all fronts. His limbs refused to obey no matter how hard he tried to move his arms and legs. And he knew why and who caused it.

Eleanor.

The witch hadn't bothered to keep her name from him. In fact, she had been most forthcoming in telling him all about herself. As soon as she'd mentioned she was on the Coven's council, Braith knew his foe was formidable.

No one questioned Eleanor. Not the witches at her command, and certainly not the overweight man doing his best to keep up with the rest of them.

While Braith fought against the icy fingers surrounding him, he let his mind drift back to analyze what he could remember in the hopes that he could break through whatever magic the Coven used on him this time.

He recalled how he'd been all too aware of how Eleanor quickened her pace. He was shocked that a woman of her age managed such swift speed. Then again, she was a witch.

For hours, he'd listened to her drone on about the greatness of the Coven. The less impressed he looked, the more she talked. He tried to ignore her, but she never took the hint. He walked ahead of her, but she quickly caught up. He even attempted to lag behind, but not even that worked.

Braith kept putting one foot in front of the other, all while taking note of the eight witches and cataloguing which ones seemed to fear Eleanor the most. He knew once he developed his plan that his very last target would be the man. It wasn't as if Walter moved very fast.

When Leoma reached him—because Braith refused to even consider that she was gone—they would unleash Hell upon Eleanor and her witches.

Braith itched to feel the weight of his sword in his hand, to heave it at Eleanor's neck and watch the blade slice through skin and bone.

Her persistent talk of the Coven and how wonderfully grand they were was driving Braith daft. Each of her words was like a knife being plunged into his body. He took it until he couldn't listen anymore.

Since she made sure to remain near him, it was no great feat for him to maneuver beside her. As she spoke of how all witches would soon beg to be part of the Coven, the last of his control snapped.

He reached over and locked his hands around her throat and squeezed. He was bombarded with magic. It slammed into him from all sides, but he didn't release his hold. He turned Eleanor and forced her onto her knees as she clawed at his hands.

Pain exploded through his body. But it was the look of fear in her gray eyes that gave him the most satisfaction. Even with his strength failing from the onslaught of magic, he tightened his fingers.

Suddenly, he was forcefully hit in the chest by something cold. His fingers slipped from Eleanor's thin neck as he was propelled backward. Wind rushed around him, drowning out the bellows of the witches.

And then everything began to tilt so that he was looking up at the sky before he crashed into something. His breath left him in a whoosh, but an instant later, his head slammed against something hard.

Darkness dotted his vision as Eleanor stood over him. She said something as she held her hand over him. And that was the last thing he remembered.

Until now.

Until the cold.

"Can you hear me?"

He tried to pull away from Eleanor's voice, but his body was still not his own.

"Ah," she said with a laugh. "You can. That was a good attempt to kill me. A very good attempt."

He wanted to see where they were. Everything sounded different. No longer did he hear the birds or the wind. Wherever they were, it was silent as a tomb, except for the distant drips of water.

He stood frozen and began to gain back his body. To his shock, his eyes opened. It took him a moment to adjust to the darkness around him. Was it night? No, it was too damp.

Eleanor's laugh came at him as if from a great distance. He blinked several times to clear his vision and saw two small flames ahead of him, hanging on something. Torches. There were torches.

His legs abruptly gave out, causing him to crash onto his knees. Even as agony shot through him from landing on stone, he attempted to move his arms forward to catch himself. Just before his face hit the ground, his hands were there.

Braith squeezed his eyes shut and pushed himself onto his hands and knees. His body was thawing from the persistent cold, but he couldn't hold back a shiver from the dampness that seemed to sink into his very bones.

He looked to each side but saw no sign of Eleanor or the witches. What he did glimpse was water, vast amounts of it. The dark liquid rippled slightly when drops from the walls hit the surface.

Braith straightened on his knees and let his eyes wander the massive cavern. He knelt on a smooth path about four feet wide that was laid out straight before him toward a large, dark shape situated between the two torches.

On either side of the track was water. He couldn't tell how deep it was or even how far it extended. A glance over his shoulder showed a rocky platform, a doorway, and another path.

How had he gotten here? What kind of magic did Eleanor use that made him lose so much time? He pushed aside those questions because he would get no answers. Instead, he got to his feet, his attention drawn to the torches.

He knew Eleanor wanted him to walk to the lights, but he wouldn't do it. Whatever the Coven sought, it couldn't be good. And he wasn't going to be part of it.

Braith took a step back. No sooner had he moved than he doubled over and grabbed his head as images poured into his mind as if a dam had broken. They barreled through his brain one after the other, showing blood and death. Hundreds of bodies torn and ripped to pieces.

The land laid to waste, blackened by fires and dripping with blood. The sky was a deep red with dark clouds rolling in ominously. He choked from the smell of burning flesh.

Then he was walking on bones. Hundreds of thousands of them. He heard screams. Then he heard his name.

He reached out as he recognized Leoma's voice. But the image of her being burned alive made him recoil in horror. The sight of her remained in his mind even as he was shown more and more destruction.

Finally, he threw back his head and bellowed, his arms out at his sides as he dropped to his knees again.

"Braith."

He bent over and slammed his fist against the rock in utter frustration and weariness.

"I've been waiting for you."

The whispered voice was soft, seductive. He opened his eyes, and the images stopped.

"You have the power to break the pact. You, born in battle. You, who have lived amongst death, who was bathed in blood. Only you, Braith."

He lifted his head and looked at the dark shape before him.

"The dead await you. They nip at your heels, eager to pull you down with them."

Braith got to his feet. The words were coming from every-where. And nowhere. They were all around him—and in his mind.

"Your death will come not by blade, but by the hands of witches. They seek to use you. But I know what's before you. I've watched you since the moment you came into this world, screaming in fury."

"Who are you?" he asked as he began to slowly walk forward.

"I am night. I am blood. I am death. I have walked beside you all these years."

He felt the pull of whatever was ahead of him, but it wasn't magic being used. It was something more primal, something he didn't want to ignore.

As he drew nearer, the torches blazed brighter.

"*You're on a path you cannot walk away from. You were always meant to come here.*"

"I don't understand," he said with a shake of his head.

"*All will make sense soon. Trust my words.*"

He glanced at the water to see it moving on either side of him as if something were gliding just beneath the surface. But he wasn't afraid. The voice was right, he was meant to be here. He felt it.

The closer he got to the dark shape, the more he was able to make it out. A long, thick chunk of rock rested on a large, squat boulder. On either side of the slab were two massive columns that stretched high above him.

The light from the torches allowed him to see the carvings on the pillars and the altar. Each design told an ancient story whose meaning felt just out of reach.

He returned his attention to the altar and saw two hand-prints. He knew that's where he needed to be, and the closer he walked to the slab, the more certain he was.

Braith lifted his hands and laid them on the rock. Immediately, a crimson glow seemed to ignite from within, shooting light from between his fingers and around the edge of his palms.

The red light flashed in his eyes before moving toward him. It made him feel as if he were flying through the air. All he perceived was the scarlet radiance and the rocks around him.

Then he saw it. The skull. It sat in a small chamber deep beneath him on a rock, blood continually flowing from the eyes, nose, and mouth.

Braith yanked his hands away, and the light faded. He looked at his palms to see that they were covered in blood. Even now, blood followed him.

He walked behind the altar to the column on the right and traced an etching of a spiral. Then he made his way to the other pillar and traced a trinity knot.

A dull red light began to shine from each of the markings he traced. The beams met before pointing at the wall behind him.

Braith followed the light to find nothing but a wall. Yet he knew what was below, he knew what awaited him. He closed his eyes and walked forward. When he opened them again, he was in a narrow passageway. The only illumination was that of the red light that had brought him this far.

But as he descended the steps, the crimson glow grew brighter. He reached the bottom of the stairwell and turned to the left where the illumination originated. There, he spotted the skull.

"You found me."

"You still haven't told me who you are."

"Who I once was matters not. It's what is coming that you need to be worried about."

He moved toward the skull before circling it, watching the blood flow from its orifices to run down the pillar into a channel cut into the rocks that drained somewhere. He thought of the water he'd seen in the cavern and wondered if he put his hand in it if it would be blood.

"You doubt."

"I swore not to help the Coven, and yet I've done just that."

"I am but one of four pieces. One piece does not a war win."

He frowned at her words. "You want me to bring you to the Coven?"

"It is the only way for you to live. And you are needed. Leoma needs you. I need you."

"None of this makes sense," he said and looked down at his bloodied hands.

"The Coven does not know I'm able to talk with you. Nor can they. If you want to defeat them, you must trust me."

He squeezed his eyes closed a moment. "Just tell me what I need to know."

"Trust my words."

Braith stared at the skull, looking into the holes where the eyes used to be for a long time. A decision had to be made. Either he left without the skull, which meant his death—as foretold by the skull.

Or he gave it to the Coven.

Was he being duped by the witches even now? Was magic being used on him? He knew what the Coven's magic felt like, and what hovered around him now was nothing like it.

He reached for the skull and put his hands on either side of it. Dozens of voices began to fill the area in a soft cascade of reverent singing, some tones higher than others, the sound beautiful and powerful. And terrifying.

"Trust me."

Braith took a deep breath and lifted the skull.

27

The dirt was cool against Leoma's fingers as she kept close to the ground while creeping toward the rock formation. She saw nothing that would suggest it was more than a group of boulders, but she followed Jarin just the same.

The warlock's lips flattened before he swiveled his gaze to her. She came up alongside him and looked over the rim of the hill. Her gaze locked on Eleanor and her company of witches.

"The man with them is Eleanor's husband, Walter," Jarin whispered. "He's a duke, which gives her the clout she needs in London."

No matter how hard she looked, Leoma couldn't find the one person she searched for. "Where's Braith?"

"Inside."

She refused to believe that he would so easily do what the Coven wished of him. "Alone?"

"It looks that way?"

"Why?"

Jarin sighed as he looked at her. "I know no more than you."

"I have to get down there."

"There are eight witches, plus Eleanor. And just two of us."

Leoma glanced at the wolf. "There are four of us if you include Andi and Valdr."

Jarin's smile was slow as it filled his face. "The witches will be expecting you, but not me."

"We use that to our advantage, then. I'll attack first. Let them believe they've overtaken me. Then you strike."

He lifted a blond brow high on his forehead. "You trust me to have your back?"

If she wanted to find Braith, she would have to do just that. "Aye."

"Whenever you're ready, then."

She crawled back down the hill until she could stand without being seen. Leoma put her hood up and withdrew her sword. When she turned around, she saw Jarin watching her with his pale blue eyes.

"I would ask something of you," she said.

He gave her a nod. "Name it."

"If I die, do I have your word you will continue to help Braith? Will you promise me to protect him until you can find another Hunter?"

Jarin closed the distance between them. "Braith is to become a Hunter?"

"It's what he said he wants."

"Then you have my word."

Her head swung to the side when she saw something out of the corner of her eye. She stood still as the wolf came up beside her and sniffed her hand. His yellow eyes met hers briefly before he walked to Jarin.

"He likes you," the warlock said.

Leoma studied the magnificent animal. "You're lucky to have such a companion."

"Aye."

There was something in Jarin's gaze that made her frown. A sadness she didn't expect. As curious as she was about it, she didn't have time to inquire.

"We'll be ready," Jarin assured her.

She turned and walked around the hill to come at the Coven from the side. Her heart was in her throat. Of all the times she had fought witches, none mattered more than this battle.

Not only because they were after the Blood Skull, but also because of Braith. He was decent and kind and...special. He was strong and imposing, resilient and fierce.

And he held her heart.

No matter how many witches or councilmembers she had to fight, Leoma would not leave him to face whatever was within the boulders alone.

She kept her gaze on Eleanor as she approached. The witches noticed her immediately, but it was Eleanor who smiled as if excited by the prospect of their encounter.

Leoma stopped and faced the eldest witch. Though fear slid icily through her veins, she refused to let it take her. Too much was at stake.

"You're too late," Eleanor said with a grin.

Leoma looked into the lined face of the councilmember, keeping her expression impassive. It was imperative that no emotions be revealed in her face, eyes, or tone. "For what? You're still here."

"Braith is ours," a witch said.

Eleanor jerked her head to the side and hissed at the witch, her mouth forming a contemptuous sneer. After the witch lowered her head in deference, Eleanor's gaze returned to Leoma.

That small display of reprimand showed Leoma just how

controlling Eleanor—and most likely the rest of the council—was of the lesser witches. It was just as Edra had said it would be, but seeing it firsthand was eye-opening.

Eleanor lifted her chin to look down her nose at Leoma. "You have no magic, child. Why would you come after us?"

"Someone has to stop you from killing innocents and taking children."

"The children are a necessity," Eleanor said.

Calm. She had to remain calm. "Why?"

"That's Coven business."

"It ends now."

Eleanor laughed as she walked to Leoma. "I might be tempted to find a use for you, Hunter. Lay down your sword, and I'll allow you to live."

"I'd rather die than serve you and the Coven in any capacity."

"That's a mistake you will regret."

Leoma dove at an angle to the right before Eleanor finished speaking. As Leoma got to her feet, she shoved her sword up into the stomach of the nearest witch.

There was an instant of shock from all around her, and then pandemonium ensued. Witches shrieked in outrage, magic came at Leoma from everywhere. She used her sword to block as much as she could, but it helped little.

The power weakened her so that she was soon on the ground, holding herself up with one hand. A witch leaned close, smiling in triumph. Leoma wanted to lift her sword, but it felt as if an entire mountain were pushing her down into the earth.

Then, above it all, she heard the cry of the falcon.

There was a blast that sent the witches tumbling backward. Leoma ducked her head to avoid the worst of the reverberation. When she looked up, Eleanor still stood before her.

Jarin jumped from the boulders to land between her and Eleanor. His arrival halted the magic being forced on her, which allowed her to jump to her feet and take out two more witches who were still trying to get up from the blast of Jarin's magic.

The wolf came from out of nowhere and latched on to a woman's throat, tearing her to shreds. Leoma quickly stepped between Valdr and another witch. With one thrust of her sword, Leoma ended the witch's life and turned to the wolf. Only to find him gone and the witch dead.

That barely registered in Leoma's mind before the falcon swooped in and clawed out another witch's eyes. Leoma glanced over to find Eleanor and Jarin staring at each other, neither making a move.

Leoma heard a growl and turned in time to see a witch coming at her. Valdr took down the witch with one pounce. Leoma quickly turned her attention to the last witch.

"Brigitta was my friend," the woman said.

Leoma shrugged indifferently. "She chose the wrong side. Just as you have."

"I'm going to make you scream in agony."

As soon as the witch came for her, Leoma ran towards the boulders. She put one foot on the rock and jumped off it, turning as she did with her sword pointed downward. She watched the witch's eyes bulge right before the sword came down.

Leoma landed on the ground and pulled out her blade. Valdr came up beside her as Andi flew overhead. During all of this, Eleanor and Jarin had yet to move.

There was movement behind Leoma. She turned to find Walter cowering and sweating profusely. Leoma ignored him and turned her attention back to Eleanor.

"Warlock," the elder said, disgust dripping from that one word.

Jarin's pale eyes were alight with a fire that gave Leoma pause. He raised his staff as the tip began to glow white.

Suddenly, an intense crimson light filled the area. It was so vivid, Leoma had to shield her eyes. As she looked for the source, she noted that it was affecting Eleanor and Jarin, as well.

The first thing Leoma saw was boots. She blinked, trying to keep her eyes open long enough to see who would appear. Oddly, the light was warm as it washed over her.

"Leoma."

She turned towards the sound of Braith's voice. The crimson glow dimmed enough that she was able to see. Only to find him walking from an entry in the boulder she hadn't noticed before. He held something in his hands.

Braith continued in her direction, stepping over bodies without a glance at them. She straightened in confusion as she looked around at the others—even the wolf—who averted their gazes.

Her sword lowered when Braith stopped before her and slid his hand around the back of her neck. When his head lowered, her eyes slid shut as their lips met.

The taste of his kiss made her melt against him. After such worry, he was now back with her. Whatever the Coven wanted was out of their hands. Against all odds, they had won the day. The only thing that could top it was Eleanor's death.

Braith ended the kiss and looked down at her. "Trust me."

"I do," she said with a frown.

"Trust me," he repeated.

Her frown deepened when he released her and stepped back. Then he turned toward Eleanor. Leoma could only watch in horror as Braith made his way to the Coven elder and grasped her arm.

He looked back at her and mouthed, "Trust me," again.

And then they were gone.

When the red light faded, Jarin straightened and turned in a circle, scanning the area for Eleanor. "Where is she?"

"G-g-gone," came a voice behind her.

Leoma turned to Eleanor's husband. "Where did they go?"

Walter shrugged and wiped at the sweat on his brow. "I-I don't know."

"You need to try harder than that," Jarin said as he stalked toward the rotund man.

While Jarin questioned him, Leoma made her way to where she had seen Braith exit the boulder. She stepped inside, her eyes adjusting to the darkness.

The sound of water dripping could be heard. She walked down the few curving steps until she was surrounded by the dark. Leoma continued on until she stood on a wide circle of rock. A narrow path with water on each side led out to something far ahead, where two torches burned.

She didn't turn around when she felt someone behind her. Jarin came up on her left, and the wolf moved to stand between them.

"Braith found the Blood Skull," Jarin said.

She inhaled, shock still weaving through her. "He didn't just find it. He gave it to Eleanor."

"He spoke with you."

Leoma knelt and peered into the water. "He kissed me."

"And?"

She dipped her hand into the liquid and held it up to see something dark slide from her fingers. Jarin moved his staff toward her, the end lighting up to reveal blood on her hand.

"Born of blood," she murmured.

Jarin held the staff out, the light revealing that it was blood on either side.

Leoma straightened and looked toward the torches. As she and Jarin stood there, the blood began to recede, being sucked in somewhere else until there was nothing left. Not even the dripping she'd heard upon entering.

She looked down at her hand. "Braith told me to trust him."

28

There was blood everywhere. As soon as Braith lifted the skull, the world was drenched in crimson. Yet, he no longer found it distasteful or repulsive.

It was calming, comforting. As he carried the relic, he heard a single drum beating a steady cadence in time with his steps. And while he couldn't explain it, if anyone had asked, he would have said it felt as if an army were at his back, waiting for his command.

The darkness around him was no more. He was bathed in light. A red light that cocooned him. Protected him.

Then he strode from the cavern and saw Leoma. His joy at discovering she was alive made his knees weak. Until he recalled what was in his hands. He wanted her with him, but he couldn't chance her life where he was going. There was so much he wanted to tell her, so much he needed to share. But there was only time for a kiss.

"Trust me," he told her.

She searched his face, her brow furrowed in confusion when she saw the skull. There was no time for him to tell her that he fought for her, for everything she stood for. For their love.

The skull pulled him toward their destination, an endpoint he couldn't ignore. Braith reluctantly walked away from Leoma and made his way to Eleanor.

As soon as he touched the old witch, the scarlet light dimmed enough for her to see what he held. Eleanor's smile was joyous, her gray eyes glittering with success.

But Braith hesitated. He was meant to be with Leoma. Of that he was certain. Without her, he was nothing. She was the only one who could get him through what he had to do. He met her dark gaze and urged her once more to trust him.

Then he let the skull take him where it would.

The moment he left Leoma behind, a piece of him died. Despite all the men he'd faced in battle, his beautiful warrior had the power to destroy him like no one else.

As soon as their destination was reached, Braith dropped his hand from the Coven elder. Eleanor repulsed him, and even being so near to her made him want to skewer her with his blade. But he held to the course that the skull had shown him after he took it in hand.

The old, gnarled trees that made a wide circle around them grew so close together that it was impossible to tell where one ended and another began. Their thick branches were laden with leaves as the tops curved away from the circle as if trying to look away.

In fact, the more Braith stared at the trees, the more it appeared as if they had linked branches to shield the rest of the world from what the Coven did there.

"I knew you wouldn't fail me," Eleanor said as she faced him.

She reached out a hand and placed it on the skull to try

and take it from him. Instantly, she jerked back with a hiss, her face contorted with pain.

Braith smiled when he saw the smoke wafting up from her burned hand. The witch would soon discover that no magic could heal the injury. Ever. He somehow knew this as fact.

"What just happened?" Eleanor demanded.

He tilted his head. "Should you not ask after your husband?"

"I've more important matters to deal with."

"You mean you brought him along, as you always do, in the hopes that he'd get killed."

Eleanor raised a gray brow and shrugged, nonchalantly, refusing to admit anything as she held her injured hand against her.

"Why not just kill him?" Braith asked.

Eleanor lifted her chin and glared at him. "It was part of our marriage bargain. If he swore never to come to me for sex, I vowed to never kill him. If either of us broke our pact, we would both die."

"I take it Walter added that condition to ensure you held up your end."

The witch cut her eyes away. "Aye."

"He was smart. Too bad he wasn't smart enough to stay away from you."

Her head swiveled back to him. "Give me the skull."

Braith smiled and held it out. "You think there will be a different outcome than when you first touched it?"

"Why are you not hurt?"

"I was born in blood, remember?" he told her and brought the skull back against him.

Her gaze narrowed dangerously. "You act as if you have control of the Blood Skull. That's not possible."

"Then why didn't you get it yourself?" he asked, even as he knew the answer. But he wanted her to admit it.

Eleanor's lips pinched, showing lines of age around her mouth. "Because only a direct descendant of the one who placed the skull in the cavern could retrieve it."

Braith looked down at the skull. The voice had told him as much once he touched it—as it had imparted so many other things.

"The Blood Skull is meant to be mine."

He raised his gaze to the witch. "The skull belongs to no one. You would know that if you listened to the warnings given to you by other witches."

"I need the relic."

"I know."

Braith held back his smile when shock fell over Eleanor's face. It was likely the first time in a very long while that anyone had surprised the witch. And he was just getting started.

"How do you know?" Eleanor asked in a hushed tone as she turned slightly away from him.

"You, who sought the Blood Skull of the first witch, ask me this?"

Eleanor stared at the relic, her chest rising and falling rapidly. "It couldn't know.

"*She* knows."

Aging gray eyes snapped back to his face. "I brought us here."

He let her believe the lie. The skull had known the witch's destination from the beginning. It was what brought them to the wood.

Eleanor pointed to the middle of the area. "Set down the skull."

"You think you'll be able to touch it if I'm not holding it?"

he said as he walked to the spot she'd indicated and lowered the relic to the ground.

The moment he released it, blood began to trickle from the eyes again.

Eleanor kept her gaze on him as she walked around the skull to put him at a distance. She then knelt before it and reached out her uninjured hand. Just before she put her fingers on the skull, she pulled back.

"I, too, am bathed in blood," she said to Braith.

He clenched his hands into fists. "You were not born of it."

"Of course, I was."

"I would advise against touching it," he warned.

Eleanor sneered and grasped the skull. For a moment, there was nothing, and then spirals of smoke rose from her hands. The witch began screaming, yet she couldn't release the skull.

Braith took a step back when blood gushed from the skull to pool thickly on the ground. Eleanor was so focused on her hands burning that she didn't realize she was sinking into the dirt.

"Blood is how you've lived. Blood is how you will die," Braith told her as the ground sucked her in deeper and deeper until nothing but her head and hands remained.

Soon her face—and her screams—were gone. Her fingers peeled away from the skull as if grasping for something. A moment later, her hands curled into themselves and were taken by the earth.

Once Eleanor was gone, the blood stopped pouring from the skull. Braith then unsheathed his sword and walked to stand before it.

He knelt and brought the flat side of his blade to his forehead and then turned the sword tip down to thrust it into the ground.

"What the bloody hell just happened?" Jarin demanded after the blood drained.

Leoma looked at him. "You're the warlock, and you're asking me?"

His nostrils flared as he looked around the cavern. But she had seen enough. She strode outside and saw the faint marks from where the dead witches had burned.

"Did he tell you where they were going?" Jarin asked as he came to stand beside her.

"I told you all that he said."

The warlock slammed his staff into the ground. "We've no idea where they could've gone. I had Eleanor. I could've killed her."

"Braith didn't betray me," she stated and faced Jarin.

"How can you say that when he has the skull and went with Eleanor?"

She shrugged and turned away. "I don't kn—"

Her words halted when she saw the crimson beam shining straight up to the heavens. Somehow, she knew that was Braith.

"Jarin, do you see it?" she asked, pointing to the light and glancing back at him.

He looked to where she indicated and shook his head. "I see nothing but clouds."

She whirled around to face him. "You don't see the red light?"

"Red?" he repeated with a frown. Then his brow smoothed as he looked at her anew. "You see red?"

"Aye. Just like the light that blinded us."

"Blinded me. It didn't hurt you."

She thought back. "It did at first. Then Braith came to me."

"And kissed you," Jarin said with a grin.

"Why is that important?"

The warlock smiled and whistled to the wolf and falcon. "Find your horse, Hunter. With a kiss, Braith allowed you to find him. You and only you."

Leoma didn't have to be told twice. She ran to the stallion, who was munching on a shrub. Once mounted, she turned the horse around and headed toward the light, ignoring Walter as he shouted for them not to leave him.

Why hadn't Braith told her what he planned? Why hadn't he said more? She intended to ask him that as soon as she found him.

"How far is the light?" Jarin asked as he ran beside her.

She kept the horse at a slow gallop. "Farther than I'd like."

The wolf suddenly darted out in front of the stallion, causing the animal to rear as she yanked back on the reins not to cause a collision.

The horse danced around in a circle, agitated. After she'd gotten him calmed, she turned her head to Jarin. "What was that?"

"I had to get your attention."

"You have it. What was so important that you couldn't just tell me to stop?"

He stalked to her. Everything moved in slow motion as she was pulled from the horse. She saw Jarin's staff fall against his chest while his arms lifted. She met his pale eyes right before his hands cupped either side of her face.

Her head exploded with agony as she felt someone—Jarin—inside her mind. She was powerless to get him out. Her body was frozen, gripped with pain and magic.

He finally released her. Leoma fell to her knees, gagging at the nauseating throbbing of her head. She heard retching behind her and turned to see Jarin bent over with his hands on his knees.

"I should...kill you...for that," she said between gags.

He wiped his mouth and turned to her. His face was as pale as death, his eyes more white than blue. "I apologize. I didn't want to give you a chance to refuse."

She batted away the hand he held out to her and climbed to her feet. Her legs were wobbly, and she hastily grabbed hold of the horse for balance. "What did you do?"

"I got into your mind to see the red light."

"Did you not believe me?"

He turned his head, a sheen of sweat covering his skin. After a moment, he looked at her. "I needed to know how far. It's days away. Days we don't have."

"Unless you can fly, we don't have another choice."

His face was grim. "Actually, we do."

Her stomach rolled so that she put a hand to her mouth. "Why do I get the idea that the process is as painful as what just happened?"

"Because it is. But we'll be there in moments instead of days."

A lot could happen in the span of an hour. She had to get to Braith. And soon.

Leoma nodded reluctantly. "All right."

29

Blackglade

S he could always tell when Armir was behind her, and Malene didn't need magic for it. Her skin prickled with awareness as she looked out the window, every nerve ending coming to life in excitement.

Which was understandable since he was her only companion. It was by her own hand, but that was why she'd become so...aware...of him.

Malene looked down at her right palm, rubbing her left thumb over the faint blue light that matched her other hand. The swift and potent increase in her power left her dizzy. And reeling.

To put it simply, she was terrified.

"My lady."

Her eyes closed at the sound of Armir's voice. There were times he simply stood next to the door of her tower like a silent sentry. Then there were days he pushed her to increase her magic and accept her role among the Varroki. It was never enough that she was inside the tower at Blackglade. Armir wanted more from her.

And she was afraid that she had reached her limit.

She didn't know if he had brought her down from the top of the tower, or if she'd lost time, regardless, she wasn't ready to share her new discovery.

She turned her head to the side to address him. "Aye?"

There was a long pause of silence before he said, "Jarin's falcon hasn't returned with a message."

Jarin? It took her a moment to sort through her memories to recall Armir telling her about the warrior who was tasked with tracking Eleanor.

"You fear he and the Coven elder clashed?" she asked and faced him.

Armir's green eyes were locked on her face. "I've already checked with the Quarter. The four seers sense his life force."

There was much she'd learned about her people over the years. Armir was extremely protective of his warriors. He was a demanding, exacting leader, but there was no one more loyal to them than Armir.

He never doubted their abilities when he sent them out on a mission. Nor did he waiver in the knowledge that they would complete their assignment and return home.

For the few warriors who never made it back to Blackglade, Armir was the first to discover what went wrong. And while he tried to keep his travels quiet, she knew when he left to track down a particular witch to dole out his special brand of justice.

So, while his words about Jarin were nonchalant, Malene knew he was worried. "Tell me," she urged.

His gaze shifted to the side for a moment as he took a deep

breath. "Jarin is one of our best. If he wanted my position, he could take it."

"He's that powerful?" she asked, surprised that she was just now learning such information.

Armir's lips compressed briefly. "Aye."

"Which is why you sent him to follow Eleanor."

He gave a nod of his blond head. "Jarin is first and foremost a Varroki, but he does not always get along with others. He prefers solitude with his wolf and falcon."

Malene recalled meeting the warrior during the first year of her reign. She folded her hands together and walked toward Armir. "Do you want to find him?"

"Nay," he replied instantly.

"Your words say one thing, but your eyes say another," she pointed out.

A muscle ticked in Armir's jaw. "Jarin is a close friend, my lady. His assignment was a treacherous one. Then I asked him to find those from your vision."

"Give him another day. If there's no word, then you will discover what has become of him," she stated.

His lips parted as a frown formed. "I'm not to leave your side."

"We both know you've done it before. This time, I'm not only giving you permission. It's an order."

His pale green eyes studied her for a long moment. "You're different."

"Because I'm acknowledging something you've attempted to keep secret?"

He closed the space between them, his long strides eating up the distance. He halted before her. While he didn't touch her, he was close enough that she could feel the heat rolling off him.

"Do you trust me?" His voice was soft, barely above a whisper.

But his eyes blazed with unease and a healthy dose of annoyance. As well as sadness. It was the dejection that surprised her.

She licked her lips and nodded. "I do."

"Then tell me," he urged.

With three words, she had her confirmation that he was the one who'd brought her from the roof and put her in bed. In many ways, she was relieved that he knew her secret.

But it was the other part of her that recoiled in desolation and despair. For he had touched her again, and she hadn't been awake for it.

Ages ago, a Varroki leader and her commander had an affair. The leader renounced her title and made plans to run away with her lover. Since a new leader can only be found after the death of the current one, it left the Varroki vulnerable.

The warriors were forced to pursue the lovers. When the couple refused to return to Blackglade, the warriors had no choice but to kill them. The fallout from the event nearly destroyed the Varroki.

A new rule was quickly enacted that the Lady of the Varroki was not to be touched. Malene understood why the decree was there, but for someone who craved another's touch, it was the worst kind of torture.

She held out her hands between them. Then, slowly, she turned them, palms up.

Armir's gaze remained on her face for a heartbeat before his eyes lowered. His visage remained impassive. She was so focused on looking for any emotion crossing his face that she almost missed his hands lifting. His fingers came within inches of touching her, but he dropped them at the last moment.

She nearly cried out, almost begged him to put his hands

on her, but she managed to keep it inside somehow. A little more of her died then.

Armir thought she fought her role with the Varroki. When in fact, she was withering inside. A slow, agonizing death she suffered alone.

Malene lowered her hands and returned to her spot at the window. There, she could look across the sea and imagine a life where she had no magic, where she met a man and fell in love and had a family.

Every day she built upon that fantasy, the story unfolding in her mind. It was the only thing that got her through the unending days. And it was a secret she would keep from Armir. He knew nothing but the Varroki way of life. He didn't understand what it meant to want something more.

"Are you in pain?" he asked.

She squeezed her eyes shut and fought against the sudden sting of tears. She was suffocating, the pain slashing deeper every day. But that's not what he referred to.

Malene took a deep breath and opened her eyes. "There is no pain."

"But there is fear. I hear it in your voice."

She whirled around to face him and held up her hands. As her anger rose, the blue radiance got brighter. "Look at these! I've spent the morning researching the other Ladies of the Varroki. None of them had both palms glowing. Only the left. What does this mean?"

"That you're more powerful than the others before," he said as he walked slowly toward her. "That there is much more planned for you."

She dropped her arms and shook her head. "Nay. I don't want any more. I've reached my limit."

In a blink, he gripped her wrists in his hands and leaned

his face close. "If anyone can handle this, it's you. *You*, Malene. Only you. Your potential is limitless."

"You can't feel the power rushing through me. I have no control."

"You do." He released her wrists, but he didn't move away. "Don't keep these feelings bottled up. You need to talk to me, and if you cannot, or do not wish to share with me, then I will find you someone you *can* talk to."

She let her arms drop to her sides, and she smiled ruefully. "I don't know how long you looked for me years ago, or even how you found me. There were times I hated you."

"I know," he stated in a flat voice.

"And times I couldn't survive without you. You've helped me to stay on the path the Varroki need me to follow. You've even helped me walk the fine line of my position. But all of your wisdom and guidance cannot help me with what's in here," she said as she pointed at her chest.

"And what is in there?" he asked.

She fought the urge to touch his chiseled face. "Do you remember the first night we met and what you said to me?"

"To follow your heart," he replied with a nod.

"I thought it would be an easy way to find my way in this role, but it has only made things more complicated. I know what I want, but it goes against everything I'm supposed to do. I have an entire city looking to me. Not to lead them, because we all know that you do that. But to protect them, and to keep Blackglade thriving."

Armir's face folded into a frown. "You are so much more than that. You are the beacon that reminds our people who they are."

"They don't need me for that."

"But they do," he insisted. "Why do you think they look to this tower every day, hoping for a glimpse of you? Why do you think magic is revered so? Not because it is handed down through our blood to our descendants, but because of your hands. That blue light makes you royalty to our kind."

She ran her thumbs over her fingers as she felt the light of her palms warm at his words.

"You remind them of how great our people are, of how we survived eons of both worship and persecution. You signify what was forged in flame long ago. Magic. Power. And it courses through you so fiercely that I can see it."

"I want to be all that you say and more."

"Then do it," he stated. His green eyes stared at her, filled with a fierce light, daring her to do as he said.

Malene looked down at her hands, turning her palms to face each other so that the blue light reflected back onto itself. "You know what the second light means, don't you?"

"Aye," he said after a long pause.

And he hadn't told her, which meant he wanted to keep it from her for a reason. Normally, she would have demanded to know the facts, but not tonight. It might destroy her, and then there would be nothing Armir could say or do that would fix her.

She lifted her gaze to him. "Keep me informed about Jarin. I want to know the moment you get word from him. Or if you don't."

His eyes searched her face, the worried frown smoothing away. "Aye, my lady."

"If Jarin is...no longer with us, then I will accompany you to confront Eleanor."

Armir's lips parted in shock, a scowl in place. "You cannot be serious."

"But I am. I may be everything you said a moment ago, but I'm also here to fight witches, specifically the Coven. After the vision I had, it might be better to have this confrontation now rather than later."

"Malene, please. You do not even know what this extra magic can do."

"Then we'd better make sure I'm prepared," she said and lifted a brow.

"It's going to hurt."

Leoma gave Jarin a baleful stare and petted the side of the stallion's face when he put his head over her arm. "Worse than what you just did to my mind?"

He hesitated before shrugging. "Aye."

"Great." Leoma let out a breath as she faced the horse. "And the animals?"

"I'll send Armir a message, telling him what is going on. As for Valdr and the stallion, they must be left behind."

She closed her eyes and rested her forehead against the horse. "I cannot just leave him out here."

"Valdr will ensure that the stallion is safe."

"A wolf guarding a horse."

Jarin blew out a breath. "I must tell you that travelling with magic is not without risks."

Leoma faced the warlock. "Braith is standing among the Coven. Alone. I told him we would fight them together. I'll not leave him by himself. Regardless of the risks," she added.

"It will take me a few moments to prepare the message."

She took the horse's reins and led him a short distance away. There was no magic within her that allowed her to communicate with animals, but she had to tell the stallion what was happening.

Gazing into the creature's large, dark eyes she said, "I'm going to get Braith, but you cannot come. Valdr, the wolf, is going to stay with you. Now, Jarin has assured me Valdr won't harm you, but if, at any time, you feel threatened by the wolf, feel free to kick him. Just to keep him on his toes. I don't know how long it will take, but I plan to bring Braith back to you."

The horse blinked at her and returned to eating. Leoma turned and found Jarin and Valdr a few feet behind her. The warlock was grinning, letting her know he had heard every word.

"Consider Valdr warned," Jarin said.

Leoma glanced at the wolf. "Good. This horse means a lot to Braith."

The smile dropped from Jarin's lips. "Valdr will guard him well. I can assure you of that."

"Thank you."

He gave a nod and turned on his heel. A moment later, he issued a loud whistle and held up his arm while looking at the sky. Leoma found herself searching the heavens, as well. It didn't take long for her to see a dark shape flying high above them.

The falcon dropped down and perched on Jarin's arm. Leoma saw no quill and ink as the warlock unrolled a small piece of parchment that appeared out of thin air.

Jarin's lips moved, but she couldn't make out what he said. Then he rolled up the paper and tucked it into the holder on the falcon's leg. The next instant, the bird was in the air, and Jarin was looking at her.

"Ready?" he asked.

Her stomach still wasn't settled from her last encounter with his magic. "I think."

She was reaching for the waterskin when he said, "You may not want to do that."

Leoma met his gaze and decided against drinking—or eating—anything for a while. "How weak will we be when we arrive?"

"More or less as we were after I read your mind."

She forced a smile. "Wonderful. And how close will we be?"

"We'll have time to collect ourselves before we face the Coven," he replied.

The fact that Jarin didn't look any more prepared to do this magic than she was to experience it helped her gather some courage.

The warlock knelt, and the wolf walked to him. Jarin rubbed his head against the wolf's in some kind of silent message. After a few more rubs and soft whining from Valdr, the wolf loped off to the woods and lay down in the brush.

Jarin stood and motioned to her. Leoma knew that Braith would do whatever it took to get to her if the tables were turned, and she would do the same. She came to stand before the warlock, who held out his arms. After clasping his forearms, and him wrapping his fingers around hers, she met his gaze.

"You trust Braith completely," he stated.

She frowned, unsure where he was going with his assertion. "I've said as much, aye."

"You keep your trust. I'm going to prepare for a betrayal."

Leoma swallowed past the lump of emotion in her throat. "He's a good man."

"Good men can be influenced by evil."

She knew that all too well, but she couldn't let doubt into her mind—or her heart.

Jarin said, "Stay alert and be wary. Of everything. It won't take the witches long to sense the connection you and Braith have. They'll use it against you."

"You forget, I've fought witches before."

"Not like this. Training will only get you so far, and let's hope those who readied you gave you all the skills you'll need. If you fall into a trap, I may not be able to reach you."

Her mouth went dry. "Understood."

"If Braith is as steadfast as you claim, you'll be the only one who can reach him. I'll have your back."

How had she begun this journey not trusting anyone to find herself with a knight who'd stolen her heart and a warlock she was prepared to hand her life to, in the hopes that he didn't betray her?

Jarin's pale eyes held her. "It's going to be all right."

"You have to stop saying that. I get no comfort from it."

His lips turned up in a grin. "Keep your cheeky wit, Hunter. It's a good asset."

Before she could reply, his head tilted back, and his hands tightened on her arms. The wind picked up, tangling their cloaks around their legs. She turned her head and squinted to keep debris from her eyes. But the wind only increased, pushing and pulling against her until her hands clung to Jarin in desperation.

When he lifted his head to look at her, his eyes were glowing white. Leoma glanced to her left, but it was nothing more than a blur as if the world were spinning around them so fast that she grew dizzy. She had to shut her eyes.

Nausea rolled in her stomach. She pressed her lips together so as not to be sick. Suddenly, she felt as if something grabbed hold of her midsection and yanked.

"Open your eyes, Leoma. Breathe. Breathe!"

She parted her lips and sucked in a large mouthful of air, the same time she opened her eyes to find Jarin standing over her looking ashen and sweaty.

Her fingers sank into earth. Almost immediately after that, her stomach rebelled. Leoma rolled onto her side and emptied her belly. Beside her, Jarin collapsed to his knees, his head hanging.

When the retching finally ceased, she rolled onto her back and looked at the sky. Her entire body ached as if someone had battered it for hours. How in the world was she going to fight feeling like this?

"You don't look quite as green," Jarin said as he sat back on his haunches and put his hands on his thighs.

She turned her head to him. "I feel horrid."

"It'll wear off."

"It better." She closed her eyes and concentrated on her breathing.

But knowing that Braith was waiting for her had Leoma getting to her hands and knees, and then her feet. She turned in a circle and found the red beacon behind her. It stood bright and vivid, only a little ways ahead of them.

Jarin used his staff to help him get to his feet. He stood beside her. "Is the light close?"

"Aye."

"Then I know where they're at," he said with a sigh.

Leoma cut her eyes to him. "A Witch's Grove?"

"Worse."

"Worse?" she repeated, trepidation gnawing at her.

A shadow of unease ran over the warlock's face. "It is their Temple."

"A structure?"

"Not as you would imagine. This place is where witches

are initiated, where the council gathers to send out their wishes to the others. It's a place where wills are broken, and unholy alliances are made."

She held back a shudder—barely. "It sounds like a place I'd rather not go."

"*I* don't even want to go there," Jarin said. "The Coven will have the advantage. It's their consecrated ground."

"You're not making me feel any better about going in there."

He shot her a crooked grin. "But think of the entrance we can make."

Despite the dire situation, Leoma found herself smiling. It faded as she looked back at the crimson light Braith was shining for her. She never expected to live to a ripe old age, not while hunting witches. And if she were going to die for what she believed in, then dying not just to save those she cared about, but also for love was a good way to go.

"Shall we?" she asked Jarin.

The warlock smiled. "Oh, aye."

They moved through the trees like ghosts. They made no sound, left no sign of their presence. She led the way, her gaze locked on the light shining straight up into the sky.

The closer she got to it, the more the forest changed around them. The leaves were beginning to change colors, indicating that the trees were alive, but they seemed lifeless. As if they were merely enduring each day with their heads down.

And just like a Witch's Grove, Leoma knew the instant she crossed the threshold into this Temple, as Jarin called it. Her heart hammered against her ribs, her breaths coming quick and hard.

There was no time for pain or discomfort, no time for rest or repose. Her mind was focused on Braith and the upcoming battle. She would need all her wits about her.

Every morsel of training ever given to her would need to be at the ready.

Without a doubt, the witches would outnumber them. Not only did her foe have the advantage of the terrain, but also numbers. Any commander would know the disadvantage and withdraw from combat to face the enemy on another day.

But she didn't have that luxury.

Death might await her. For all she knew, Braith had already been killed, but that didn't matter. She was still going to the Temple to fight. Because it's what she did.

It's what Braith would do.

She pushed aside those emotions and any others that made her forlorn. There was no room for such feelings in battle. There was blood, and there was death.

There were losers.

And there were victors.

She slid to a halt when she came to a barricade of trees that seemed to reach far into the sky. The trunks had grown together like a wall, the limbs tangled like a maze.

"I've never seen this before," she whispered.

Jarin was breathing heavily as he looked unhappily at the trees. "We're here."

"How do we get in?"

The warlock began to climb the tree. Leoma rolled her eyes. He could have just said that. She threw her cloak over her shoulders and started after Jarin.

Soon, they were ducking and crawling through branches, moving ever inward toward the light. The woods seemed to go on and on, their interlocking canopy never wavering.

"I see a red light," Jarin whispered from up ahead of her.

She crawled faster before grabbing hold of a branch and using it to jump. Leoma landed on a thick limb beside Jarin.

She knelt and peered through the boughs to see a man on one knee before a sword.

Braith.

"The promise I asked you to make me before we fought Eleanor still stands," Leoma said as she looked at Jarin.

The warlock glanced at her. "This battle will only have two outcomes. Either we both die, or we win."

"I prefer to win."

Jarin's smile was slow. "Me, too."

31

He knew the moment Leoma reached him. Braith opened his eyes and looked at the skull. The ancient witch had given him the ability to sense when Leoma was near. If the Blood Skull had such potent magic as a relic, he couldn't imagine what the witch had been like while alive.

But it wasn't just knowledge of Leoma that the Blood Skull gave him.

He got to his feet and pulled his sword from the now dry ground. The blood that had run so freely while drenching the ground was gone, but the magic had been absorbed into the steel of his weapon.

Finally, he had a blade that could kill witches. And his sword couldn't wait to bring retribution to the Coven.

Braith turned his head toward Leoma. He didn't see her among the dense branches, but he didn't need to. He also detected another with her. Most likely the man who'd wanted to battle Eleanor at the cavern.

"Not yet," he whispered to Leoma.

It wasn't time for her to reveal herself. Not until the

others arrived. Even though the skull had shown him a glimpse of what was to come, Braith still fought not to go to Leoma.

He wanted one last chance to hold her, kiss her. To feel her body against his. To open his heart and allow himself to think of a future with her by his side. It was the one dream he'd never allowed himself to consider through all his years of war. Then Leoma had unexpectedly come into his life and turned it upside down.

Leoma. His beautiful warrior.

He turned his back to her lest he forget everything the skull had shown him. He was a battle-hardened knight, a man born of blood. A killer, who offered death to all.

The hilt of his sword warmed—a warning from the Blood Skull. It hadn't spoken to him since the cavern, but the witch communicated in other ways. It was because of her that he had a distinct advantage over the Coven. That advantage was what would save Leoma.

He set the tip of his sword on the ground and rested both hands on the pommel. His gaze was directed in front of him to where the trees began to moan, and the ground vibrated. A great yawning divide opened in the woods as the trees leaned away from each other and a path was revealed.

Mist rolled over the pathway like the breath of a great beast. It billowed out once it reached the vast circular area he stood in. The fog remained along the edge, wrapping around the base of the trees and waiting.

Braith knew what it was like to be in the mist. He recalled how alive it felt, how it had wanted to hurt him. Just as it did now. But it was controlled by masters who kept a tight leash on it, at least for the moment.

His attention moved to the figures that formed out of the cloying whiteness on the path. The delight he saw on the witches' faces reminded him of his enemies across the battle-field. He had defeated those foes.

And he would annihilate these.

Five witches took positions around the area. He ignored them since his true targets had yet to show themselves. Braith kept his gaze on the path as an eerie hush fell over the area.

The woods had been quiet before, but this was different. This was a precursor to evil.

He tightened his grip on his sword. Heat flashed on his palms from the metal pommel an instant before he felt breath on his neck.

"A gift," a woman purred behind him.

Out of the corner of his eye, he saw fingers unfurl with long nails that were black in color. The nails, filed to points, grazed his face.

He remained calm as another whispered in a singsong voice in his other ear. "Such a handsome gift."

With both witches stroking his face and neck, Braith remained still and calm. The storm had yet to arrive.

Leoma was still reeling from hearing Braith tell her that it wasn't time yet. As if he had known she was about to go to him.

She hadn't been the only one to hear it either. Jarin hadn't questioned it, merely grabbed her arm to stop her from moving.

"Wait," Jarin urged.

She looked Braith over and saw that he hadn't sustained any injuries. In fact, he looked healthy. But there was something different about him. She couldn't pinpoint what it was. Yet.

"What's he doing?" she asked when Braith put his back to them and rested his sword tip on the ground.

Jarin unfastened his cloak and let it fall from his shoulders. "There's no sign of Eleanor."

"I'm glad of that."

"Aye. But an elder only comes to the Temple when they're all to meet."

Leoma jerked her gaze to the warlock. "Are you telling me the rest of the council will be here?"

He nodded his head slowly.

Dread filled her as she returned her eyes to Braith. "He'll never survive. As good as he is, he doesn't have a sword that can kill witches. And he's too far away from me."

"He has the Blood Skull."

She frowned as her head swiveled to him. "That the council wants."

"Leoma, any bones from the first witch are powerful. But the skull is twice as strong. There's a possibility that the Blood Skull chose him."

"For what?" she demanded.

Jarin shrugged and shook his head. "I could not even begin to imagine. One of the Varroki long ago used to tell stories about how if the Blood Skull were found, she could choose a Warden."

"Is this Blood Skull good or evil?"

The warlock glanced at Braith and the skull that lay on the ground. "There are varying stories of the first witch. Some say she was good. Others, evil. Still others say she was a mix of both."

"This isn't making me feel any better about this scenario."

Their conversation halted at the loud groaning that came from across the space. Leoma watched in wonder as the trees bent away and mist came pouring in.

Jarin held out his hand and whispered something as the mist reached them and began to climb up the tree toward them. Whatever the warlock said halted the mist.

She began to thank him, but Jarin put his fingers to his lips then pointed toward Braith. Leoma unhooked her cloak and turned her head as witches filed out of the path opened by the trees. There were five in all stationed along the edges of the forest.

Leoma sucked in a breath when a witch suddenly appeared behind Braith. She had long, red hair that fell past her hips. No sooner had the witch materialized than a second joined her. This one had blond curls that hung down the middle of her back.

"Elders," Jarin whispered.

She frowned and glanced at him. The witches weren't aged as Eleanor was. These women were young and vibrant and beautiful.

He leaned close and said, "Each elder uses their magic in different ways. Trust me. They are the council."

"How do you know?"

"Look how the others bow their heads."

Leoma let her gaze roam around each of the other five witches. "We're missing two elders."

Jarin exhaled, his expression flat as he returned his gaze to the others.

Restlessness settled over Leoma. Everything inside told her to withdraw her sword and jump into the fray. But she held back, waiting for the right moment, even though it went against every instinct she had.

"Ladies," a husky voice said. It filled the area and sounded as if the women were standing right next to Leoma.

That's when she spied mist gathering together at the

pathway and swirling faster and faster as it grew taller. The mist fell away to reveal a woman cloaked in black.

Braith stared at the new arrival as she reached up and grasped the hood of the cloak with both hands and drew it back over her inky black hair. Her beauty was almost impossible to look at for more than a few moments at a time.

She smiled and came to stand a few feet in front of him with the skull between them, her black eyes locked on his face. "I'm Angmar. That is Matilda and Catherine behind you."

He didn't bother with a reply.

Angmar's lips curved into a smile. "I sense no fear in you. At least, not about us."

Matilda ran her long nails against his cheek again. "I want a taste of him."

Catherine leaned close and inhaled as she ran her nose up his neck. "I smell desire." The smile in her voice died when she added, "For someone else."

Angmar raised a thin, black brow. "Eleanor vowed she would deliver the Blood Skull. However, I wasn't expecting to find you along with it."

"Eleanor couldn't touch the skull," Braith stated.

Angmar's head cocked to the side at hearing that. Then she squatted before the skull and studied it. "There is no blood."

"There was."

The witch's dark eyes jerked to him. "Why did it stop?"

"You'd have to ask it."

Beside him, Catherine laughed. "It's a relic. It cannot talk."

"It has power," Angmar said with her hand hovering over the skull. "That means it could talk. To the right person."

Braith waited for the witch to touch the skull, but she lowered her hand to her side and stood instead. Angmar must be the leader of the council. Already, she showed she was smarter than Eleanor.

Angmar moved to him. As she drew near, the other two moved away. Angmar put her hand on his arm as she walked around his back to his other side, her fingers trailing over his shoulders and back. "You brought the Blood Skull here."

"You know I did."

"Where is Eleanor?"

Braith shrugged as he looked at her. "You'd have to ask the skull."

"I would know if Eleanor was dead. I'd feel it."

He leaned to the side, putting his face close to hers and said, "You should've left the skull alone."

Angmar parted her lips to reply when she and the other two elders gasped. Angmar's black eyes widened as she whispered Eleanor's name.

There was a strangled cry that rose up from the ground before it was cut off. A shockwave blasted outward and knocked everyone down but Braith, the force originating from the skull.

His eyes were locked on Angmar. The witch wore hatred and fury like the wings of reckoning. She climbed to her feet, joined by Catherine and Matilda on either side of her.

"You killed Eleanor," Catherine declared.

Braith smiled. "Actually, I didn't. But I do plan on killing you."

Matilda started laughing. She pointed to him and asked, "With what? We're witches, you imbecile. We cannot be killed."

"You will feel the full force of the Coven's wrath," Angmar stated as she raised her hands above her head.

Braith grasped his sword and spun around, lifting the

weapon to block the magic directed at him. He smiled at Angmar when his blade halted the spell directed at him. "You should've left the Blood Skull in peace. Now, you will pay."

The scream of the witches deafened Braith as he swung his sword toward Angmar. The witch sucked in her stomach as she curved her back. He watched in slow motion as his blade cut into her black gown but missed her.

32

The time had come. Leoma leapt from the trees, tucking her body into a roll to land with bent knees. She straightened as she unsheathed her sword and spun to face one of the five lesser witches that came at her.

She swung her blade, but the witch was quick and ducked before coming up with a hand on Leoma's back with an added punch of magic. Leoma gritted her teeth against the pain and tried to keep her feet, but her knee buckled.

A pair of boots suddenly landed beside her. She saw the end of the staff slam into the ground. A moment later, the witch screamed and burst into flames.

Leoma jumped to her feet and gave a nod of thanks to Jarin before turning to the next attack. She wanted to get to Braith since he was alone with the three elders, but the other four witches came straight for her and Jarin.

She heard a witch running up behind her. Leoma reared back and slammed her elbow into the witch's face. Leoma then ducked when the second witch sent magic toward her. The blast slammed into the first witch, who convulsed and fell to the ground as her skin began to burn.

"I'll kill you for that!" the second woman screamed. "She was my sister!"

Leoma jerked up her sword to shield herself when she saw the ball of orange flames come at her. She batted the first one away, but the second grazed her right thigh. The sting of the magic was instantaneous, but she couldn't let it stop her. Not now, not when they could end the Coven once and for all.

She heard a bellow and glanced over to see Braith impale the blonde elder on his sword and lift her over his head. He tossed her away, her body burning by the time it hit the ground.

Shock reverberated through Leoma. Somehow, Braith's sword had been spelled—and the only one who could've done that was the Blood Skull.

"Leoma!"

Jarin's yell reminded her that she was in the midst of battle. She turned, but the witch was already upon her. Leoma grabbed the flat side of her blade with her other hand and held it before her as the witch slammed her back against a tree.

Flames licked perilously close to her face. She smelled burning hair and knew it was hers. Only her sword stopped the witch—but it wouldn't halt the magic.

Leoma peeled back her lips and pushed against the witch with all her might while the woman smiled in triumph. Sweat dropped from Leoma's face as the heat of the fire singed her. If she remained, she would burn.

She jerked up her knee, ramming it into the witch's stomach. At the same time, she shoved the woman to the side and dove away. When she got to her feet, the tree she had been held against was burning.

Leoma ran to the witch as she got to her feet and plunged

her sword into her stomach. The witch's eyes widened as the magic she had been casting in her hands faded with her life.

Leoma kicked the witch off her blade and looked over to find Jarin putting out the fire on the tree with his staff. She spotted the two witches he had been fighting burning, as well.

With those four dead, she turned and ran to Braith. She reached him with Jarin at her side, but when they tried to attack one of the elders, they were thrown back.

She rose up to see a greenish-blue dome around Braith and the elders.

"We cannot help him," Jarin said as he stood.

Leoma climbed to her feet. She couldn't take her eyes off Braith. He fought like a man possessed. His movements were fluid, effortless. His raw, visceral rage matched his lust for death—and it was conveyed in every action.

Her stomach clenched, as she was helpless to do anything but watch him confront two elders. Her hand tightened around the hilt of her sword, eager to join in the fray. But this fight wasn't hers.

His sword sang with blood. It rolled down his blade as he held his weapon with both hands, ready to end another elder's life.

Braith stepped and swung his sword. The two remaining councilmembers blocked him with magic. Out of Angmar's hand shot a thick length of silver that looked like a whip. It wrapped around his sword, sizzling from the contact.

His lips peeled back when she tried to yank his weapon from his hands. Braith spun towards Angmar and kicked Matilda in the chest.

In the next breath, Angmar stood before him, her face

inches from his with her magic whip crackling between them. "Join us."

How she repulsed him. "I'm no witch."

"The power of one flows through you. The Blood Skull is using you."

He scoffed at her. "You understand nothing."

"Then tell me," she urged.

"All you want is power."

Her dark eyes flashed. "I do this for my people."

"Nay, witch. That's a lie you feed others, but I can see the falsehood on your lips."

"We're growing stronger every day," Angmar said. "More witches come to us."

He gave a loud snort as he glared down at her. "You mean other than the ones you force to join you? I saw your witches bring another to a Grove. I heard them say 'join us or die.'"

Angmar shrugged indifferently. "Some need a little push."

"You disgust me."

"I can kill you. Right here. Right now," she threatened. As if to accent her words, the silver whip grew brighter.

He twisted so his back was to Angmar. He gritted his teeth and put all his strength into yanking his sword free of her whip. There was a snap, and behind him, he heard a surprised inhale. Braith lowered his sword and slowly turned to face the elder.

Angmar looked from his sword to her hands, but there was no sign of the crackling whip. "What did you do?"

"Your time is up, witch. Prepare to die."

"Nay!" Matilda said as she rushed him.

———

Armir read Jarin's message and rushed to the tower. He threw open Malene's door without knocking and found her standing in the middle of the chamber with her palms facing each other and blue light emanating from both.

As well as her eyes.

"Armir," she said, her voice coming out as a husky whisper.

Her eyes were directed at him, but he knew she wasn't seeing him. He gradually walked into the tower, unsure what was happening. This wasn't something he'd ever seen, especially not in a Lady of the Varroki.

"I've news from Jarin," he said.

"He's in battle."

Armir frowned as he glanced at the parchment in his hand. He wasn't sure how she knew such a thing. Then he looked at the blue light in her hands. "What do you see?"

"The Coven. And elders."

"So the council is there," Armir murmured. He took a step closer. "I should go to Jarin."

Malene blinked slowly, the blue glow in her eyes broken for just a moment. "There is a Hunter with him. And someone else, someone using very powerful magic."

Armir dropped the hand holding Jarin's message and kept his gaze on Malene. He didn't know what was happening to her, and while it could benefit them, he was worried about the repercussions. Because power such as this came at a price. "Jarin said the Blood Skull was found."

"Aye," Malene said as her blue light grew brighter. "The skull has found a Warden."

At her words, Armir remembered one of the many tales of the Blood Skull. It was said that it had a Warden, but since no one knew where the skull was, he figured that account to be nothing more than myth. It appeared that wasn't the case.

"The Warden is strong," Malene said. "Formidable."

"Can he defeat the Coven?" Armir asked as he moved closer.

Malene cried out suddenly, her back arching. Without thought, he dropped the missive and rushed to her, catching her before she hit the floor. He held her in his arms and smoothed back her hair as the glow faded and returned to her palms.

Her troubled eyes, now once more their usual soft gray, met his. "That has never happened before."

"You were there, at the battle."

"I saw it as if looking down upon them. I wanted to help them. The Warden...he's in trouble."

Armir nodded and gathered her in his arms. "You need to rest."

When he stood and glanced down at her, her eyes were closed. It didn't go unnoticed that carrying her to bed was becoming a habit.

And one he liked.

But what worried him more were the changes he saw in Malene. Her magic was growing swiftly, and if she didn't control it, it could easily rip her apart.

Leoma yelled a warning when the flame-haired woman rushed Braith. The force of the witch's magic against him shattered the dome surrounding them and sent his sword flying from his hand.

When Leoma tried to go to Braith, Jarin wrapped his arms around her and held her back. She struggled against him, but he yanked her close and hissed, "Wait for the right moment."

Braith winced as he hit the ground hard, but he immediately rolled toward the skull. He grasped it in his hand, lifting it as he lay on his back. Then he shoved it at the black-haired elder's face.

Her screams of pain pierced the air.

Leoma looked at Jarin. "We can take them. Now."

Jarin gave a nod and released her. They rushed the trio as the redhead kicked the skull from Braith's hand and wrapped her arms around the other witch. The mist swarmed them, but by the time Leoma got there, the elders were gone.

She slid to a stop beside Braith and dropped to her knees. Smiling down at him, she took his hand, noting the blood that covered him. The problem was, she didn't know if any of it was his. And she had a sick feeling that he was dying.

"My beautiful warrior." Braith's fingers wrapped around hers, strong and tight.

She heard the pain in his words, and her heart jumped into her throat as she fought not to let her worry show. "How bad is it?"

"I tried to get them all for you."

Leoma shook her head. "That doesn't matter. Tell me where you're hurt?" She looked behind her. "Jarin!"

The warlock hurried over to them. Braith glared at him then turned his eyes to Leoma. "Did you replace me?"

"Never," she told him and brushed his hair from his face. "He's a warlock who came to help me find you. I wouldn't be here without him."

Braith rolled his head to Jarin. "My thanks."

Jarin nodded, but his gaze was moving over Braith's body. "Where are you injured?"

"Leoma, there is so much I want to tell you," Braith said, refusing to answer Jarin.

She licked her lips. "There will be time for that. We need to heal you first."

Braith closed his eyes, his pain evident. When he opened

them, he gave a nod to her wounds from the battle with the witches. "You're bleeding."

"And I'll take care of it as soon as we see to you." Her throat clogged with dread and regret. She had seen plenty of people die, and she knew that's what was happening to Braith.

He smiled at her. "The elders were exact in their strikes. There is no helping me."

"I don't believe that." She couldn't. There was no way he held the Blood Skull and fought so valiantly only to die this way.

She wiped at a tear that escaped and looked around for the skull. As soon as she saw it, Leoma jumped up and ran for it. Even though she knew how it had burned the witch, she still grasped it.

It was warm in her hands as she rushed back to Braith and held it out to him. "Take it," she insisted.

He reached for it. As soon as his hands made contact, blood rushed from the skull. Jarin jumped back, but Leoma remained beside him, holding the skull with Braith's hands over hers.

His gaze held hers before his eyes slid closed. She watched in dismay as the blood coated him from head to foot. The longer she waited for him to move, the more anxious she became.

"Braith!" she called. "Braith, please."

The blood suddenly halted, and Braith's hands fell away. Leoma stared in shock.

"He's gone," Jarin said.

Leoma shook her head. "Nay. He cannot be."

Jarin tried to take the skull from her and jerked back when it singed his hand. He frowned at it and looked between her and Braith. "Set the skull on him."

With nothing else to lose, Leoma did just that. Her mouth

parted in alarm when the blood began retreating back into the skull. When there was not a drop left on Braith, Leoma leaned forward and touched his face.

"Born of blood," she whispered. "Died in blood."

Suddenly, Braith's eyes opened.

"Reborn of blood," Jarin said.

33

Breath never tasted so sweet. The world had never been so bright. Braith gazed at the Blood Skull before grabbing it with his hands. His heart beat solidly in his chest, but he could still vividly feel the sensation of it slowing and—finally—halting.

All the while, his thoughts had been on Leoma.

His gaze moved to his side and clashed with dark brown eyes. The sight of those beautiful orbs filled with tears unmanned him. He reached an arm out for her and pulled her down against him. The soft, ragged inhale he heard made him hold her tighter.

"I thought I lost you," she whispered.

"You did."

She straightened and slid her gaze to the skull in his other hand. "Her blood brought you back."

"Her blood gave me life," Braith said as he sat up.

"As enjoyable as this reunion is, we should go."

Braith turned his head to Jarin before glancing at the many

places of scorched earth from witch deaths. "The warlock's right. Angmar and Matilda could return at any moment."

"You know their names?" Leoma asked.

He got to his feet and took her hand. "I know a lot more than that. I'll tell you all of it, but we need to get clear of this place."

As Leoma stood and strode past Jarin she said, "I told you he wouldn't betray me."

Jarin's pale blue eyes met Braith's. "I told her to be prepared for anything."

"It was wise council," Braith admitted as he rolled to his knees before getting to his feet.

He glanced at the path the witches had formed. He found his sword and retrieved it, returning the weapon to its sheath before he followed Leoma. Braith didn't need to look behind him when he heard the trees moaning again. He knew they were forming another barrier.

With the Blood Skull in his hand, they approached the trees where Leoma and Jarin had been hiding. The branches suddenly shifted, sliding from their knots to clear a narrow path riddled with thick roots protruding haphazardly from the ground.

"It's better than trying to climb through the trees," Leoma said and glanced at Jarin.

The warlock shifted his staff into his other hand. "Don't look at me. I didn't do this."

Braith watched as they both turned to him. He lowered his gaze to the skull. "Time and death didn't fade her magic."

He was the first down the trail with Leoma behind him. As soon as Jarin passed, the branches knitted back together behind him. Braith held the skull close against him. There was no denying he felt very protective of it.

"What happened to Eleanor?" Jarin asked.

Braith was curious about the warlock. Somehow, it had never entered his mind that men could also have magic. All Leoma had ever spoken about was female witches. But that was a discussion for later.

"The Blood Skull killed her," Braith replied.

Leoma let out a soft whistle. "I would've liked to see that. How did the skull do it?"

"Blood," Braith told them. "She filled the ground with so much blood that it pulled Eleanor under. There, the skull held the witch until the other elders arrived. Only then did it—she—kill Eleanor."

Jarin grunted behind them. "That's what I felt then. The elders did as well since they screamed."

Braith exited the entwined trees and waited for Leoma and Jarin. As he walked past, the warlock bent and retrieved something from the ground. Jarin shook out the material to reveal a cloak.

"Where to now?" Leoma asked.

Jarin leaned the staff against a tree and fastened his cloak before wrapping his hands around his thick, wooden staff. "The council will be coming for Braith—and the Blood Skull. There is nowhere he can hide that they won't find him."

"Let them come," Braith stated as he tucked the skull against him.

Leoma's eyes widened at him. "I don't hear any fear in your voice. They just killed you."

"He's now the Warden of the Blood Skull," Jarin said.

Braith looked at the warlock without replying.

Leoma glanced between them before throwing up her hands. "And what's that supposed to mean?"

"It means the Blood Skull has chosen me to keep it out of other's hands. No one else can touch it," Braith said.

There was a brash smile on Jarin's lips. "Really? Why don't

you ask Leoma how the skull was placed on your chest where it then saved you?"

Braith moved his gaze to Leoma, shock reverberating through him. "You touched it?"

"I had to," she replied with a shrug. She looked warily at the skull. "Something told me to get it to you."

He was so stunned by the revelation that he could hardly believe what he was hearing. "The skull told me anyone else who touched it would be burned. It's an injury that cannot be healed, even with magic. Are you hurt?"

Leoma lifted one shoulder. "The skull was warm, but it didn't harm me."

"The answer is obvious," Jarin said as he walked between them. "But if neither of you can figure it out, I'm not going to tell you."

Leoma rolled her eyes and let out a long-suffering sigh. "He's quite full of himself. However, he saved my life and got me to you."

"I knew you would come," Braith said.

They turned as one and trailed behind the warlock. Having Leoma beside him again felt wonderful. Perfect. He never wanted to be apart from her again, and after everything they had been through, he wasn't going to wait to tell her how he felt. He just didn't want an audience when he did it.

"Where's my horse?" Braith asked after they had walked a good distance.

Jarin said over his shoulder, "Being guarded by my wolf."

Braith frowned and jerked his head to Leoma. "Did he just say wolf?"

"Aye," Jarin replied.

Leoma grinned. "Valdr is Jarin's companion. He's quite beautiful and very capable of killing witches. We fought together."

Braith smiled at her before turning his head forward. "It seems there is much I missed."

"Us, as well," Jarin said as he came to a halt and faced them. "You said the Blood Skull spoke to you."

Braith nodded once. "She did. You sound surprised."

"I am," the warlock, admitted. "My people—"

"And who are your people?" Braith interrupted.

Jarin grinned as they stared at each other. "We are the Varroki, an ancient race of witches and warlocks."

Braith looked to Leoma. "Did you know of them?"

"Nay, not until I met Jarin," she answered.

Braith shifted his gaze back to Jarin, but before he could ask another question, the warlock said, "I was tasked with watching Eleanor. The Varroki have been avenging and protecting those wronged by witches for centuries. We also catch and bring witches who harm innocents with the purpose of causing fear or doing evil to justice."

"You've failed with the Coven," Leoma said.

Jarin put both hands on his staff, his gaze lowering to the ground for a long moment. "The Varroki aren't as mighty as we once were. We do our best with the resources that we have. We learned from a witch we caught years ago who the elders were. Finding the councilmembers, however, hasn't been easy. They are rarely together. And no one has ever gotten close enough to attempt to assassinate one."

Leoma smiled. "Until Braith."

"I was only able to do it because of the skull," he corrected them.

Jarin shrugged as he dropped one of his hands to his side. "It matters not how you were able to do it. What matters is that the Coven has taken a mighty blow this day thanks to you and the Blood Skull. Yet the repercussions will be swift and substantial."

"We should get to the others and warn them," Leoma said to him.

Braith jerked his chin to Jarin. "How long have you known of Leoma and the other Hunters?"

"Not long. I just learned recently. Malene, our leader, had a vision of them standing against the Coven and requested that I attempt to find one." Jarin's eyes went to Leoma. "Malene knew one of your kind would be following the Coven."

Leoma walked to Braith's side. "You said we needed an army. If we join forces with the Varroki, we could have that."

"I cannot and will not speak for my people," Jarin said. "Malene makes our decisions. She told me to find you. It was my choice to help you since we had a common goal, to end Eleanor. Now, I must return."

Braith asked, "Where?"

Jarin's lips curved slightly. "To my home. Do not worry, Warden, I will make sure your stallion is returned."

A strong wind began around the warlock. Braith let Leoma pull him back a few steps. Within a heartbeat, Jarin was gone.

Leoma shuddered. "I'm glad he didn't offer to take us with him. The last time he used magic to transport us, I thought I was dying."

Braith wiped blood from the side of her face. "It's good to have you with me again."

"I'm sorry," she said and put her hand on his chest. "I should never have gone after Roger at the castle. He wanted us separated, and I gave him exactly what he desired."

"Do not blame yourself. One way or another, they would have separated us."

Leoma glanced at his chest. "I killed Roger."

"That saves me having to return to Falk Castle."

"You do understand that the skull has made you into a weapon?"

Braith nodded slowly. "I felt it as soon as I took the relic into my hands. The first witch asked me to trust her. She told me what the Coven planned to do with me, and she showed me what I needed to do to keep you safe. She also told me you would be there."

"What are you going to do with it now?"

He adjusted the skull against him. "I'll guard it for the rest of my days. In exchange, she spelled my sword."

Leoma let her hand slide down his chest before it fell to her side. "I suppose we should head toward the abbey now."

"Aye."

She turned and began walking. Braith fell in step beside her. They covered ground quickly as she told him all that had occurred with Jarin, including how the warlock healed her after Roger threw a dagger at her.

Braith's fury was substantial, but he seemed appeased by the knowledge that Leoma had punished his old friend. She'd questioned them going to the castle. Next time, he would listen to her.

Once she finished her tale, he began his. Relaying all that happened with Eleanor and the Blood Skull was hard enough, but reliving the battle with the Coven elders was challenging.

He had known that he would die by their hand, but it only strengthened his resolve to deliver as many blows to them as he could.

It was nearing dusk when they found a place next to a lake to bed down. Leoma was silent as she gathered wood and started a fire. He set aside the skull and watched her, utterly enamored. And it was time he told her.

He returned from hunting to find her in the water. And while he wanted nothing more than to join her, he sat and waited until she finished her swim. She walked to the shore with her hair wet and her skin gleaming from being scrubbed. Their eyes met briefly as she halted at the edge of the water.

Braith rose and undressed, never taking his eyes from her. He walked to stand beside her, shoulder-to-shoulder as he faced the water, and she the land.

He wanted so much to pull her into his arms, but first, he needed to wash off the smell of battle. He walked a few paces and dove into the chilly water before scrubbing himself clean. After he'd rinsed, he turned to make his way back to shore and halted when his gaze landed on Leoma who now faced him.

He walked to her, stopping before her. She linked her fingers with his, and they walked from the water together. His mouth watered at the sight of her damp skin. She bent to gather his clothes before she shot him a seductive smile.

After he'd grabbed his boots and sword, they returned to the fire. With each step, desire rose, and need burned. He hungered for a taste of her, craved to run his palms over her silken skin.

Longed to join their bodies—and hearts—once more.

He'd lost everything, yet he'd found the most precious thing of all. Leoma.

34

The time had come. Leoma put her hands on Braith's bare chest. She looked into his indigo eyes while his fingers slipped into her wet hair and held her head.

"The morning we woke at the castle, I told you I wanted many more such days," he said.

Her heart leapt at his words. "I remember."

"There was more I wanted to say, more I would've said." He drew in a deep breath. "I never envisioned myself with a family. It seemed like it was out of the realm of possibility, so I never contemplated looking for a wife."

She smoothed her hand over his chest, her body hungry for him. "I had the same feeling."

"Had?" he asked.

Leoma parted her lips but hesitated when the words began to form. She had never spoken anything like it to another before, and it frightened her. It also motivated her.

"My heart broke when I saw you with Eleanor," Leoma said. "I knew magic was being used, and I didn't think I would ever be able to get to you to break it. I should've known you were stronger than that. I should have realized you would see through it on your own.

"I thought I got you back at the cavern, but then you were gone again. You were days ahead of us, and I could imagine all sorts of things happening to you. Then Jarin used his magic."

One side of Braith's mouth lifted in a smile. "He brought you to me."

"And I saw you fight. I was in awe of you. Then my heart was ripped out of my chest when you died. You would never hear of the feelings I was too afraid to share. I wanted to stop time and have the opportunity to tell you."

His gaze bore into hers. "Tell me what?" he urged.

Leoma rose up on her tiptoes and pressed her lips against his for a soft kiss. "That I love you. With all my heart, with all that I am."

His mouth was suddenly on hers, his tongue slipping inside her mouth while his arms held her tightly against him. Passion exploded between them. He lifted her in his arms before dropping onto his knees and laying her on the ground.

The feel of his skin against hers was heavenly. She wrapped her legs around him and gazed into his eyes. With one thrust, he filled her, joining their bodies. She dug her fingers into the flesh of his shoulders and arched her back at the exquisite sensation of him inside her.

"I love you," he whispered reverently.

She sighed and looked at him as he pulled out and drove back inside her.

"I've never said those words before, but I feel them all the way to my bones," he said.

"I never want us to be apart again."

His hips shifted, and he once more filled her. "Never."

Her eyes closed, and desire tightened low in her belly as his rhythm quickened.

Jarin made his way to the tall black gates. Valdr walked by his side as Andi soared above him. As he reached the gates, he rested the tip of his staff against them and let his magic spread outward into the iron.

The massive doors swung open, and he strode inside. His gaze immediately went to the cliff where the tower stood. Varroki came out of their cottages to watch him as he began the journey through the winding streets to the tower.

He saw a spark of blue light from one of the top tower windows. Malene. Few had seen her since her arrival five years prior. Jarin had been one of them, but the meeting was brief. In fact, he could go the rest of his life without ever laying eyes on the Lady of the Varroki again.

Andi called loudly above him. No one stopped him or spoke. A Varroki warrior spent most of their lives in solitude. They kept to the shadows, watching enemies and relaying reports. And they fought.

All died in battle eventually.

It was a rite of passage that began with their Viking ancestors and continued in the Varroki culture hidden on an isle in northern Scotland. And just as the Norse welcomed their women fighting beside them, so did the Varroki.

When Jarin finally reached the base of the tower, he wasn't surprised to find Armir waiting for him.

"She said you were alive," Armir stated.

Jarin cocked his head to the side. "Who?"

"Malene."

"I didn't know peering through another's eyes was one of her powers."

"It isn't," Armir said. "And she didn't. She saw the battle with the Coven elders as if watching from above."

Jarin's frowned at the news. "That is...significant."

"And just a bit of what's been happening. She wants to see you."

He nodded to Armir as the commander led the way up the stairs. Valdr yawned and lay down at the door where he would wait until Jarin returned.

Halfway up the stairs, Jarin said, "You seem worried."

"Concerned," Armir corrected. "Malene hasn't asked to see anyone since she came to Blackglade. Whatever you see inside her chamber—"

"I'll keep to myself," Jarin interrupted.

Armir glanced over his shoulder and nodded.

Jarin smoothed out his frown when they reached the top of the tower. Armir knocked twice and opened the door. Jarin stepped inside and came face-to-face with one of the most beautiful beings he had ever laid eyes on.

"Hello, Jarin," Malene said with a smile.

He was awestruck by her soft gray eyes and long, flaxen hair interwoven in an impressive array of braids that pulled back one side back while the rest hung free. She stood with her hands held together before her, gowned in sky blue with a silver ring girdle around her hips that dropped down the front of the dress.

Belatedly, he realized he was staring. He bowed his head. "My lady."

"I saw you found one of those I wished you to seek out."

"Her name is Leoma," Jarin explained. "She calls herself a Hunter."

Malene raised a brow, her interest clear. "A Hunter," she repeated. "Did you find out more?"

"She was raised by a witch who fights against the Coven. Whoever trained Leoma, did a fine job. She's very skilled. Even for one without magic."

Armir asked, "What does she do when she finds a witch? It's not as if she can kill them."

"Actually, she can. Her sword was spelled by her witch guardian," Jarin said.

Malene turned, her long, pale yellow tresses swinging out behind her. "How did she react to you?"

Jarin glanced at Armir. "Leoma was hesitant to trust me at first, and to be honest, I still don't believe she fully does. And she was shocked to learn I was a warlock."

"We should change that," Malene said. "I believe we're going to need these Hunters. And they're going to need us."

Leoma was giddy. It was the only word she could come up with that came close to describing the emotions running through her. The night with Braith held many things, but sleep wasn't one of them.

They made love and dozed, only for her to wake and reach for him again. They talked and ate and made love some more. Except the next time, he was the one to rouse her. And so it went until dawn when they dressed and set out for the abbey.

"Will they accept me?" Braith asked with a frown.

Leoma smiled and nodded. "They will welcome you with open arms. Not only are you a skilled knight, but you're also the Warden of the Blood Skull. Not to mention, you saved my life."

"Only after you saved mine," he said with a wink.

She thought she might burst, she was so happy. They kept off main roads and traveled quickly across the country. Though they tried to keep to the trees, there were vast open spaces that offered no shelter. They teased and talked, walked and ran.

And the closer they got to the abbey, the faster Leoma walked. She couldn't wait to get home. Not only to bring Braith into the fold, but there was so much information to share with the others, as well as preparations to be made.

Braith grew quiet as he followed her through the forest. She looked back at him and grabbed his hand as she came to stand before the entrance to the abbey.

"I don't see anything," he said.

She tugged him after her as she walked beneath an arch of ivy that had grown over the stones. Once through the barrier, the magic hiding the abbey was gone, and the structure visible.

Braith turned around in a circle, taking it all in. Leoma watched him, recalling how awed she'd been the first time she saw the ruins. Except it was no longer crumbling. The abbey had been rebuilt and was a spectacular sight of arches, peaked roofs, and life.

"Leoma!"

At the sound of her name, she turned and spotted her family. The younger children rushed her, throwing their arms around her while Edra, Asa, and Ravyn made their way over a bit slower. Behind them on the steps stood Radnar, staring at Braith.

As Edra approached, the children scattered. Leoma gazed into the blue eyes of the woman who had assumed the role of mother. Edra still looked as young and beautiful as the day she plucked Leoma off the streets.

"Leoma," Edra said and opened her arms.

Leoma rushed to Edra and hugged her. "I've so much to tell you. But first," she said and stepped back. "This is Braith. He's a knight who..."

Her words trailed away when Edra left her to walk to Braith, her gaze on the skull in the crook of his arm.

"My love?" Radnar said as he strode to Edra and put an arm around her.

Braith bowed his head to the couple. "Sir Radnar, I've looked forward to meeting you. All of you. Leoma has told me so much about you. I may have begun life as a knight turned earl, but my calling is with you, fighting witches."

Leoma moved to stand beside Braith. "Braith has become the Warden of the Blood Skull."

Edra gasped as she jerked back. "It's not a myth, then?"

"Nay," Braith said. "I'm proof of that. It helped kill an elder of the Coven and spelled my sword so I could kill another."

Radnar's brows snapped together. "Two are dead?"

"By his hand," Leoma said proudly. "And he learned the names of the other two while fighting them."

Edra looked between them before asking Braith, "That's impressive. Are you sure you want to leave your world behind to join us?"

"I've found my calling, and I'll not be parted from Leoma."

"I see," Radnar said in a low voice.

Leoma smiled at the man who had been a father to her. He raised a brow in question, silently asking her if she indeed loved Braith. She nodded, letting her love shine on her face for all to see.

"We can certainly use another knight," Radnar said and held out his arm.

Braith clasped Radnar's forearm as the two men smiled at each other.

Edra turned so everyone could hear her. "Our ranks have grown again. Braith is now welcome among us as a Hunter."

Radnar leaned close to them. "If you want any privacy,

then I suggest you take him the back way to your quarters, Leoma. We'll see you later where you can tell us your story."

Leoma flashed Radnar and Edra a smile and grabbed Braith's hand. They were laughing as they ran through the abbey, turning this way and that, running up stairs and down long corridors until they came to her chamber.

She flung open the door and turned once inside. Braith walked in slowly and shut the door, then he set the skull down and made his way to her where he drew her against him and gave her a long, slow kiss that made her knees weak and curled her toes.

"You never answered me this morning," he said as he nuzzled her neck.

She unfastened his cloak and let it fall away. "You actually expected me to give an answer when you were giving me such pleasure that I couldn't string two words together?"

"It's why I'm asking again. Will you be my wife? Will you carry my name, our hearts and bodies bound for all eternity?"

Leoma smoothed her hands over his face, his whiskers scraping her hand. She slid her fingers into the cool strands of his hair and felt her heart bursting with so much love and happiness it was almost overwhelming. "Aye. There is nothing I want more."

His indigo eyes blazed with happiness and love. "I hope they don't expect us for dinner because you're not leaving that bed once I get you in it."

"Is that a threat?" she asked with a grin as she backed out of his arms and began to undress.

"It's a bloody promise," he stated, stalking her.

Her vest dropped to the floor. "Then come and get me."

Three days later...

"That's quite an adventurous tale," Radnar said as he paced the area they had turned into a dining hall. "And you're an earl?"

Braith rested his arms on the table and looked at the knights, Hunters, and the others of the abbey. "There were times I didn't think I would survive, and times I didn't want to."

"But he did," Leoma said. "We both did."

Edra rose from her seat to stand with Radnar. "When I was running from the Coven all those years ago, I came across a witch who told me a tale of the Blood Skull. We're fortunate the Coven didn't get their hands on it, but what worries me more is their plans."

"Your arrival got me thinking," Radnar said to Braith as he glanced at Edra. "Now that I know you hold a title, my thoughts have turned down a particular path."

Braith nodded. "I have land and a keep, if that is what you wish to know."

"I'm more interested if you know others who might join us?"

Braith reached over and linked his fingers with Leoma's. "I do. I told Leoma that your coven needs an army. However, I've been doing some thinking of my own."

Leoma frowned at him, a question in her dark eyes.

He squeezed her hand, letting her know that it was time to let the others know. He turned his attention to Radnar and Edra and took a deep breath. "The two of you may not have birthed Leoma, but you are her parents nonetheless. As you might have guessed, I love her, and she loves me. I ask your permission to marry her."

"If that is Leoma's wish," Radnar said.

Edra smiled widely when Leoma nodded her head.

But Braith couldn't smile, not yet. He waited until everyone quieted down from their excited cheers before he swallowed. Leoma moved closer to him and put her other hand on his arm, giving him the courage to voice what they had agreed upon the night before.

"What you have here is special," Braith continued. "It needs to be protected and kept secret. As long as I'm alive, I will be the Warden of the Blood Skull. After what I did to the Coven elders, they will be coming for me. If I remain, they will find this place."

Leoma said, "This isn't a decision we came to easily, but we both want to ensure that the abbey and everything the two of you began continues, so we all have a chance against the Coven."

"I'll be able to find the men we need for the army," Braith added. "Leoma and I can also be a link to the outside world for anything you need."

Edra and Radnar looked at each other and smiled sadly. It was Edra who turned to them and said, "We accept your decision and appreciate the concern and consideration you've given all of us. Will you hold the marriage celebration here, at least?"

Braith laughed and nodded. Within moments, Leoma was dragged out by the women to begin preparations. He waited until they were gone before he rose and walked to Radnar and the other knights.

They had much planning to do. And it started now.

Angmar stared at the reflection of her face in the bowl, fury burning inside her. She slapped at the water and turned away. No magic she conjured could heal or hide the burns on the left side of her face put there by the Blood Skull.

She was marked now.

Matilda sharpened her nails as she reclined on a chair. "Retaliation. It's our only choice. They killed two of the council."

"As long as Braith has the Blood Skull, he can harm us."

Matilda lowered her hands and shrugged. "Then we kill him."

Angmar smiled as an idea formed. "I've something better in mind."

"Oh," Matilda said as she sat up. "Do tell."

"He was with a Hunter. Perhaps the Hunter becomes the hunted."

Matilda threw back her head and laughed as she rubbed her hands together.

Angmar touched her ruined face. If she couldn't get to Braith, she would hurt those he cared about.

EVERKIN

Read on for EVERKIN, the short story previously only
available in ebook!
And look for the next Kindred book
Spring 2018

1

England, 1334

Battle had a way of damaging not just the body, but the mind, as well. Radnar gripped his right wrist as he flexed his hand. He'd taken a nasty hit two weeks prior, and there were times his fingers went numb.

Not a good sign for any knight, much less one who earned his keep by his sword.

He blew out a breath and leaned a shoulder against a wooden beam as he watched the blacksmith work on a new shoe for his horse. It was something Radnar could ill afford, but if his horse weren't properly outfitted, he was as good as dead. So here he was, spending his last bag of coin.

Life was one meaningless battle after another. He'd fought alongside some of the best knights of the age, and had even trained in techniques from a foreign land.

A few of the nobles he'd fought in service for had asked him to remain at their castles, but something kept driving him onward. It was as if there weren't a place in all of England he felt he could call home. Or even wanted to.

His travels were taking him to an earl, who was building up his army to invade.... Someone. Somewhere. Radnar didn't know who the earl was attacking, and he didn't care. There was coin waiting, meals, and a way to release his love of battle.

It was the sights, the sounds...the smell...of battle that sustained him. There was no family to call him home, no lover who beckoned.

His mind drifted to years earlier when he was just a squire. Though his life had been hard, he hadn't minded. Sir Gregory was fair, if heavy-handed at times. Gregory, unlike some knights, was more than willing to help Radnar join their ranks.

It was during that time he first saw her. Edra.

He pushed away from the post he leaned against and walked to his horse, rubbing his hand down the stallion's neck. More and more often lately, Edra had entered his thoughts.

No matter how much time passed, her face remained as clear in his mind as the day he'd first met her. There would never be another who had her bright blue eyes. No matter how hard he looked, there wasn't a woman whose hair could match the honey blonde of Edra's.

Her smile had the ability to melt away his cares. Her laugh had given him contentment. Her sexy voice could have him hard and yearning with just a few words.

The three months he'd spent with her had been the best of his life. He'd fallen in love with her and had promised to make her a lady just as soon as he earned his spurs. They'd made so many plans.

Their passion had run hot from the instant they met, so it was no surprise that within a month, they were lovers. The gift of her maidenhead wasn't something he'd taken lightly. He would've done anything for her.

So when she'd left without a word, he was devastated.

All he'd wanted to do was drown himself in ale, but Gregory didn't give him a moment's peace. Though Radnar hadn't realized it at the time, the old knight had been looking out for him. He'd given Radnar something to focus on to quell his desolation. And when his misery turned to anger, Gregory had given him the opportunity in battle to become a knight.

After he had been knighted, Radnar lay awake, staring at the stars, wishing he could celebrate one of his goals with the only person he loved: Edra.

Sometime over the years, that anger had dissipated and shifted into longing. It settled in his chest, consistently tightening. It kept him moving from place to place, but he knew why.

He was searching for her.

Radnar knew he was a fool. If Edra had really loved him, she wouldn't have left. But his heart wouldn't listen, no matter how many times he tried such reasoning.

He rubbed the black's velvety nose. "Easy, boy," he murmured when the stallion flicked his tail in agitation.

Suddenly, Radnar stilled, his heart pounding. He turned in the direction where he'd seen the flash of honey blonde hair out of the corner of his eye. He was about to rush after the woman when the blacksmith called his name as he finished shoeing Radnar's horse.

Radnar fished out a coin and tossed it to the blacksmith before taking his stallion's reins. He leapt atop the horse and gave him a nudge with his knees that sent his mount into a trot through the streets.

He was so intent on looking for blonde hair that he nearly missed her. The woman was light of foot and wore a cloak with the hood up, preventing him from seeing her face as she zigzagged through the streets. But the cloak moved just enough that he saw a long, honey blonde braid.

Just as Radnar started to call out to her, he noticed the woman glance hastily over her shoulder. He pulled on the reins to slow the stallion as he looked in the direction the woman had gazed. He saw two more cloaked women striding purposefully after her. One in red, the other in green.

He clicked to his horse, following the blonde as she diverted toward the forest. It was a smart move. There was more cover within the trees, but if she needed help, there would be no one to hear her.

With a sigh, Radnar dismounted and dropped the reins. His horse would remain there until he returned. His other two horses, along with his armor, were hidden a few miles from the village. He didn't like leaving them so long, but he couldn't, in good conscience, abandon the blonde.

He kept the other cloaked women within sight as he followed discreetly. The fact that they didn't quicken their steps as the blonde began running worried him. Only someone who was sure his or her quarry would be caught projected such confidence.

His gaze jerked ahead, past the blonde. Years of battling and planning attacks had honed his instincts. Someone was there, waiting to capture her. He could feel it. He quietly slid his sword from the scabbard at his waist and twirled it once.

On quiet feet, he trailed the women through the forest. Thunder rumbled in the distance, and the smell of rain hung heavily in the air. The women didn't look away from their target or falter in their pursuit.

It was their stony countenance that set his teeth on edge. He knew what killers looked like. He'd seen enough of them in battle, and that's exactly what these females reminded him of. It was an odd thing for the fairer sex.

His grip on the hilt of his sword tightened when the blonde jerked to a halt. The hood of her cloak fell back, revealing a wealth of honey blonde hair. He quickly ducked behind the trunk of a tree.

Then she turned around.

His heart missed a beat as he found himself staring into a face he saw every night in his dreams. Edra. He drank in her hauntingly beautiful eyes and her stubborn chin. His hands ached to caress her creamy skin along her jaw to her cheek-bones. He longed to feel her plump lips against his.

His mouth parted as his blood pounded in his ears. The joy that erupted within him quickly soured as he saw two other women come up behind her.

Just as he'd suspected. She'd fallen into a trap.

"You shouldn't have run, Edra," said the woman in the deep green cloak.

Edra squared her shoulders and lifted her chin. "My answer was nay years ago. It is nay now, and it will be nay for eternity."

The one in the red cloak threw off her hood to reveal her midnight locks. She laughed as she shook a finger at Edra. "We warned you. We told you what would happen if you refused us."

"Someone would die," said a third woman in a brown cloak.

A fourth woman, wearing a black cloak smiled widely. "Someone close to you."

If Edra's eyes could kill, all four of the females would be lying dead upon the ground. "You killed her."

Radnar frowned when he heard the tremor in Edra's voice. There was violence in her words and in her bearing. The soft-spoken girl he'd known had grown into a fierce, defiant woman.

And it set his blood aflame.

"Of course, we did," said the first woman.

The second cackled loudly. "You can keep running, but we'll continue to follow."

"And kill those you help," said the third.

The fourth woman rubbed her hands together in anticipation. "But we have you cornered. I say we deal with your disloyalty now."

To his shock, Edra calmly smiled before she said, "I was hoping you'd say that."

He stood, awestruck, as she flung open her cloak and shifted so that she could see all four women. Her stance was that of a warrior, one ready and willing to face her enemies.

His first instinct was to help her, but something held him back. Edra appeared more than capable of handling herself. Even against four. It shouldn't be possible, surely, and yet what he saw said otherwise.

"You want to take us all?" asked the one in the red cloak, disbelief etched on her pretty face.

The woman in green held up her hand for silence. "This is the very reason we wanted her in our Coven."

That drew Radnar up short. Coven? As in...witches? His gaze jerked back to Edra, who appeared unfazed by the word. He crept closer, needing to know more.

"I'll be leaving here," Edra stated as she looked at each of the women. "Alone."

Black cloak gave a loud snort. "We've not tracked you all over England these past years just to allow you to get away."

"You actually think you caught me?" Edra asked, a small smile about her full lips. "How...naïve."

"I told you," brown cloak bit out as she took a step back,

putting her body at an angle as her hands went up in front of her.

Radnar had no warning before the woman in brown lifted her hand up higher in the air as words he didn't understand began to tumble from her lips. A greenish glow appeared and took the form of flames.

Edra, on the other hand, appeared to know exactly what was going on. She leaned to the side as a branch, aimed right for her, tumbled from a tree.

It was when Edra turned, and her cloak billowed that he saw the glint of steel. She pulled out a sword and plunged it into the heart of the woman in the black cloak. The shock on the impaled woman's face mirrored that of the other women.

"Get her!" shouted the one in green.

Red rushed Edra, but Edra whipped her head around, her arm outstretched and her fingers curling inward as if she were wrapping her hand around something. The woman slid to a halt, her hands clawing at her throat as she gasped for air.

Radnar was so stunned that he could only stare in wonder at what he currently witnessed. Surely his eyes were playing tricks on him—women were burned for less than what Edra now did.

The wind suddenly whipped into a frenzy, sending leaves swirling and raining upon them as the trees swayed viciously. His gaze landed on Brown and Green to find that both were chanting something. They stared at Edra with fury burning in their eyes.

There was a loud creak above him. He lifted his head and watched a large branch break off and swing straight for Edra. He bellowed her name, but nothing could be heard over the wind.

He thought for sure she would be impaled, as she never looked in the direction of the limb, but right before it struck her, she said something and moved the arm holding the sword toward where Brown stood to her right. The branch slammed into the woman with such force, he heard her bones shatter, even over the gale.

"I'll kill you!" Green screamed and lifted both arms. She spread her fingers and faced Edra, palms out.

Radnar watched in horror as Edra went flying backward, slamming against a tree before crumpling to the ground. As Green and Red approached her, he came up behind them.

"It's time we finish you once and for all," Red said to Edra as she rubbed her throat.

Edra was laughing when she lifted her head. "Beatrice, do shut up."

She then dove forward and grabbed her sword as she jumped to her feet. Radnar pulled back his arm and thrust his blade into Green's back the same time Edra shoved her sword into Red's stomach.

Red reached out to Edra, more of the words he didn't understand reaching him on the wind before she stumbled back a step and fell to her knees.

"What have you done?" Green said as she looked down at the tip of Radnar's sword protruding from her chest.

Edra took a deep breath and looked at Green as the gusts died away. "I did what had to be done."

He withdrew his sword as Green turned and speared him with black eyes before she gave a bark of laughter. "His blade can't hurt me."

"Aye, it can," Edra said as her focus shifted away from Red. "I spelled it long ago."

Red fell to the side unmoving as Green coughed, blood trickling from her mouth. She pointed at Edra and shouted hoarsely, "Hunter!"

As the word faded away, Green crumpled to the ground, dead.

Radnar lifted his eyes to Edra and their gazes clashed. She stood bold and glorious with her hair falling from its braid. There was so much he wanted to say, but suddenly, he had no words.

"Hello, Radnar."

2

She'd always known her past would catch up to her. Eventually. It's why Edra had finally stopped running from the Coven and decided to face them. But she'd been wholly unprepared for Radnar.

Of all the people she imagined she might eventually run into, she'd never expected him. Hoped for, but never anticipated.

"Is it really you?" he asked.

She swallowed and nodded, her heart aching at having him so near after so long. It had killed her to leave Radnar, but she'd done it to protect him. There had been no other way. She knew since she'd searched for any kind of solution.

"Where have you been?" he asked.

Edra didn't want to leave any bodies to be found. She whispered a few words and heard the hiss of the bodies right before they began to burn from the inside out. She ignored it as she cleaned off her sword and sheathed it. Her gaze went to Radnar often, taking in the changes she saw there.

He'd always been tall, and the years had honed his muscles

and filled him out nicely. His dark brown hair was pulled back in a queue at the base of his neck with a leather strip. She saw the faint lines of a scar along his cheek, and the deep lines on his forehead as if he wore a perpetual scowl.

It was the guardedness she saw in his dark eyes that made her sad. At one time, he'd gazed at her as if she were all that mattered. It was his love that had given her the courage to stand up for what she knew was right.

Unfortunately, that had brought doom upon all who knew her. Which was why she left.

She started to walk past him when his long fingers reached out and grabbed her arm, stopping her in her tracks. Edra turned her head to look at him. So many times, she'd wanted to find him, to take comfort in his arms, but she'd stayed away to keep him safe.

"Edra," he murmured.

"I'll answer all your questions, but we can't stay here."

He stared at her for a long moment, then gave a nod as he released her. "Follow me."

They didn't exchange another word as they trudged back through the forest until they came upon a big, black stallion grazing. Radnar whistled, and the horse lifted its head before neighing and walking to them.

He mounted the steed and then held out his hand for her. She hesitated only a heartbeat before she grasped it and allowed him to hoist her up behind him.

She'd intended to keep her hands to herself until the horse began to gallop, but once he did, she had no choice but to grab hold of Radnar's waist.

His anger burned between them, so intense she could feel it, but she didn't fault him for that. He had every right to be furious. She would be in his position. She wasn't looking forward to his questions. Or her answers.

He didn't mention anything about the magic. But that didn't matter. It would come out anyway. She wasn't worried that he would turn her in. Radnar had an innate morality that didn't always go along with the current politics or policies.

It wasn't long before they came to a stream and a secluded meadow where two other horses loaded down with his armor and other packs grazed. He grabbed their reins as they rode past and kept going.

It was another hour before he finally stopped. He swung his leg over the stallion's back and slid to the ground. Then he reached for her. The fact that he wouldn't meet her gaze let her know that things were only going to get worse.

"We'll camp here tonight," he said as he dropped his hands as soon as her feet were on the ground. Then he began unsaddling the destrier.

She looked around to find a river close and trees to give them shelter. A glance behind her showed that it would be hard for anyone to come upon them by surprise. These were things she'd learned out on her own.

While he worked with the horses, she searched for firewood. She felt his eyes on her often, but still, he didn't speak. He'd changed in the seven years since she had last seen him.

The time had changed her even more.

Radnar used to be impatient, and could, at times, be reckless. No doubt the recklessness was still there, but he'd harnessed the impatience with a firm, steady grip.

When she came back with an armful of wood, Radnar was nowhere to be seen. All three horses foraged nearby, so she knew he hadn't gone far. She set about building a fire. Once it flared, she sat back and listened to the wood as the flames devoured it.

She was on her back, looking at the clouds passing overhead when Radnar returned, carrying a brace of hares. She sat up and took one of the animals to clean.

"Why did you leave?" he asked in a soft voice devoid of anger or resentment.

The silence had gone on so long, that when he spoke, she was so surprised that she looked up from her task. She gazed into his deep brown eyes and saw the pain there, no longer hidden but raging for her to see.

"The women you saw today. They approached me a few weeks before I left you. They wanted me to join their Coven."

"Coven? As in witches?" he asked.

She gave a quick nod. "My magic was a secret I kept my entire life. I don't remember my mother, but I know everything about the magic she showed me while she was still alive. Afterward, while I lived with my aunt, I kept it to myself until I could get out on my own."

"How did the women know how to find you?"

"I don't know. I was surprised when they discovered me, but excited. I knew with them that I was safer than alone."

A look of indignation filled his face. "Because you didn't feel safe with me?"

"That's not what I meant," she said with a sigh. "I'm a witch. You know what they do to women who are even suspected of witchcraft"

"Is that why you didn't tell me what you were?"

"I didn't tell you, to protect you."

He gave a grunt and then took her unfinished hare and quickly skinned it before putting both over the fire to cook. She cleaned off the knife she'd used and tucked it into her boot as she settled before the fire. He was looking off in the distance at the horses.

It was time he knew all of it. Edra took in a bracing breath and said, "As soon as I went to the Coven, I saw that they weren't the type of witches I wanted to be around. They harmed people. Killed them. I refused to be a part of that."

"So you ran away." He looked at her before promptly shifting his gaze.

"I told them that I wasn't interested. They had seen us making love. They threatened to kill you if I didn't join."

His head turned to her, a frown wrinkling his brow. "You should've told me."

"You don't understand the power they have. I put the entire village and castle at risk. Everyone who knew me, anyone I even looked at would have died if I'd remained. They would have killed everyone until I joined them. So I left."

He stared into the fire but said no more.

"A year after I left, I heard that you'd become a knight. I returned and snuck into the castle while you slept. That's when I spelled your sword so that you would always have a defense against a witch."

"What do you mean you spelled my sword?"

She loosened the binding of her braid before running her fingers through her hair. "Most witches will cast a protection spell on themselves. They can be injured, but it takes something special to actually kill them. Every witch has a weakness. For some, it's a certain type of wood that can kill them, some it's metal, some it's flowers, and the list goes on and on. But with a sword empowered by a witch, you have the ability to kill any of us, no matter our protection."

"You could've woken me. With my sword spelled, I wasn't in danger anymore."

"Everyone else still was. It's why I kept on the move. But it didn't matter where I went because they always found me. Sometimes, I sensed that they were coming and got away in time. Others, they took me unawares."

He turned the hares over. "Who did they kill?"

"I found a girl of about ten summers. She was alone in the woods, eating berries and bark to stay alive. I fed and clothed her. I came back one day to find her dead. By the angle of her broken neck, I knew it was magic."

"Is that when you decided to confront them?"

She lowered her arms to her lap and stared into the red-orange flames. "After running for so long, it felt good to stop. I knew they'd never guess what I had planned."

"It was four against one. They would've killed you," he said, irritation deepening his voice.

"Maybe. But they didn't." She looked into his eyes. "Thanks to you."

He looked away as he reclined back on one forearm. "What will you do now?"

"What I'm supposed to do. Someone has to fight those evil witches. I intend to hunt them."

"So that's why she called you a hunter." He drew in a deep breath and slowly let it out.

Her gaze was drawn to him, as it had been from the moment they first saw each other at the market. It had only taken her days to fall in love with Radnar, and she had gladly given him her heart. Being away from him all those years had been the most difficult thing in the world.

"I never stopped loving you," she said.

The fire popped, and a log broke in two, the only thing breaking the silence. She hadn't expected him to believe her, but some kind of response would've been nice. His hurt ran deep, she knew this. When people loved as they did, the pain of abandonment sliced into the soul.

"What are your plans now that the Coven has been killed?" he asked.

She blinked back the threat of tears that burned her eyes.

His utter dismissal of her words cut her profoundly. "Those four were only part of the Coven."

He sat up and checked on the hares. "Will they continue to try and bring you into the group?"

"Their intent will be to kill me now."

"You did kill four of theirs." He tested the meat with his fingers.

"Three. You killed one."

His dark eyes slid to her as he licked the juices from his hands. "Are you suggesting they'll know that I was part of it?"

"Each witch has a different set of skills. Some are more powerful than others. It's better to think the worst and be prepared."

"Do you really expect me to go on the run with you."

She shook her head, doing her best to hide how much his words stung. "I'm warning you to be cautious. You won't know you're facing a witch until it's too late. They'll come at you when you least expect it, and you won't want to fight them because they're women."

"I'm not the man I was."

"The core of you hasn't changed, no matter how much the outside has."

He took one of the hares off the spit and pulled apart some meat before he held it out to her. "You'd be surprised how much someone can change."

The meat burned her fingers. She blew on it to cool. "I stand by my assessment. I know the man you are."

"You knew me. There's a difference."

Firmly put in her place, Edra began to eat. She was grateful for the meal, and though she wouldn't point it out, the fact that he had helped her, sheltered her, and now fed her, spoke volumes regarding the kind of man Radnar was.

She was enjoying her time with him, even if it wasn't

exactly pleasant. But it also hurt more than she'd expected. He was a reminder of what she'd had, what she'd lost—of the life that had been offered to her.

The life she'd had to walk away from.

Because of what the Coven had done, it would've been easy to allow hate to fill her and corrupt her soul. There were times when it nearly had. Then she would think of Radnar, of the way he'd tenderly held her and the passion they'd shared.

Her love for him got her through each day. Which was why it might very well break her when he departed. Because she had no doubt that he would.

There was no action she regretted when it came to him. Not giving him her body outside of marriage, not falling in love with a squire, and not leaving him. Everything she had done, she'd done out of love and to protect him.

And she would keep doing it.

She looked his way when he handed her another piece of meat. As she accepted it, she saw the wounds on his hands. As a knight, he had obviously seen many battles. He was alive and whole, and that overjoyed her. But she could only imagine the injuries he'd sustained.

Who had seen to his wounds? Who had helped him recover?

Edra's stomach churned so that she was barely able to swallow the food in her mouth. She might've remained alone because her heart belonged to him, but that didn't mean he'd done the same.

She watched his face as the light from the fire danced over him. A man like Radnar drew women. He wouldn't be alone. Not now. Not ever.

3

Radnar noticed when Edra stopped eating. He offered her more meat, but each time, she waved it away. She kept staring off into the distance as if her mind were somewhere else.

He kept going over her words, trying to reconcile them with everything he held dear. Witches were real. He couldn't believe it. No matter what the church said, he'd always thought it was just fanatics going overboard with their beliefs.

Now he knew Edra's truth. And it was a big one. The fact that she'd shared it with him so easily was astounding. He literally held her life in his hands, but she didn't seem worried. In fact, Edra appeared more than capable in all aspects.

Then again, she'd learned to survive on her own before her aunt had found her. Then after, Edra had done whatever she could to keep food in her stomach and a roof over her head. She knew what it meant to work hard, but she'd never complained. No matter how badly her hands had hurt from kneading the bread at the baker's. Coin was coin, and she'd needed it.

He'd wanted to take her away from that harsh life. It irked him that she had done it on her own...without him. Though, to be fair, she hadn't had a choice. If he could believe her.

What was he saying? Of course, he believed her. All those years of hating her when her actions had been done out of love. She'd been right not to tell him. He would've done something stupid and confronted the Coven, which would've gotten him killed.

He eyed her gown. It was clean but frayed. No doubt she'd had it for a while. Her cloak was no better. He couldn't imagine her out on her own. The world was a cruel, unforgiving place for a woman alone.

It wasn't much better for anyone not of noble birth.

"You still haven't told me what you plan to do." He hadn't intended to bring it up again, but he had to know her thoughts.

It was more than that. Now that he'd found her, he wasn't keen on letting her get away from him again. He moved his gaze from the fire to her face.

She had her legs crossed with her hands in her lap. The hilt of her sword peeked out of her cloak. Someone had taught her to fight. He hated that it hadn't been him. When he thought of her years without him and all that she'd seen and done, he was jealous of anyone who had been with her when he couldn't.

"I need my own Coven."

Her words made him frown as he sat up. "You're going to persuade witches to hunt other witches?"

She smiled as she looked at him. "I might be able to convince a few, but then I'd be giving up my intentions. I'm thinking about another kind of Coven."

"A hunter's Coven," he guessed.

"Precisely."

Intrigued, he leaned to the side, braced on his hand. "Where do you propose to get these hunters? You'll be putting your life in jeopardy if you recruit knights or anyone, really."

"I know. That's why I'm going to raise my hunters using orphaned children."

He gave a shake of his head, smiling despite himself because it was just the sort of idea she'd come up with. And it would work because Edra was that sort of woman.

"Is that approval I see in your eyes?" she teased.

"It is. Are you surprised?"

She gave a small shrug. "A little. You're taking all of this well."

"I wish you would've told me years ago. I would've kept your secret."

"I know, but it's also a burden. And you already had so much to carry. I'm proud of you for becoming a knight, but I never had any doubt."

He couldn't look into her blue eyes anymore. "I hated you for a long time."

"I don't blame you."

"I missed you." The words left his mouth before he could stop them. And once gone, his throat clogged with emotion. "I missed you so much it felt like someone had ripped out my heart."

He saw her crawl to him out of the corner of his eye. When she raised her hand, he squeezed his eyes shut because he both ached for her touch and feared it. It had taken him so long to get past the pain of what she'd done, that he refused to be put there again.

Seconds passed, and he didn't feel her. Finally, he opened his eyes to find her sitting back on her haunches, staring at him with deep sadness in her eyes.

"I left my heart with you," she said softly. "The last thing I ever wanted to do was hurt you. Perhaps it's better if I go."

She stood and turned to leave, and he reached up and grabbed her wrist more firmly than intended. She looked back at him, waiting.

"Don't," he whispered. "Don't go."

"As long as I'm with you, you're in danger."

He looked down at his hand holding her wrist. "I don't care. I can't be apart from you again."

He lifted his gaze to her face before standing and caressing up her arm to her slender neck. Then he sank his fingers into her glorious hair to cup the back of her head.

Slowly, he pulled her to him. His heart slammed against his ribs, his blood pounded through his veins. Only one woman had ever made him feel such overwhelming desire, and he'd finally found her again.

"Say you'll stay with me," he urged, their lips only breaths apart.

Her eyes slid shut. "I've always been yours. I'll always be yours."

With those words, he covered her mouth with his. He groaned at the taste of her. The passion within them exploded, consuming them. Their tongues dueled as their hands roamed over each other's bodies.

Within minutes, they had discarded their clothes, and he had covered her body with his. He feasted his gaze on her lovely body and perfect, pink-tipped breasts. His hand skimmed down to the indent of her waist and then her flared hip.

"Don't make me wait to feel you inside me," she begged breathlessly.

He looked at her swollen lips, his body eager to fulfill her wish, to fill her. She spread her legs and reached for him. From the very beginning, she'd amazed him by how she gave herself to him so freely. She hadn't questioned the passion between them, or their need to be joined. Maybe that's what made it so easy to love her.

With their eyes locked, he found her entrance and groaned at how wet she was. He guided his cock inside her. The feel of her tight, slick walls gripping him was pure heaven.

Inch by inch, he filled her. Her fingers dug into his arms as her breathing hitched. Once he was fully seated, she was the one who rocked her hips.

His need, the driving hunger to claim her again had him teetering on the edge of climax already. The way her blue eyes darkened didn't help, the desire there burning brightly. His cock jumped, and his hips moved of their own accord.

He bent and wrapped his lips around a nipple as his tongue laved at the turgid peak. The louder her cries became, the faster he pumped his hips.

He rose over her as he thrust harder and deeper. Her legs wrapped around his waist while she called out his name. His balls tightened. He didn't know how much longer he could hold back his orgasm.

Then he felt her body jerk, her mouth falling open on a silent scream. A heartbeat later, he felt her walls clutching him. He pumped his hips faster, prolonging her pleasure as he closed in on his.

When he tipped over the edge, he thrust deeply as the climax enveloped him. The ecstasy was everything he remembered from before—and everything that had been lacking with other females.

He pulled out of her and moved onto his back. Edra rolled to the side and rested her head on his chest. Both were breathing harshly. For an instant, it felt like those years separating them had never happened.

But then he felt the numbness in the fingers of his right hand, and he knew it was only an illusion. Radnar closed his eyes and held onto Edra tightly.

"I won't leave you," she whispered.

Her words brought a smile to his face. "Good."

"But I will continue to hunt the witches."

"Then I'll hunt with you," he stated. He opened his eyes when he felt her rise up.

Her blue gaze searched his face as a small frown puckered her brow. "You aren't going to ask me what I'm going to do?"

"I can, but I know you'll tell me when you're damn good and ready. You're a strong woman. It's what pulled me to you. I admire and respect you for it. You know witches. I don't."

She smiled and gave him a quick, hard kiss. "I'll teach you. And you can teach me to fight."

"We're going to need somewhere to hide."

"I know the perfect place." She settled back on his chest and released a deep breath.

Radnar understood that a woman such as Edra would intimidate many men. He wasn't threatened. Her fortitude and conviction made *him* stronger both mentally and physically.

He opened his eyes and put his other arm behind his head as he watched the sky darkening as night drew near. Hunting witches wasn't going to be as easy as it sounded, but the idea thrilled him.

The band that had constricted around his chest was gone. No longer did he feel the need to wander. Because he'd found what he'd been seeking. And now he had a purpose.

All the worries of before were gone as if they hadn't weighed upon his shoulders for years, threatening to crush him. He was free from all of that, but that didn't lighten the situation.

He was going to have to learn quickly because Edra wouldn't be hunting the witches alone. He'd be right beside her every step of the way.

Witches. Magic. His thinking would have to change, as well. Not his battle skills, but the witches were different than an army of knights. His strategy would have to adjust. Though he wasn't looking forward to one-on-one battles with them—even with his spelled sword.

4

"Where are we going?"

Edra glanced at Radnar over her shoulder and smiled. They had made love several times throughout the night. After a quick wash, they were on the move shortly after dawn.

"Don't you trust me?" She held back a laugh at her teasing. Ahead, she saw the rooftops of the village.

"I just like to be prepared."

She rode one of the extra horses while he sat astride the stallion. His dark locks were loose and falling down his back. She'd run her fingers through his thick hair last night as he'd fallen asleep with his head on her stomach.

After all the hardship she'd endured, all the torment and agony, it seemed almost too good to be true that Radnar was back in her life. But she wasn't going to tempt Fate to take him from her again.

"The village up ahead has something I need to pick up," she said.

She heard the sound of hooves as he galloped the stallion

even with the horse she rode. As he stared, she rewrapped the reins of the third horse around her hand.

"I know that look."

She shrugged and gave him an innocent smile. "What look?"

"The one that says you're preparing for something, and you're going to get your way regardless of who tries to stop you."

Edra blew him a kiss. "It got me you, didn't it?"

"I went after you," he said with a snort.

"You're wrong. I decided I was going to have you."

He gave a shake of his head as he chuckled. "Are you going to tell me what it is we're getting?"

They entered the village. "You'll find out shortly."

"I knew you were going to say that," he grumbled, a smile about his lips.

He let her pass, taking the rear as she rode through the village. They were almost to the other side when she caught sight of the little girl.

Edra halted the mare and dismounted. Radnar moved his horse forward so he could see what was going on, but he remained behind when she held up a hand stopping him.

She had seen the child when she was setting up the witches for battle and had been unable to stop and help. Since she had been homeless and starving at one time, she knew exactly how the girl felt.

Edra saw her huddled next to a building with her knees against her chest, her bare feet sticking out of the frayed and filthy skirts she wore. The girl's hair was matted, and she was covered in dirt.

When the child's soulful brown eyes turned her way, Edra felt her knees give. She remained upright by grabbing hold of the building. The desolation and misery that filled the girl's gaze broke her heart.

"Hello," Edra said with a smile.

The child continued to poke the stick she held into the ground. She looked away, not bothering to reply.

Edra knew the gaunt look of the starving. She had lived through it while others had succumbed. And if she had anything to do with it now, this little girl would survive, as well.

Even though Edra knew the answer, she asked, "Do you have any family?"

The girl gave a shake of her small head.

Edra crept closer by a few steps. "Are they dead?"

Another shake of the head.

At least she was getting answers. Though Edra didn't like them at all. She swallowed and took another few steps slowly. "I have food I can give you."

The child looked her way, but there was no hope or elation visible. "Why?"

"Why?" Edra repeated, shocked. She felt her heart breaking again. Lowering herself to her knees, she sat back on her haunches and handed the child some bread. "I'm offering this to you because you're hungry, and I have it."

For long seconds, the girl stared at her. Then, quick as lightning, she snatched the bread from Edra's hand and tore into it with her teeth.

Edra watched her for a moment. "I once lived just as you are."

The girl looked at her with eyes wise beyond her young years. She gave a huff that told Edra exactly what she thought of that statement.

"It's true," Edra said. "My mum died, and I had nowhere

to go. I remember being so hungry that the mere thought of food made me sick. It was the weakness I detested the most."

"I hate the cold and the wet."

Edra nodded in understanding. "My aunt found me and took me in. I had shelter and some food, but it wasn't much better than where you are now. The thing is...I want to help you."

The girl eyed her skeptically. "How?"

"How old are you?"

"Don't know," she said around a mouthful of bread.

By the look of her, Edra suspected she was around six or so. "I want to make you an offer. I want to share my home with you. I ask nothing more than that you help me with chores and that you don't steal."

The girl looked over her shoulder. "Who is he?"

"Radnar. He's a knight and my friend. My name is Edra."

The child lowered the bread as she considered the offer. "If you hurt me, I'll run away."

"I won't hurt you. And I promise that I can teach you how to protect yourself so that no one ever hurts you again."

"My family abandoned me."

With those four words, Edra wanted to wrap her arms around the girl and track down her family for retribution. She did neither. She simply blinked to keep the tears at bay. "I won't ever leave you."

"Why did you pick me?"

"Because you need me. Just as I need you."

The girl nodded slowly. "All right."

"What's your name?"

"Leoma."

Edra held out her hand, palm up. "Hello, Leoma. Ready to start a new life?"

The girl hesitated before she put her hand into Edra's.

Once she did, Edra softly closed her fingers around the much smaller ones. They stood together and turned toward Radnar. He sat, watching them intently, his expression fierce.

"Do not be afraid of him," Edra whispered.

As they got closer, Leoma pulled her hand away and walked straight to Radnar. She leaned her head all the way back and looked up at him.

"Hello, youngling," he said, gazing down at her.

Leoma tilted her head to the side and asked, "Are you going to hurt me?"

"I give you my word as a knight that I'll never harm you," he vowed.

Edra watched the exchange with interest and a smile. Then, to her shock, Leoma raised her arms. Without missing a beat, Radnar reached down from his lofty perch and plucked her up, setting her before him on the horse.

They both looked Edra's way.

She returned to her mare and mounted. The three of them left behind the small village and the horror of whatever had happened with Leoma.

"Where are you taking us now?" Radnar asked when the village was far behind them.

Edra thought back to the ruins she'd stumbled across a year prior and had quickly used magic to hide from others. "A place that will be ours. A place for us to gather and train. A place where we can hide when need be."

"You've really thought this through," Radnar said.

She shot him a wry look. "I knew I wasn't going to run from the Coven forever. I had to devise a plan."

They traveled the rest of that day, and half of the next before they came to the forest. Edra was nearly bursting with excitement. During their time together, Leoma hadn't spoken much, but she had taken turns riding with Edra and Radnar. It was enough that the child seemed to be adjusting.

But there were times when she caught Leoma looking around as if she expected to be abandoned again. Edra was prepared for the long road ahead of helping the child overcome such fears—if that were even possible. Sometimes such events had lasting effects.

Edra took them through the forest, turning toward a large rock formation. She dismounted once they'd reached the rocks. A look back showed both Leoma and Radnar looking around with interest.

She tugged on the horse's reins and walked around to the side of the rock where there was an opening. It was partially concealed, making it difficult to find unless you knew what to look for.

Once she was through, she stopped and waited for Radnar and Leoma to catch up. She smiled at them as they stood together. Then she waved her hand, removing the spell that had hidden the ruins.

Leoma gasped in surprise, and the first signs of a smile appeared. Without another word, the girl rushed up the curving stairs that had been cut out of the rock and walked beneath the vine-covered archway to the ruins.

"How did you find this?" Radnar asked in awe.

Edra moved closer to him and took his hand. "By accident."

"You're right. It's perfect. Though it's going to need some work."

"Come," she said and tugged at his hand as she began walking.

As soon as she was up the steps and beneath the vines, she felt like she was home. But it wasn't until she reached the old wooden door and stepped through it to stand in what was left of the castle that she knew this was where she belonged.

She released Radnar's hand and walked to the middle of the great hall. Most of the ceiling was missing, causing light to stream in, breaking up the shadows. She twirled in a circle, her arms out as she laughed.

When she stopped, she swayed from the dizziness. She looked around to find Leoma at the top of the stairs with her legs hanging over the side of a balcony.

Then Radnar was before her. He took Edra's hands and drew her against him. She leaned her cheek against the hand that cradled the side of her face.

"We're home," he said.

She wound her arms around his neck as she came up on her tiptoes. "Our home."

"I never thought I'd find you again, much less be together."

"But here we are. Are you sure you want to do this?"

He lightly kissed her lips and put his forehead against hers. "I'd rather be fighting witches with you than doing anything else."

"You might regret saying that," she said with a smile.

"How can I when I have my own witch?"

She laughed at his teasing. The laughter faded as they kissed. It was Radnar who broke away and raised his gaze toward Leoma.

"We have a watcher," he whispered.

Edra was about to pull out of his arms when Leoma's voice reached her.

"Are you two married?" the child asked.

Marriage hadn't been discussed, and Edra wasn't sure how to reply. She knew her love for Radnar went beyond anything a priest could sanction, but how did she explain that to a child?

"Not yet, little one," Radnar said.

Edra's gaze jerked to him. She gave him a curious look to see if he was saying that just for Leoma's benefit or not.

"You look surprised," he said.

Edra shrugged helplessly. "A little."

"I've wanted nothing more than to have you as my wife," he said. "Nothing will stand in my way now."

She raised a brow. "How about the absence of a priest?"

"Like I said, nothing will stop me now. What's your answer?"

Leoma asked, "Aye, Edra. What's your answer?"

"You know my answer," she told Radnar. "Aye."

While Radnar picked Edra up and spun her about, Leoma clapped and laughed, the sound reverberating through the ruins like the tolling of bells.

5

Radnar looked at the sky as he stood outside the ruins. Just an hour earlier, there had been a sprinkle of rain, but the skies had cleared as if they knew how important this day was.

"You're fidgeting," Leoma said.

He cut his eyes to the girl and gave her a stern frown that usually set men back on their heels. It didn't deter the child at all.

He'd wanted to marry Edra the day after they'd arrived at the ruins, but she had put him off, saying the date was important. So while he waited for her to tell him when it was time, they'd begun working.

After a month, the new roof was almost in place, and Edra, with Leoma's help, had been cleaning the rooms. Radnar had also cleared some of the vines away from the ruins. It was how he had discovered the stables. There was work to be done to make them suitable for the horses, but at least he didn't have to build one from scratch.

The biggest change had been Leoma. It had taken some

doing to get her thoroughly clean, and her hair detangled, not now it gleamed a glossy brunette with red highlights when the sun shone upon it. She also had new clothes and shoes.

He was thinking about growing food when Leoma elbowed him in the thigh. His gaze swung from her to the stairs where Edra stood.

For a moment, he couldn't breathe as he stared at her. In all his fantasies, nothing could've prepared him for the day he took her as wife.

She wore a dress of deep blue that hugged her shape before the shirts flared. A belt of pale blue wrapped her small waist twice before the ends fell down the front of the gown. Her honey blonde hair flowed down her back to her waist. Atop her head was a crown of flowers.

There was a smile on her face as she came down the steps, looking as ethereal as an angel. Her bright blue eyes never left his face as she came to stand beside him.

He faced her and took her hands. "You're beautiful."

"You're very handsome yourself," she said, running her hands over his navy tunic.

Leoma stood before them, her hands clasped before her. "How does this work?"

Radnar winked at Leoma before he grew serious as he stared into Edra's eyes. "I knew from the moment I first saw you that you were meant to be mine. You've always been in my heart, and you always will be. I vow to love and protect you for all of my days. I will stand beside you to fight whatever battles come our way. From now through eternity, you have my love."

Edra's smile was so bright it could've lit up the night. He watched as her eyes filled with tears of happiness, but she struggled to keep them at bay.

"Radnar," she said. "Our hearts and bodies were bound

long before we met. Our souls recognized that and called to each other. I freely gave you my heart long ago, and you hold it even now. No other can match you in strength, bravery, kindness, or love. You have always been my knight. I pledge that I will love and protect you always. Despite what may find us in the days and years ahead, nothing will separate us again. We're united in all ways. Our minds, our hearts, our bodies, and our souls. I loved you even before I knew you, and I love you more each day."

His heart hammered against his chest as her words filled the air. The forest was their church, and Leoma and everything around them their witnesses. The cloudless sky was a canopy of blessings of its own. Though there was no one to officiate the ceremony, it was binding nonetheless. Because it had been done before the gods and nature with hearts full of love, it would tie them together for eternity.

"Forever and always," he said.

Her lips curved into a smile. "Forever and always."

Radnar pulled her into his arms and kissed her with all the love, hope, and passion he held within him. Before the kiss could take a seductive turn, Leoma began skipping around them, humming.

They watched her for a moment before she took off into the trees. Radnar had been worried at first until Edra showed him that Leoma was a child of nature. He hadn't understood that until he saw how the forest protected her.

"The start of our family," he mused.

He pretended not to notice the sadness in Edra's smile. It had been there ever since she'd discovered that she wasn't carrying his child. But there were many more years ahead of them.

And there were witches to hunt.

"Don't go far," Edra called to Leoma. "You have training."

Leoma lifted her hand in a wave to let them know she'd heard.

"You're starting her early," Radnar said.

Edra flattened her palms against his chest. "In a world with magic, there is no such thing as too early."

Radnar chuckled, unsurprised. They turned and began to walk to the river at the back of the castle. "Leoma seems to know a surprising amount for her age."

"Aye, she does. What weapon are you going to work with her on today?"

"The bow. She did well with the sword the last two days, but she didn't like it."

"Perhaps the bow will be her specialty," Edra said as they stopped beside the river.

Radnar began to speak, but the words went right out of his head when his wife removed her crown of flowers and then her gown, followed by her shoes.

She gave him a smile as she walked to the edge of the water. "Are you planning to watch me, or will you be joining me?"

He didn't need to be asked twice. Radnar hurriedly removed his clothes, intent on enjoying the day. Who knew how many they'd have before they began hunting.

Edra laughed as he ran into the water and pulled her against him. This kind of happiness had seemed so far out of reach just a month earlier. Now, he couldn't remember what life had been like without Edra.

Their smiles died as the desire flared between them. Radnar groaned as he leaned down and claimed her mouth.

THANK YOU!

Thank you for reading **EVERSONG**. I hope you enjoyed it!

If you liked this book – or any of my other releases – please consider rating the book at the online retailer of your choice. Your ratings and reviews help other readers find new favorites, and of course there is no better or more appreciated support for an author than word of mouth recommendations from happy readers. Thanks again for your interest in my books!

Donna Grant
www.DonnaGrant.com
www.MotherofDragonsBooks.com

NEVER MISS A NEW BOOK

FROM DONNA GRANT!

Sign up for Donna's newsletter!
http://eepurl.com/bRI9nL

Be the first to get notified of new releases and be eligible for special subscribers-only exclusive content and giveaways. Sign up today!

ABOUT THE AUTHOR

New York Times and *USA Today* bestselling author Donna Grant has been praised for her "totally addictive" and "unique and sensual" stories. She's written more than seventy novels spanning multiple genres of romance including the bestselling Dark King stories. Her acclaimed series, Dark Warriors, feature a thrilling combination of Druids, primeval gods, and immortal Highlanders who are dark, dangerous, and irresistible. She lives with two children, a dog, and three cats in Texas.

Connect with Donna online:
www.DonnaGrant.com

www.facebook.com/AuthorDonnaGrant
www.twitter.com/donna_grant
www.goodreads.com/donna_grant
www.instagram.com/dgauthor
www.pinterest.com/donnagrant1

CPSIA information can be obtained
at www.ICGtesting.com
Printed in the USA
BVOW08s1152131017
497576BV00001B/1/P